boyracers

alan bissett

Polygon

First published by Polygon in 2001.
Revised edition published in 2002 and reprinted in 2005, 2008
Polygon is an imprint of Birlinn Ltd

West Newington House
10 Newington Road
Edinburgh EH9 1QS

www.birlinn.co.uk

Personal thanks to Amma Donkor, Terry Whittaker, and especially Natalie Hayes for their help
with the above.

Absolutely no thanks whatsoever to the bands, writers and publishers who made it impossible for
me to reproduce their lyrics. Anybody who wants to quote anything from this novel, contact me
and you can have it for fuck all.

ISBN 10: 0 7486 6328 2
ISBN 13: 978 0 7486 6328 6

The publishers gratefully acknowledge subsidy from

Scottish
Arts Council

towards the publication of this volume

Typeset by Hewer Text UK Ltd, Edinburgh
Printed and bound in Denmark by
Nørhaven Paperback A/S

AWARDS FOR ALL

Award For Giving Birth To And Raising The Author: **Irene and Alan Bissett Snr (love you both).**

Award For Encouragement Of The Author During Times When He Was, In Fact, Fucking Rubbish: **Mollie Skehal, the late Eileen Gibson, Thomas Tobias, Mark Docherty and Sarah Woodcock. (What the hell did you see in me?)**

Award For Advice, Support Or Help With This Novel Or For Just Generally Being Bloody Nice And/Or Excited About It/The Author: **Alison Bowden, Victoria Hobbs, Holly Roberts, Emma Darling, Mary-Anne Harrington, Anna Stevenson, Helen Lamb, Roddy Hamilton, Ronnie Bissett, Donna Bissett, Colin Armstrong, Allan Mann, Eddie Clark, Robert Shorthouse, Tony Makos, Anuradha Marwah Roy, Manju Kapur, Smita Agarwal, Peter Straus, Christine Kidney, Ali Smith, Jackie Kay, James Macdonald Lockhart, Des Dillon, Maggie Graham, Chris Small, Morvern Dooner, Meg Ferguson, Kirsten Kearney, Alan Nicholson, Chris Powici, David Punter, David Reid, Rory Watson, and everyone else in Stirling University's English Studies Department. (You might not all know you did, but you did.)**

Award For Being The Sharpest Writing Group In The World: **Stirling Writers. Thanks especially to Robert Ritchie, Cath Ferguson, Sarah Johnson, Colin Murrie and Judy Delin.**

Award To A Magazine For Publishing Extracts From This Novel: **Product, Pushing Out the Boat, Nerve, Cutting Teeth.**

Outstanding Contribution Award: **Magi Gibson, and my darling wife Caroline, to whom I owe more than I could possibly express.**

Look what we all did!

for the boys who were there, and still are

Colin Armstrong
Allan Mann
Thomas Tobias

Heddy-haw

like rebel angels, bright, restless, sensually attuned to the flux and flow of mortal Falkirk, Belinda our chariot, our spirit guide, the wind rushing up and past her face thrust against it like some wide-o Helen of Troy. The low growl of Belinda's undercarriage as Dolby shifts her into fifth and our mad singing at the dusk – mine, Brian's, Dolby's, Frannie's – Hallglen receding behind us like stars at warp speed cos it's Friday, seven-thirty, time for *Top of the Pops* and tramps like us, baby, we were born to run. The Glen Brae carrying us down down into the belly of the town, where the houses are big as two hundred grand mate, where one day we'll play pool and drink cocktails, champagne supernova, where a woman, a rich woman, is bending down to weed her garden and her arse flashes up in the air, then is gone. We whistle loudly, like a release, like the end of a shift. Frannie, in the back seat next to me, getting right into another work story, the NTL on his Rangers shirt giggling with him; he's talking about some guy in Tesco with loud Rod Stewart hair and the nickname Ace of Spads. 'Ace of *Spades* ye mean?' Dolby says, but Frannie's like, 'Naw! Ace of *Spads*. He's a fuckin nutcase, right, an he gets drunk ower in Magaluf an asks this Spaniard tae tattoo "Ace of Spades" on his face. But the guy cannae speak English, let alone write it, an this pissed-up Scotsman wi hair like Rod Stewart's no makin much sense . . .' Frannie's laughter is infectious. 'So he wakes up the next day, goes to the mirror, and finds fuckin "Ace of Spads" tattooed on his cheek!' Frannie snorts and grunts, kicking the back of Dolby's seat ('hey!'), knocking the little plastic Harrison Ford from his perch on the dashboard. 'I mean, can ye imagine it – no only gawin intae work wi Ace of fuckin Spades tattooed across yer mug, but it's no even spelt right!' Brian's mobile beeps

The Good, the Bad and the Ugly tune somewhere under the maps and the Mars Bars and the Eagles CDs and the whirlpool requisition

1

forms, muffled by the roar of Belinda's engine passing from FALK-IRK DISTRICT to STIRLINGSHIRE, Dolby trying to teach me the laws of physics with an Irn-Bru can, Frannie slobbering over a fish supper (dripping a vinegary smell from the windows) and there's streetlights. Millions of streetlights. Passing like tiny orange fish in the ocean. A Stirling

weapon, as we pass through Bannockburn, senses our Falkirkness through the walls of the car. He unfolds his Tommy Hilfiger arms from his Tommy Hilfiger chest and throws a coin at us. It hits Buffy the Vampire Slayer square on the tit on the bus shelter across the road. Buffy, hard as nails, doesn't feel a thing, just looks surly, sexy, Brian glaring menacingly back at the weapon-boy, like Angel. '*Uddy imfle bmsds*,' Frannie mumbles, not giving a shit, not really, his cheeks full as a hamster's and wet cod slipping onto his Rangers away top – '*Vuck*!' – it slides a slow snail trail.

Dolby holds up the Irn-Bru can like a teacher. 'Right,' he begins again, 'Now this can is travellin at' – the speedometer – 'sixty-six miles per hour.' '*Vixty-vix*?' goes Frannie, distressed, but not really, still trying to clean the grease from his top with Barr's lemonade and an AA map of Saltcoats. 'Whaur the *fuck's* that phone?' Brian's tutting, turning to me. 'Huv you got it, Runt?' 'Now if Ah wis tae drop this can,' Dolby explains, 'It wid land . . . . *thus*.' He lets the can go. It strikes the handbrake and springs off as if from a diving board (I almost hear it go *wheeeee!* with a squeaky cartoon voice). 'Brian Mann here,' Brian answers gruffly, finding his mobile, getting his life back. 'But why does it no land in the *back* ae the car?' I say, confused, wishing I hadn't spent four years of Physics lessons gazing at the back of Tyra Mackenzie's light-brown neck and hoping I don't end up with a job down Grangemouth, where someone's life might depend on my knowledge of the effects of speed on an Irn-Bru can. '*Cos fum feery rerariviry*,' Frannie mumbles again, swallows. 'Because ae the theory ae relativity.' Dolby shoots him a withering glance.

'Sgoat fuck all tae dae wi the theory ae relativity, dick! It's because *the can's travellin at the same speed as the car.*' 'But no while it's in the air,' I point out, 'No while it's fallin.' 'How's that likes?' Dolby's face creases like a sponge in a fist.

'Because it's no touching the car.'

'*Ih!*' Dolby's voice goes helium-high, '*Whit!*? This Irn-Bru is travellin at sixty-six miles per hour, *whether touchin the fuckin car or no!*'

Brian runs his thumb along his stubble often enough for it to catch fire.

'Aye,' he grunts into the mobile, 'Naw.'

and we know it's something to do with Smiths (the pub) (where he's head barman) (at the age of nineteen) (cos he's Brian the fuckin Mann and he takes no shit off nobody) (except birds) (except Catholic birds actually) (cos he says it feels dirtier with Catholic birds, somehow, I dunno). 'Anyway,' Frannie coughs, scrunching his fish supper into a ball and lobbing it out into the Dunipace waste, 'Guess who Ah wis oot wi last night.'

'Oot wi oot wi or *oot wi* oot wi?'

'Oot wi oot wi.'

'*Oot wi* oot wi!'

'Naw,' he emphasises, 'Just oot wi.'

'Aw.' Dolby's face falls. 'Who?'

'Scarlett?'

'*Who?*'

'Scarlett,' Frannie repeats, raking through the pile of Dolby's CDs which lie scattered: Limp Bizkit, *The Best of Cream* (Clapton's band, not the nightclub), the *Gladiator* soundtrack, Moby's *Play*, and Boney M. Boney M, I ask you. I'm convinced Dolby bought it thinking it was Eminem.

The Irn-Bru can. How it fa

lls in a moving car. The grand conspiracy that is Physics. My

3

confused Homer Simpsonness.

'Aw *Scarlett* Scarlett?' Dolby beams, 'Heddy-*haw*!'

Brian is nodding into the mobile, serious. I can actually hear the sound of his thumb rasping across his face. 'Aye,' he grunts again, 'Naw.'

'Whit did she say?'

'She said: *get yer fuckin hands aff me, ya–*'

Pit-stop. Petrol. Crisps, juice, shit. We clamour in to pay for it like a four-headed monster, Frannie up at the counter giving immediate patter to the girl serving – 'Could you tell us how to get to Aba*deen* from heeya?' putting on an English accent so fake she has to twig, but no. The girl gives him directions as best as she can, even though Aberdeen's, like, 8000 miles away or something. Then Frannie's comedy withers in the main attraction which is Brian Mann, action-movie hero. Clint Eastwood in a Rangers shirt. He strides up to the counter, imaginary spurs clicking, and the girl's eyes flick on and a smile curves round her mouth, as he slyly hands her his Curly-Wurly. Not that she could know that the cool, immaculate dude who stands before her is a man with stillborn patter. He recently tried to chat up a girl in The Maniqui with the line, 'You're a Tim, aren't ye? Ah can tell.'

I buy a can of Cherry-Coke ('for poofs' says Brian, stam

ping three glass bottles of Irn-Bru on the counter, which, I kid you not, will be gone within the hour). In the forecourt, that sharp tang of petrol making me feel, for one second, ill, Frannie beams, pleased with himself: 'She fancied me. Ye see the wee honey? Ah lightened her day right up, heddy-haw.' I glance back at the girl. Arranging the newspapers and sighing heavily. She looks about as inspired as greaseproof paper.

Back in the car. Heddy-haw. Belinda hums with satisfaction at our return. 'Whaur next?' 'Maddiston.' 'Glasgow.' 'Cairo.' Dolby and me kick-start a debate about the new Stephen King novel while Frannie

4

and Brian – the Ibrox twins – flick through the *Rangers News*, which means that in-between Dolby telling me the plot (writer finds Indian burial ground then dreams about killer clowns, or something), I keep hearing 'there's a split in the dressin room . . . Old Firm should move tae the English Premiership likes . . . thinkin aboot gettin ma hair cut like Coisty's' and then a song comes on that Frannie likes and he yanks the volume up, up, way up, as Karaoke Colin – his dreaded pub alter-ego – takes over.

> ah want tae run!
> ah want tae *hiiiide*
> ah want tae tear doon the *waaas* that *hauuud* me inside
> ah want tae reach oot and touch the

Traffic lights at red. Then a smooth sort of sick feeling on the rise into Bonnybridge, UFO land. We sight a few aliens lingering at bus-stops, bored outside chip-shops, Frannie stubbing his finger against the window, going: 'Greedo . . . and she's, hmmm, *Yoda*!' Frannie has a habit of rating women as *Star Wars* characters (even if he's been with more Jabba the Hutts than Princess Leias). 'What about her, Fran?' 'Her? *Ugh*! Did ye never see Vader when he took his helmet aff?' We start assigning each other *Star Wars* names; Frannie, we relucantly agree, being Han Solo. 'Heddy-haw,' he grins smugly, folding his arms, his work on Earth done. Brian – imposing, hairy – is Chewbacca, and being the oldest, Dolby is the natural Obi Wan Kenobi. 'Ah suppose since Ah'm the youngest,' I pipe up from the back, 'Ah'm Luke Skywalker?'

'Naw Alvin,' laughs Frannie, hurling an empty crisp-packet in my face, 'You're an Ewok.'

> whaur the streets huv nae name!
> whaur the streets huv *naaaee naaaame*!

and soon Brian's three bottles of Irn Bru to the wind, burping heroically, and Frannie's mobile's giving it *'I'm a genie in a bottle, better rub me the right way'* and Dolby's pulling Belinda over so he and Brian can pish and Frannie's got text.

He slouches in the seat, sighing. The message says:

TIMS 2
SHEEPSHGRS 0

I look down the motorway. A hundred yards away there's an old couple having a picnic on a fold-down table. Old and gentle. Maybe seen a war or two together, maybe even still in love. Cars whizz past them. The husband carefully spreads marmalade onto slices of bread, while his wife pours from a flask of tea. 'Hey!' Brian shouts at them, 'Fuckin George and Mildred!' The wife looks up to see Dolby and Brian shaking urine from their dicks. Brian points at their picnic. 'Whit sort ae thing's *that* tae be daein at the side ae a motorway, ih?'

We cruise past and they stare dumbly at us like tortoises. 'Fuckin noddies,' Brian's muttering, zipping himself up, 'Fuckin hate auld folk.' He stabs Led Zeppelin into the stereo and his head does a frustrated, funky pecking.

Dolby's eyes widen in the rear-view, furious. He's just noticed what I'm wearing. 'How many times have Ah telt ye, Alvin, *get that stupit baseball cap aff*!'

'Why?'

'Cos you make us look like boyracers.'

'Are we no boyracers?'

Both Brian and Dolby turn to me. The air gathers menacingly. 'Are we *fuck*!' Brian spits, the word curling from his mouth and landing on my shirt. I look to Frannie for back-up but his thumb's still stabbing at the mobile, which says the Rangers score. 'Dae ye see any birds in here wi bad perms?' Brian demands.

'Are there stickers on the windaes that say *On A Mission*?' Dolby.

'Are there Buckfast bottles clinkin in the back?' Brian again.

'Naw.'

'Well take that fuckin thing aff and stop actin yer age!' Brian turns, and starts singing the wrong words, off-key, to *Whole Lotta Love*.

'Boyracers . . .' he mutters, disgusted. 'Typical schoolie.'

Frannie snaps shut the mobile, dripping exasperation, and stuffs it away and runs a hand through his hair and goes: 'Whit we talkin about?'

'The gear that schoolies and losers wear.' Brian glances foully back at me.

'Aw right,' Frannie tuts, 'The Runt at it again?' Then he spies my head-gear and yelps: 'Cool! Gies a shot ae yer baseball cap!' and af

ter we leave Falkirk's skanky parts, summoned back into the tan-stocking finery of the sandstone houses, sex begins building up a head of steam under the bonnet. We talk about women and underwear, women in underwear, finally, women *out* of underwear, as we imagine rich wives hanging sheer knickers on washing-lines that flex above fresh, well-trimmed grass. Frannie regales us again with Elaine, legendary section manager who plucked his cherry when he was about, oh, Alvin's age, and then they all turn to me as if it's me alone who's keeping them from entry to the Palace of Love. 'That's your problem, Alvin,' Brian growls. 'You want tae get yer dick oot thae books and intae some wee schoolies.'

'They aw go for older guys,' I moan, then clench shut my eyes as I realise the bait I've just dangled, which – 'Whooaah!' – they clamp onto, hungrily. 'Get them roon here/Gie them ower tae me/Ah'll show them an aulder guy!' (god almighty). I'm afraid to report, however, that even if Brian has the Mann With No Name physique, the finesse was stolen and shared out between the other two. Frannie, for example, since Elaine, has been known to satisfy the urges of many a frustrated wife between shelf-stacking in Tesco's, and can you really blame some overworked woman of thirty-five, forty, for listening to a horny eighteen-year-old who tells them how pretty they are, that their man and kids don't appreciate them, all that pish, Christ, they lap the Franster up in there. Every Tesco's Christmas party we lose him after five minutes to a quick one with some wookie round the back.

Falkirk Town Centre.

The nightclub doors flung open and a tempo pounding out like jungle drums and the young – drawn from sleepy shires by chart rhythms, block-rockin beats, the call of the wild. Lipstick smoothed over lips, t-shirts unfurled down chests, tights wriggled up thighs, while shaving cuts absorb the splash and sting and

the force, luke, is what gives a jedi his power. an energy field created by all living things. it surrounds us and penetrates us, and binds the galaxy together with

the other sex's body. Midriffs, torsos, necks. The word DOLCE, the word GABBANA. Low, slow whistling from Frannie, that becomes

there's not a team like the Glasgow Rangers.

TESCO, as we ooze past, bleeds red letters down the windscreen. Frannie prays to the place that pays his wages and Brian slaps him – 'Fuck off – slaps him again – 'ya dick.' My baseball-cap tumbles from Frannie's head. John Cusack, Rene Zellweger, The Cruiser – exuding milk-white grins in the video-shop window. 'Who's read *American Psycho*?' I say, but we park, disembark, with sharp shoes clicking either side of us, with the laughter of females at dusk, with the Lads switched to automatic, pulled along in the tractor-beam of nice arses towards

Rosie O'Grady's nightclub.

At the head of the queue stand six bouncers. Twelve eyes to try and sneak beneath. Dolby turns to me.

'You bring ID?'

'Em . . .'

'Naw?'

'Naw.'

Dolby and Brian shake their heads, weary cops saddled with a rookie. They look like they should be chewing cigars and nodding at corpses. 'Right, well, here's the plan . . .' We merge into the queue. Brian and Frannie have changed from Rangers shirts into Top Man shirts. I recognise the two girls in front of us from school: fourteen-year-olds trying desperately to look fifteen. One of them starts adjusting her tiny tits in her bra. 'Tell ye whit Ah says tae her, Emma!' she seethes in her mum's voice, 'Make a fuckin choice Ah says! Ye cannae like Destiny's Child *and* the Sugababes.'

'Fuckin out of order,' her pal agrees.

'Alvin,' Dolby commands, 'Stick close tae us. The bouncer might assume yer the same age.' I shuffle into position. 'If he asks for ID, whit should ye dae?'

'Pretend tae search for it.'

'And why'll ye no find it?'

'Must have left it in my other jacket. Sir.'

'Good. Dinnae call him sir. He'll probably no go for it, but it's better than shruggin an lookin like a knob.' Dolby's tone suggests I must often look like this. 'Date ae birth?'

I reel it off, smart.

He nods, without much confidence, checking me up and down.

Shoes shined immaculate black. Shirt almost stapled into my school trousers. Hair slicked and stiff with gel. I don't feel very old. I feel that over-groomed, stuffed way you do on the morning of a cousin's wedding.

'Have ye shaved?' Brian growls.

'Aye. Twice.'

I peer through the club window. Alvin through the looking-glass. My reflected face looms ghostly in front of me, and for a second I am dislocated, hovering with the pretty faces, listening to chat-up lines from immaculate blondes over the sound of Basement Jaxx/Armand Van Helden/Geri Halliwell. Drinks glowing Mediterranean and neon, life lived in knife-like prime, while I

Stand outside.

In the grey Falkirkness.

Frannie has let in comrades from Tesco's; there are grumbles from the rest of the queue. Frannie does his MC bit – 'Andy, Mark, this is the Lads – Brian Mann, fellow Teddy Bear. *Heddy-haw.*' They shake hands with a fraternal pump. 'This is Dolby, he works for–'

'Whirlpools Direct.' Dolby taps grim cracks in the pavement with his shoe.

'An the wee yin here,' and their eyes, expecting another giant, fall, 'this is the Runt.'

The pair nod at me, unimpressed, before continuing the Ibrox banter with Brian and Frannie ('aye there's definitely a split in the dressing-room likes') and the queue shunts up

a space. Falkirk cinema across the road is showing the BLIAR WITCH PROJCET, the title arranged like broken teeth above the entrance. A picture of The Cruiser and Kidman exchanging flesh-tones has been defaced and now reads EYES WIDE SHITE. Dolby is chatting up the girls in front of us. They turn over their accents, softly stroke their fourteen-year-old curls and sigh: 'Work? Oh, uh, I work for a management consultancy firm in Edinburgh.' Q: How can you tell when someone in Falkirk is lying about their job? A: It's in Edinburgh. Seriously, have you ever met anyone in Edinburgh – batting their eyelashes, patting their ringlets – who said they worked in Falkirk? Soon Dolby-Wan Kenobi's gesticulating to the schoolies: 'Ye've no even *read* an X-Men comic? Well shut it then!' and one of them laughs – high, piano-like: 'You're so *funny.*'

The bouncer leans his meaty head out like a truck-driver in traffic. I duck, fearful, then try to position my shoulders that sort of Liam Gallagher way, so that I look older, harder, cooler, but my shirt feels too big for me and the creases in my trousers could cut paper. The queue shuffles

up. A gaggle of girls roam past in pinks and lilacs and my stomach starts flopping like a fish on a deck.

'Ye awright, Alvino?' Frannie frowns. 'Look a bit pale.'

'Ah'm fine,' I swallow. 'Too much, em, Irn-Bru.'

'*Too much Irn-Bru,*' one of Tesco's splutters, '. . . *the wee man.*'

Inside, Daft Punk segues into the new Radiohead single, something about jumping in the river with black-eyed angels. A brave choice. The floor empties in protest then the DJ panics and sticks on some dance choon that goes, 'Ooh-*ooh*! Ooh-*ooh*!' and the place goes barmy.

'Ye've never seen *Gregory's Girl*!' Dolby is choked, crimson. 'Ye've *never* seen *Gregory's Girl*?!' One of the girls pats his hand and sighs, 'Isn't he funny?'

'Have ye seen *Aliens*?'

'No.'

'Are ye *alive*?'

They're still laughing! And I'm wondering where the hell I'm going wrong with women. And all along the queue people are tapping at their mobiles, reading texts, grinning, tapping, grinning, reading, squawking, raucous, then a random, hip-hop snatch of thoughts: how did The Cruiser feel about the world seeing Nicole Kidman's tits?

Will the government shut Falkirk down as a non-profit-making industry? What if The Cruiser and Kidman, right, were walking down the street, right, and I just walked up to him and asked to see her tits, would he let me? Would he let me, do you think? Date of birth, date of birth.

'So you've read Stephen King?' Dolby's urging, 'Clive Barker? *Enid fucking Blyton*?'

We are four people away from the head of the queue now. Three. Three steps to Heaven, Valhalla, Mount Whatjimacallit (the Greek one). I can feel the music trembling in the base of my teeth. And the Lads. Look cool. As Gods.

Would The Cruiser let me, do you think? See Nicole's tits, that is. But, like, what's the difference if she's in a film? What difference does it make? These things keep me awake. What difference does it make? Mobiles ringing semitone chart-hits, digital love arriving up and down the queue, the Lads' patter, girls, and I sometimes wonder if it's really, truly, genuinely fine for someone my age not to take drugs, I mean will it stop me from getting a job in the future?

The bouncer, eyes like flints and his smile a tiny razor cut, turns away two hopefuls (older than me) with a malevolent, 'Back to the nursery, boys.'

Has anybody noticed I'm wearing a girl's deodorant (Dove)? Does Dad really believe that Mum's coming back? Is Dolby stuck at Whirlpools Direct forever? Could Spider-Man kick Batman's ass since Batman has no superpowers, just a really cool outfit? Why doesn't Tyra Mackenzie *fancy* me, for fuck's sake!

'There must be a law against it.' Brian is discussing Wonderbras with the Tesco's boys, and Fran responds with his Ali G impression: '*you fink you is gettin sumfin an then you don't get it.*' Dolby will not give up on his crusade to educate these schoolies. 'Whit aboot *Hellraiser*?' he demands. 'The Old Firm should join the English Premiership,' says Brian, and everyone mutters, agreeing, 'Scotland's

deid for Rangers' and the Chemical Brothers kick into life and Rosie's
howls and stomps bright colours and I look on, a child at Santa's
grotto

> hey girl
> hey boy
> superstar Djs
> here we go

'You're dead, ya fat fuckin bastard!' the spurned ravers are yelping at
the bouncers as they retreat, the word GAP stark and black on their
chests, Newmarket Street cold and loveless and eerie as a graveyard;
the further away they get, the more they look like vampires. The
bouncer raises a nasty smile and his middle finger. I am swallowing,
hard.

> hey girl
> hey boy
> superstar Djs

'Four? *Four*? You've seen *Hellraiser IV*? And no the first one!'

Does my breath smell of Wrigleys? Do I look like a girl? *Why*
doesn't Tyra Mackenzie fancy me? Do I put too much gel in my hair?

I do, don't I?

When I get nervous I start to run lines from *Top Gun* in my head
but the only one I can remember is, '*You screw this up, Maverick, and
you'll be flying a cargo plane full of rubber dog-shit out of Hong Kong.*'
The two girls younger than me breeze past the bouncers with a
professional tinkle of their fingers. 'Evening, ladies.' Their perfume
dances happy on the air and

> here we go!

the place starts jumping.

'Movin oot tae California this year, boys,' Brian informs us, his resolve Made In Scotland From Girders. It is my hair-gel, isn't it? What if Tyra's in there and my hair's stiff as an Oriental sculpture, my palms slick with Asda-brand gel? What then? What if I don't even get *in*? Will the Lads stop letting me hang about with them? '*This is what I call a target-rich environment*,' The Cruiser's boasting in my head in his pristine-white naval uniform and I've just remembered that The Cruiser and Kidman actually split up and Dolby

(shit)

strolls past the bouncer

(what's my date of birth?)

who nods his head politely, almost reverentially, then Frannie, Brian, his well-pressed shirt graceful with Tommy Boy, then

(*what's my date of birth*?!!!!!)

The bouncer stops me. His hand firm on my chest.

And the world.

Slows.

Down.

'Whit age are ye, son?'

The words sound machine-distorted. A bomb threat. Arnie in *The Terminator*. '*Vhaat. Age. Uh. Yoo.*'

The eyes of the people of the queue. Older, dressed-up folks, itching to enter once this schoolie gets his Poundstretchers-clad arse out the way. Brian lingers, holding open the door, and beyond it are giggling, tipsily dancing beautiful ones. A guy with a roving mike and a lion's mane of blond dreadlocks is barking at glittering party-dresses. The barman throws drinks like The Cruiser in *Cocktail*. The Cruiser and Kidman have split up and all of this moves across me in waves. In slow, swimming-pool motion.

'Eighteen,' I cough, trying to make my voice sound deeper. 'Nineteen next month.'

'Date of birth?'

(*Your ego's writing cheques your body can't cash!*)

I tell him confidently.

The bouncer frowns. An actual frown, with the mouth pulled down at the corners. His skin is pock-marked, rough, and I imagine him stubbing out his own fags on it. A badge on his bomber-jacket names him THE OUTLAW JOSEY WALES.

'So you're fifteen?'

'What?'

He fiddles absently with something between his teeth, like a lion after a meal, not looking at me. And I don't believe it.

I've given him my real date of birth.

'That date of birth makes you fifteen years old, son.'

I try to laugh, but it comes out choked, constricted. 'But of course Ah'm no *fifteen*!'

The Outlaw Josey Wales starts ushering in another two pubescent girls, raising his tabloid-sized hand. They wink at him gratefully. 'Mibbe no,' he mutters, bored, 'But yer no fuckin eighteen either.'

Brian hears this. Nods. Lets the door swing and flit on gold-plated hinges. I watch him join Fran and Dolby at the bar, mouthing to them:

'*The Runt lost it.*'

Then I turn from the throng, braving taxis that vomit more Ben Sherman gear out into the street. I decide not to bother going to the pictures on my own, laughing on my own, hiding behind a box of popcorn at the scary bits on my own. I head for home. And the music dies behind me like a whale sinking beneath the sea.

In the High Street: WH Smith, Burtons, Virgin, Boots, The Body shop. All empty, stark and flat. Their products stand regimented and still as if preparing an invasion. A drunk wearing a Scotland shirt asks me for/demands a pound for the phone, which I give him. He puts it in his pocket and walks away, straight past the booth. I stand and watch the numeral X become trapped by the hand of the steeple. Its legs are silently pleading, released, making me spring awake. Startled. Vaguely terrified.

Crashed and burned, huh Mav?

Alone as a figure in a ghost story, I trudge up the Glen Brae. Infrequent cars soar past in a billow of night air. To cheer myself up, I start thinking of funny things to say to the Lads in Belinda tomorrow. And fail. And content myself with hoping they get laid tonight.

When I get in, Dad is sleeping on the couch, and Davina McCall is Streetmating a rugby player with a poet in Colchester. I switch it off, knowing they won't match (who does?) then throw a cover over Dad and go to bed (half-past ten) to read some of *Pet Semetary*, the bit where the little boy gets killed by the truck, then fall into sleep with *The Dark Side of the Moon* still playing and have a lush dream about Tyra Mackenzie and the Lads and me all at a Pink Floyd concert in Paris and during 'The Great Gig In The Sky' Tyra moans, reaches over, says '*Alvin*', gently touches my lips with her lips and I

slip un

der

to

when Mum was there.

I'm very small, and I'm looking at a big Phillips atlas spread on the kitchen table. Sunlight tearing at the curtains. My straw sidled in a glass of Orangina. *Byker Grove* on the telly. Dek coming in, going out.

16

Things like that. Home. Mum as a phantom memory – roaming the kitchen, taking things out of cupboards, putting things back in cupboards. The ethereal scent of her perfume. The crinkles in the back of her blouse. The *smeck!* sound she and Dad make as they kiss. But I can't remember her eyes. I wish I could remember her eyes. I follow my Dad's finger on the atlas, marvelling more at the hairs on his knuckles than the countries he's pointing out to me. So far away, they might as well be Narnia.

That's America. Ken, whaur Mickey Mouse comes fae? . . . an that's Russia, whaur they wear thae big broon overcoats . . .

Ra-ra Rasputin, Dad?

Eh, aye son. And see – that's Spain. Mind whaur yer pal next door went on his holidays?

Spain! He says there's swimming pools ootside and everyhin!

Aye well. We cannae afford it. Anyway, see that magic wee place there? He taps a tiny purple head, jutting awkwardly at the top of Britain. *That's Scotland. That's whaur ye live.*

I look at it. I have to lean in and squint in order to look at it.

That? I say.

That *is the finest country in the world, son!* my Dad boasts, a bit too magnificently.

There is hardly room to fit the word *Scotland* on it. The letters spill out into the North Sea, swimming desperately away towards the Netherlands.

That? I say again.

An right in the middle, he makes a dot with his pencil end just between Glasgow and Edinburgh, *that's . . .*

Falkirk

I focus on the dot, trying to relate it to the vastness of the rest of **EUROPE,** that seems to consume it, make it invisible.

That's the town whaur ye live. And see if you look right intae the centre of that dot, he goes on, bringing out a magnifying glass so that, if I hurt my eyes, I can make out the tiny ridges of the pencil marks on the paper. *That's whaur we are the now. Me an you an Derek an yer Mum. That's us.*

Then he rubs the dot out.

I wake up every day with the Sex Pistols.

Usually it's 'Holidays in the Sun', which means Dad in his dressing-gown, straining his vocal chords through his nose and slashing at an invisible guitar. Today it's 'Pretty Vacant'. Which means nothing good. I dra

ag myself from bed, a prehistoric thing rising from the sludge. Patch of sunlight pining outside Dek's old room. Pick up toothbrush. Put down toothbrush. White paste slugs on the tap. Bleary eyelashes of rust round the bathroom mirror. Shower water revolving down-wards at the bottom of the bath like in *Psycho* and we're so pretty, oh so pretty

my bare feet

make the floorboards groan. Downstairs, Dad is arranging pieces of toast on old chipped plates. He nods, gives a perfunctory 'morning' as I drip through the back pages of the *Daily Record*, find the lazy Rangers defeat. Hearts. I see Frannie zapping barcodes on the morning shift, muttering the name.

I finger some toast into my mouth and offer Dad the paper, which he refuses.

'Did Ah ever tell ye . . .' His eyes alight on the sparrows on the garden fence and I know what's coming, 'That yer Mum an me saw Elvis Costello?'

'Elvis Costello? When?' I have to keep sounding surprised each time he mentions this. The floorboards are moaning beneath my feet, as if there's someone trying to sleep down there, or maybe they're just

18

fed up with the Elvis Costello story too.

'1979?' he shrugs. '1980? It was at The Maniqui.'

I dump a carton of orange juice on the breakfast bar – installed during Mum's formica phase in the eighties. Never removed. A tiny nail polish smudge decorates one end. A quick image of Mum spilling it, her mouth an 'o' of horror, the *Only Fools and Horses* theme playing in the background.

'Elvis Costello in The Maniqui,' I marvel woodenly.

'Well it was called Oil Can Harry's back then,' he continues, 'But it used tae attract a lot ae big acts. Costello, The Jam, The Buzzcocks. Nae artists that stature playing Falkirk now.'

'Nope.' I start pulling on my Simpsons socks, then my trousers (the same ones I wore to Rosie's), glancing at the clock. 'Was he, um, any good?'

'Aw aye,' Dad begins to nod, a toy sheepdog in the back of a car on a long, long trip. 'Very good. Very good indeed.'

'Elvis Costello in The Maniqui,' I repeat. Dad's mind and mine are dancing druggedly round each other, as they do every morning. When I cross to the fridge, there is a pause in the conversation which seems as fraught with danger as an Arctic journey. 'The Jam as well?'

'The Jam as well.'

'And the Buzzcocks?'

'And the Buzzcocks.'

'Uh-huh.'

'Just goes to show.'

'Yup.'

Dad takes a pensive sip, transporting himself back to the fag-end of the seventies, where he is gayly destroying phone-boxes with some punks. I'm waiting to see if there's more of the Maniqui story to escape those coffee-tinged lips. Queuing for tickets in the rain? The interrupted kiss on Mum's doorstep? But no, he is treading towards the stereo, searching indecisively for the off-button. '*We're so pretty, oh*

19

so pretty,' Johnny Rotten whines, '*We're vac–*'

The portable TV on the kitchen chair. The chair's nude aluminium legs. Ghosts flicker on the TV screen, slide, merge into images of a cricket match, a great white shark, an awards ceremony, Lorraine Kelly. Dad glowers and taps the box. '*brad pitt . . . it . . . yit . . . table tennis,*' Lorraine stutters, gleeful as a kid, '*Banan . . . wit . . . fib . . . huddersfield.*'

We both slurp, waiting for her message. I LOVE MY COFFEE, Dad's mug declares, like a placard raised at some pro-caffeine rally.

I thread my tie through my collar, recanting Mum's dim instructions from my first day at school, '. . . *the fish swims round the rock . . . into the cave . . . down the hole . . .*' Her words seem to burble up from the bottom of the ocean.

'See you fell asleep on the couch,' I mention, for conversation's sake more than anything else, but Dad quickly tries to justify it. 'Aye,' he coughs, 'em . . . Ah wis watchin a film.'

My third-year blazer constricts my fifth-year shoulders. In the mirror, I'm a passport photo, scissored off at the chest. Not whole.

'Aw aye? Which one?'

Dad takes a long gulp from his coffee mug, his eyes like pinpoints on Lorraine Kelly.

'*Clash of the Titans,*' he mumbles eventually.

'Good movie,' I shrug. 'Good special effects for its day.' Mum and Dad's wedding video is perhaps half an inch further out than the rest in the cabinet. 'I like the bit with the army of skeletons.'

'That's *Jason and the Argonauts,*' he replies, not missing a beat, and maybe he did watch a film after all.

I muse about the kitchen for a bit. The tap is working again. I have come to the conclusion that Dad is not going to the Job Centre today. Or the doctor's. I move the lid of the breadbin up then down, noticing the tiny beige crumbs that have accumulated over the years.

'*And later we'll be making a picture of Ronan Keating,*' says Lorraine

Kelly, '*Using needlecraft!*'

'Whit did you dae last night?' Dad calls from the living-room.

My reflection shrugs in the dirty mirror. 'Stayed in at Brian's,' I reply with a composure I should have reserved for the Rosie's queue, 'Watched *Saving Private Ryan*. Played the Playstation. You know.'

'Are you no too auld for Playstations?'

Dad is still on his haunches, still in his dressing-gown, still tapping the box for a better picture. I suddenly can't bear what a sad old fucker he is and have to get out.

'Are you no too young for GMTV?' I say.

A wry little snort shuffles out from his beard. 'There's a postcard there for you from Derek.'

On my way out the door, cold sunlight spreading plague-like across the scheme, I hear 'Pretty Vacant' rumble back to life.

Graffiti on the bus-shelter saying: FRANNIE + ~~GREEDO~~

~~JABBA~~

JAR-JAR BINKS!

and funnily enough I end up sitting on the bus next to a girl who looks just like Carrie Fisher. Skin white as a china doll. Hands folded neatly on her lap. I am about to try and talk to her when she suddenly leaps to her feet and shouts, '*Davey? Ya fuckin knob ye!*' and throws a Coke can down the bus.

The *Blade Runner* soundtrack on my personal stereo drowns out the hordes. By the time I fish out Dek's card I am calm as Buddha.

On the front is a red London bus. In one of the windows, Dek has drawn a stick-Alvin wearing a personal stereo, carrying a book of HORROR STORIES. The bus runs over another stick figure, spurting ink blood. Stick-Me is smiling merrily at this gruesome death. Dek thinks I'm warped because I read Stephen King and listen to *Dark Side of the Moon*. A lot.

DEAR FLOYD-LOVING FUCK

ALL WELL IN THE BIG CITY. LONDON A BITCH THAT HAS BEEN FINALLY BROKEN. HOPE TO GRACE HASH-GLEN SOMETIME SOON. GIVE DAD MY FONDEST AND MRS GIBSON, AS THEY SAY IN BRIXTON, 'REESPECT'.

DEK

PS. YOU KNOW

that moment in films? When the boat's bobbing to a shore decked in metal. Or the helicopter descends to the roof of the jungle. Or the police van draws up outside the drugs bust. The faces of the men. Mouths doing frantic chewing. Bodies locked on rifles. Eyes steel and hard, as little things itch imperceptibly in the skin, then

GO!

the bay doors open and they stream out like gas pissing from a main into bombs and bullets and shouts and stabs and glory and death and

Anyway.

Sorry.

See when our school bus rolls up at the gates?

That's what it's like.

School's a war movie. All these kids from all these different homes all stuffed into blazers, a pen in their hand and a stencil-set in their bag and told to go fight the good fight. A common enemy: each other. A common goal: good marks. Some are shot on the first day. Never rise again. Some go on and become heroes, immortal in gold leaf on the mahogany standard in the foyer. Dux. Their names we shall remember.

Look from the window of the staff room out onto the quad, with your coffee cup and your EIS protection, and tell me it's not a war. We arrive in first-year with our eyes shining like blue gems, our new maroon blazers coming down past our arms so we can grow into them. By Christmas we're just doing what we can to stay alive, desperate to think of something funny to say in front of the in-crowd and

she's employed where the sun don't set

growling at the smallest in the corridors, lest we be growled at ourselves, nipping out during double French to either smoke hash or buy clothes, depending on which part of Falkirk we're from, and the whole time our whole lives are dependent on every single thing we do, every book we (do not) read, every exam we can('t) be fucking arsed to turn up to, and there's MPs on the telly and soon we're all going to have internet access. In my second year, a bottle fight erupted in the quad. Plastic bottles right enough, but hurled with enough force to break the spectacles on any dozy sods caught in the middle. Camelon lined up one side, Hallglen lined up the other. A no man's land in between where

she's the shape of a cigarette

emptiness breathed, as barren as the Somme. Everybody finishing their Blue Kola and Limeade and Orange, slyly smirking at the opposition. The occasional shot fired, but most wary of Melville standing like an implacable god at the staff-room window, his eyes picking out the sinners the way a hawk hunts mice. But then the bell rang and

she's the shake of a tambourine

a hundred bottles whistled into the air, spinning, aerobatic. Leaving defiant grins behind. And the beauty of the sight – like birds in flight, or a display of aeroplanes – poised, hanging, buoyed briefly on the

23

momentum of scrawny teenage muscles. The sheer amount that filled the air meant they couldn't finger anyone for it. And it's that same kinetic force I feel in the pit of my gut as Belinda transports the Lads and me from Hallglen to places where we can be heroes, just for one day.

I'm in fifth year now. I've been looking for Private Ryan for five whole years. Stopped caring about finding the cunt now. Stopped caring about punnies for swinging on my chair, clothes I can't afford to wear, being chairman of the debating society, editor of the school magazine, head boy, head girl, or listening to the hash-heads yak stonedly about Bob Marley, *OK Computer* and

she's the colour of a magazine

Trainspotting. Stopped caring about quadratic-equations and French past-participles and whoever's Scotland's First Minister now and the Lib-Lab-paddywhack-give-a-dog-a-bone-type-alliance or whatever, and the only thing I can really find any sort of enthusiasm for is disappearing from the babble of this world into an eternal dream where

she's in fashion.

she moves through the crowd like rarified air. Her hair bright as sunlight. She takes her seat beneath the *Midsummer Night's Dream* poster. Words in delicate script above her head: '*Now, fair Hippolyta, our nuptial hour draws on apace . . .*' Her hand tanned and smooth. She leans. Her bag: PRADA. Her throat, speckled and lightly undulating as she swallows. Her mobile phone: NOKIA. It plays the love song to *Titanic.* I imagine her asleep, moaning softly, her hand folded back on her forehead, her eyelashes flickering like pencil marks on paper. Mrs Gibson is reading from *The Great Gatsby.*

24

Outside, a bee bats against the illusion of the glass, and Tyra's eyes flick over at me, then away. A pen works lazily between her fingers. I write, and in some way it is an intercourse:

They. Cannot. Touch. Her.

The classroom is warm, and frequently I find my head nodding further down my hand, the room floating in and out of consciousness, seeing me, Frannie, Dolby and Brian in Rosie's, laughing and ordering girls from a menu. Dolby's finger runs down the list and he muses, 'Hmm, I'll have the redhead. Lightly tanned and easy on the feminism,' and Brian agrees, 'Excellent choice,' and then the waiter turns to me, for some reason angry, and barks

'*What foul dust floated in the wake of his dreams!*'

Mrs Gibson skelps me on the head with a copy of *Gatsby*. I jerk awake. The whole class is laughing like that bit from *The Wall*

Poems everybody! The laddie reckons himself a poet!

except Mrs Gibson's alright about it, so I mumble something about cough medicine Miss, um, makes you drowsy. She lets me off; guardian angel, fairy-godmother, good witch of the north, etc. I glance over at Tyra, blushing. Gibson starts talking about the theme of 'Desire and the American Dream', somehow seeming to know fine

who's going to be Gregory's girl?

that I was out till one in the morning last night, cruising car-parks in Stirling and talking about Schwarzenegger movies with the Lads and I don't care what Brian says, *Predator* is a much better movie than *The Terminator*.

Tyra Mackenzie's eyes swim with amusement. It occurs to me just how much she looks like Buffy. Tyra was the first in our year to pass her driving-test, get a Mazda from her folks, start driving it to school

25

with the window down and sixties songs playing, but she's always been pretty nice to me. I used to sit beside her in Computing Studies and she would lend me her pen every week, the one that had her initials on it. Maybe she's attracted to me because I'm obviously, you know, a bit of rough.

Gibson scratches something on the board about symbolism or something, roses meaning blood and love and blah blah blah, like who couldn't work that out? Connor Livingstone, meanwhile, is staring at me, imperious and cool. Wealth oozes from him. He does not fall asleep in class. He does not drag-race in car-parks. He has not a zit. Since his first year at Falkirk High he's been getting private tuition three nights a week, because he has the pushiest parents and an assured future in the paid-thousands-to-sign-cheques-for-millions industry. His neck suggests rugger, and when he speaks his accent glides all the way down from Windsor Road. Probably reading Tolstoy while I was watching *Predator*. Still, when Mrs Gibson asks a question and Connor's hand shoots up like an excited toddler, it's me she turns to.

'Now that you're awake, Mr Allison, how would you summarise Gatsby's character?'

I pause, aware of the eyes of the whole class: Connor's (burning) but especially Tyra's. I pat my pen against my teeth rapid-fire. Look Catalogue-Model Livingstone up and down and sneer:

'He's fake. He's all surface.'

Mrs Gibson cocks her head. The class waits for her reaction, pens poised. Then she scrawls in huge letters up on the board THE SURFACE IS FANTASY and everyone writes it down. Even Tyra! She floats obvious respect my way, as cladding falls in pieces from my heart, and I write

how i wish
how i wish you were here

and draw the cover from *Dark Side of the Moon* on my jotter. I am a thin ray of light, refracted through Tyra. Mrs Gibson starts prowling between desks, the novel open in one hand, the other trailing the room like a silk scarf, and whenever she reads from *Gatsby*, she seems to bristle with magic. She should be carrying a fucking wand. My brother Dek confessed it was the only reason he ever went to English, that Irish intensity in Mrs Gibson's voice, injecting little boys with prose. The short sound of her breaths, in, out, pausing at the commas, released in a breathless sigh in the vowels.

The heat of the classroom makes me drowsy again. I see Tyra's reflection in the thin of the window. I watch Mrs Gibson's mouth shape the words:

> *we were content to let their tragic arguments fade with the city lights behind. Thirty – the promise of a decade of loneliness – but there was Jordan beside me* (and I find myself thinking about Belinda, the Lads), *who, unlike Daisy, was too wise to ever carry well-forgotten dreams from age to age. As we passed over the dark bridge* (hope Dolby's bought the new Travis album) *her wan face fell lazily against my coat's shoulders and the formidable stroke of thirty died away with the reassuring pressure of her hand* (the places we might go, the girls we might meet, the patter) *and so we drove onwards* (Brian owes me a fiver) *through the cooling twilight* (might buy a Chinky!) *towards*

the sky, fast, lit like a huge dragonfly, the road out of Falkirk before us and Radio One doing Ibiza on the car stereo, Sara Cox addressing the glorious San Antonio sun setting over the sea (which would be ruined, for me, by some pixie-like presenter sticking a microphone in my face to ask if I was 'Avin it laaaaahhge!', but there you go). Every time she says the word '*Abeefa!*' invisible ravers go ape-shit in the background and there's this joke that Frannie told us once: a Rangers fan dies and

27

goes to Heaven (!) and the angel Gabriel is pointing out all the Ibrox legends. Scot Symon, Davie Cooper, Willie Waddell. But the guy spies Ally McCoist, and he's like, 'Wait a minute! Coisty's no deid!' 'No, that's God,' replies Gabriel, 'He just likes to pretend he's Coisty.' Seems to me that joke says as much about the teller, with Frannie-boy giving it his best (worst) McCoist patter tonight. There's only one god here. He's in the mood, and not for dancing. And while I try to tell Dolby about falling asleep in class, Mrs Gibson skelping me awake, Connor Livingstone sniggering at me, and all about Tyra's chest, again, Frannie keeps leaning out of the car window and whistling at girls and blowing them kisses.

'Hey! Hen! D'ye think Ah look like Ally McCoist? Dae ye? Ih? *Aye, same back, ya boot!*'

Brian is on a shift at Smith's. Our chances of any Kate Bush are limited without him. The Franster is trying far too hard to compensate for the Mann's absence, hoping to prove to disinterested Bainsford scrubbers that tonight, Matthew, he's Super Ally, and, sure enough, he soon gives up and inexplicably starts singing 'Sweet Caroline' to every girl he sees instead, at the top of his voice, till one of them (obviously called Caroline) waves back, making Frannie yell '*Heddy-haw!*' and Dolby beam with shame and laugh and screech into the tarmac as the lights turn

Red.

Men stumbling from The Big Bar. The most imaginative pub name in Scotland. It has a big bar. The old guys croak and groan, crossing in front of us. A line of brown tweed drapes the windscreen for a while. The three of us watch and are appalled. There was one night we found all of our fathers in Smith's at the same time. They were sitting there at the bar (my Dad gently tapping his foot to 'Anarchy in the UK'), and they don't really know each other except through us, anyway, they ended up discussing football, music, the telly, all the things we usually talk about together. Except sitting there, they looked like the cast of *Cocoon*. Grey. Spent. We sort of realised what this meant collectively, the horror of it seeping over us like graveyard air. We put down our pints (well they did, I put down my Britvic), and walked out, shocked, as if we'd been given six weeks to live from the doctor. And Falkirk never seemed so dead and wasted and dustbin-lid grey as it did then.

My brother Dek in London. The Las Vegas-like vista from his window and beautiful, intelligent *Cosmopolitan* models in every elevator, in every restaurant, while

We. Are parked. Outside The Big Bar.

Dolby turns to me. His eyes are clear and hard. He jabs a finger at the pensioners. 'I swear that'll never be me. Shoot me if that's ever me.'

'Ah'll shoot ye,' Frannie muses, his fingers making a gun shape, 'Say the word.'

(amber) AZAD video on my left hand side, Tom Hanks grinning cheesy (I've been told I look like him) (*and* the wee poofy guy out *The Breakfast Club*), becoming elongated as Dolby starts (green) to gather speed and unfold away from the traffic lights behind us and the old bastards who yell incoherently at the noise from our getaway across the skin of Central Scotland making Frannie shout 'Fuckchoo, man!' like Al Pacino in *Scarface* (or *Carlito's Way* or *Serpico*, it doesn't make much difference) as we hit the open road like a snake attacking a rat, fangs glinting, shedding the sight of the old guys from the Big Bar like a skin cos

we

are

the

fucking

future

and the world is the striped legs of that wife in *Tom and Jerry* that I race past but I'm well aware, at this point, right now, that I have no

29

idea at all what it must be like having sex or being drunk, having sex *and* being drunk – the booze-soaked fumbles which everyone seems so icky about the next morning ('*Ye dinnae look at the mantelpiece when yer stokin the fire*' is Frannie's fat-bird escape clause) and I'm in no hurry, but Frannie, for some reason, has never let this lie, as if my virginity somehow emasculates *him*. 'Runt,' he turns to me, 'There's a night in Smith's comin up.' His fake Rolex glisters a dull silver. 'You gonnae start gettin pished wi the Lads soon?'

I imagine being strapped to a seat, having Superlager poured down my throat, and being made to sing 'Hello, Hello, We Are The Billy Boys,' like some grotesque *Clockwork Orange* experiment.

I imagine Mum is stumbling across a road in some pissy Scottish town. Paisley, Penicuik or Perth.

'Nope.'

'No even Bacardi Breezers?'

'No even Bacardi Breezers.'

'Fuckin toddlers can drink Bacardi Breezers, man. Dolby,' Frannie sighs. 'Tell him, he listens tae you. Although fuck knows how cos ye talk shite . . .'

Dolby grimaces, as if being told a favourite son is gay (which I'm *not*), and I resent his tone (a bit) when he sighs:

'Are ye sayin ye'll *never* drink?'

'Never,' I insist.

'*Never?*'

'Never!' I repeat.

'Ye can never say never.'

'Never! Never! Never Ah say!'

'Why?'

No.

I'm not going to tell them about Mum. It's none of their business. But I might tell Dolby about the awful sound of that first glug of vodka, those drugged, slurred maternal words, the day she left, and I came home from school to find

But I'm not telling Frannie or Brian. Those bastards would just tell me to grow up, I know they would, they would say:

'Alvin, you truly are a poof.'

'Aye whatever, Fran.'

Belinda rolls on. The world rolls under her. Sometimes the sky is the colour of tears, the sound of air broken only by Frannie coughing, and I'm not a poof. I just don't shag. I don't see any reason for it. Shagging seems like something elephants should do, not people, so I just pick up

the copy of *FHM* in the back seat, next to *Autotrader* (Dolby has ringed a Renault Megane, yeah right), flick through moodily, scan the interview with crap Bond girl Denise Richards, as Belinda curves into Stenhousemuir, purring gently, as Frannie spots the girl – 'Queen Amidala' – that Brian claims to have shagged at the back of the Maniqui last Christmas (still annoyingly stunning). They list drinks I might actually like, while I look at Denise Richards posing naked with a snake beneath the words EDEN BETTER THAN THE REAL THING and the Lads start pissing themselves at a vision of me wandering the pub, gassed on lager-shandy, beerily asking girls what their favourite Narnia books are, but I don't care, so instead Dolby starts rhapsodying about the new Clive Barker novel as Belinda floats across a ri

se before Laurieston (Frannie has covered his face with the *Rangers News* in boredom) and Dolby thinks it is, but I know it isn't, a sequel to *Weaveworld*.

'How did the boy Barker write *Weaveworld*?' he gasps. 'Imagine havin brought somethin like that intae the world. Imagine bein, like, Whitsherface K. Rowling! Or the guys that directed *The Matrix*?'

'I totally agree,' I say, totally agreeing (although Dolby said 'matrix', rather than '*may*trix', and I decide not to correct him, cos the first time I saw the poster I said 'matrix', until Doc at school, who can be a bit like that pedantic pony-tailed comics guy out *The Simpsons*, pointed out it's '*may* trix', and he's right – in the film Keanu definitely says '*may* trix'). 'Why dae somethin if it's no a masterpiece? Why live if ye dinnae want tae change the world? If yer gonnae make a movie, it should be *The Matrix*. If yer gonnae record an album, make it *Dark Side of the Moon*. If yer gonnae write a book, write *Harry Potter and the Sorceror's Stone*.'

'If yer gonnae talk shite,' says Frannie indignantly, 'It should be diarrhoea. Whit the fuck are yese on about?'

'It's *Philosopher's Stone*,' says Dolby.

'It's *Sorceror's Stone*,' I correct him.

'Don't fuck wi me, Runt, it's *Philosopher's Stone*.'

'Anyway listen,' I say, suddenly passionate, '*We* should dae somethin! We should write a film . . . or form a band . . . or go tae Ibiza . . . or drive roon America.' In our future, I see a bold 'I' emblazoned across the sky. A powering into the fray. A fist thrust into the buzz and crackle. Weakness is not permitted. Pain is discarded like litter by the roadside, as we speed forth, we speed forth, we speed forth and multiply. *We* are the kings of our own world, and nobody, I realise, is listening to me. Frannie asks if anyone's seen the size of Brian's nipples.

'Ah have,' says Dolby, 'An they're *huge*!'

'Like plates!' Frannie agrees.

They are very much the nipples of a pregnant woman. I'd often wondered why Brian never took off his top when he was sunbathing, until Frannie told me those nipples don't go *at all* with his Dirty Harry image, and soon we're singing another spontaneous verse of 'Born To Run' (like cats injected by testosterone by a med-student who missed the class on 'Injection Procedure') and as Frannie opens the sunroof to belt out the chorus, Dolby asks me:

'Alvin, whit d'ye think ae the name Uriel?'

'As in the angel?'

Dolby has a thing about angels. Frannie has a thing about Ally McCoist, Brian has a thing about Clint Eastwood. Dolby has a thing about angels. Especially archangels. His bedroom's a weird fucking sight, I tell you: Playboy bunnies, Lee Marvin, *South Park*, and a huge print of the angel Gabriel bearing the words, '*Let there be light . . .*' This from the man who calls me poof.

Actually, the picture isn't there any more. Not since Brian drew a speech-bubble on it saying: '*No that's God, he just likes to pretend he's Frannie.*'

'As in the angel.'

'Hadn't really thought about it,' I shrug, 'I always preferred Raphael.'

'And all the other Turtles,' Frannie moans. Angels, alternate worlds, things that go bump in the night: not Frannie's scene. His idea of fantasy, he told me, is a bed, a line of checkout girls, and a Rangers video playing in the corner. The nine-in-a-row one preferably.

'Uriel,' Dolby raptures, gazing at himself in a mirror, wearing a silken kimono, a flute of Absolut Vodka held in a manicured hand, simpering about like the killer in *Silence of the Lambs*. '*Uriel,*' he says again.

'Sounds like a fuckin washing-powder,' Frannie grunts. In his head, even now, he's probably kicking a Sharon out of bed as a Tracy gets in, as Rangers secure their ninth title on the trot.

'Cos,' Dolby murmurs, fiddling with the volume as if he doesn't actually want to us to hear him say:

'Ah'm thinkin ae changin ma name.'

Silence in the car. Damon All-Bran singing, '. . . *love's the greatest thing.*' A slight bum-bump as Belinda flattens the corpse of a cat.

Frannie says:

'Tae whit?'

'Forget it.'

'Tae Uriel?' The corners of Frannie's mouth start rising. 'Or Persil? Or Radion?'

'Ah kent *you* widnae understand, ya dull fuck!' Dolby broods, 'Ah just happen tae like the name—'

'Uriel,' Frannie finishes his sentence, sniggering. 'What about, em, *Muriel*? Or *Urinal*?' and I can see him revisiting this in the queue for Rosie's already. '*Awright ladies, huv you met ma friend Urinal? Ach, he always seems to be pished!*' that sort of thing.

Dolby's idea isn't as unexpected as you might think. You'll be browsing the Sci-Fi/Fantasy section in WH Smith when he'll suddenly exclaim, 'D'ye no think if ye had, like, *pink eyes*, the women would totally go for you!' Or be paying for petrol in some rural backwater and he'll whisper, 'Ye ken these places often have strong werewolf legends,' and look about, warily, almost praying for things lurking in the bushes to spring forth and transform him and

It's a lot to do with why I like him. To be honest. I recognise that need.

Dad and Mum screaming at each other – I must have been only about six – the walls ringing with their spite, and Dek ushering me upstairs to watch *Spider-Man* cartoons, and while the air was pierced with accusations ('Did ye drink it? That's aw Ah want tae know. *Did ye fuckin drink it?*'), I'd imagine myself above the Manhattan skyline, web-slinging, the air soaring through my ears.

I can't remember if he punched her or not. Sometimes she would hit herself and claim it was him.

It's definitely *Sorceror's Stone*.

'Aye awright Fran,' Dolby's muttering, his skin starting to hiss with the Uriel-ribbing. 'Anyway, who's this *Connor* cunt, Alvin?'

'Um . . .' I tell Dolby about the antagonism that goes back between Connor Livingstone and me since I beat him in an English test in first-year (I could always think up better metaphors . . . I was a metaphor factory) and not just that, him and his club of rich acolytes, his advantages, how he claims to have tried charlie ('Charlie fuckin who?' says Fran), his working Mum (Strathclyde University), his working Dad (Chartered Accountant), his entirely, as it happens, working fucking family. Dolby pauses to consider this, his hands casual on Belinda's wheel. 'What you wanna do' – he starts mimicking Harvey Keitel in *Reservoir Dogs* – 'is break that sonofabitch in two.'

'Naw, seriously.'

'Seriously?'

'Aye.'

The car screeches to a halt.

Outside Tyra Mackenzie's house.

Her door has frosted glass panels. Marigolds, tulips, chrysanthemums round it. The number **9** is in the centre of the door in bright, untarnished gold.

'Ally McCoist's shirt number,' Frannie breathes. '*It's a sign.*'

Now this is some shit. My Dad has a great story of how he met my Mum. It was at Oil Can Harry's (later The Maniqui, presently Storm – from punk to disco to *The X-Men*) which according to him was the best punk venue in Scotland. I still have visions of motorways clogged by youths pierced with safety-pins, desperately trying to get to Falkirk to see the Drunk Fuckpigs or something. Anyway, he told me and Dek this story, out of the blue, on a family holiday to Butlins. We were perched on a rock on Irvine Beach or Girvan Beach or wherever, surrounded by greetin weans, and he tells us how he saw Mum for the first time. 'A vision, she wis. Green eyeshadow. Blue hair. She wis wearin this New York Dolls t-shirt. Ah mean, the New York Dolls! No even the Pistols or the Clash. Classy . . .' He sighed. The waves crashed against the beach in doomed, grey battalions. A child's name was eradicated by the tide. It was getting cold. Me and Dek kept glancing at each other, awkwardly. 'Ah could see this other guy gettin

35

ready tae ask her tae dance, and he could see me thinkin the same thing. The two ae us went for her at the same time. Some skinheid battered intae the poor fella an knocked him ower, so Ah reached her first.' He beamed proudly. It all sounded a bit too *Back To The Future* to me. 'Just think,' he said, and this was the chilling part, 'if it wisnae for that other guy, you pair widnae be here.'

There you go. Born of the failure of some pissed skinhead.

I have to be able to scare my own son shitless like this. I have to sit him on a rock in the middle of Irvine or Girvan Beach and say, '*If ma mates had never parked ootside yer Mum's door that night . . .*' and make him realise that through these accidents are fucked-up teenagers made.

Dolby and Frannie's telekinetic stares try to push me from the car, up the path. 'No!' I repeat (thinking

Tyra Mackenzie!) as Karaoke Colin starts murdering 'Sweet Caroline' again and Dolby's asking, 'How wid this Connor react tae you walkin the corridor wi *that*?' He points to the upstairs window, where Tyra is leaning to water the flowers in her window-box. I duck out of sight. 'Nae way,' I stress, my heart starting to retch at the thought, but strangely in love with it. 'Ah'm *no* makin a fool ae myself ('*Hauns . . .*' Frannie croons) jist for *your* entertainment!' 'Alvino,' Dolby says. 'How wid he react?' 'Naw.' ('. . . *touchin hauns . . .*') 'How would *you* react then?' 'Um . . . well,' I sigh, 'mibbe be a bit . . . envious.' '*Env*ious!' Dolby rolls the word around his mouth, savouring its quality ('. . . *reachin oot . . .*'), 'Shut the fuck up, Frannie. So ye gonnae go tae the door or no?' 'No!' 'Are ye a pussy?' 'Whit?' 'Are ye a pussy or a Lad?' 'Ah I'm a . . . pussy.' ('. . . *touchin me . . .*') 'Meow.' ('. . . *touch-in yooouu . . .*!')

'Frannie, *gie it a fuckin rest, eh*!'

'SWEET CAROLINE! DI-DEH-DEH-DEH! GID TIMES NEVER SEEMED SAE GOO–'

Dolby clamps his hand over Frannie's mouth.

'Alvin,' he urges, 'don't be a runt all your life.'

And I think:

I'm taking advice from someone who wants to be called Uriel?

But these guys have done it. Lived it. I've had no Queen Amidala round the back of The Maniqui, no Elaine Section Manager propped against the tins of baked-beans in the Tesco's stock-room.

Belinda chugs, quietly listening, and it's almost her I feel I cannot let down. Not the Lads (though I look forward, thank-you-very-fucking-much, to my promotion from Runt), not even myself, really. Belinda's the closest I've ever been to something bearing a woman's name. Without her I would still be staring from my bedroom window at drizzly Hallglen roofs and fridges dumped in back-gardens, softly mumbling along to 'Comfortably Numb'. Yet here I am, outside Tyra Mackenzie's house, heart performing mad choreography, the girl herself, perhaps, dreaming *right now* of a knight who will ride along in a shiny steed to save her from her ivory tower. 'Okay boys,' I bre

athe deeply, thinking about my parents' eyes meeting across a room of headbanging bodies, and say

'Ah'm gonnae fuckin dae it!'

Heddy-haw! explodes in the car like a flare. They start shaking my hand, slapping my back, as if me and Tyra are already married and the birth of our beautiful baby boy announced in the Society press. 'There's a good runt!/Gaun the wee man!/Ye'll make a Bluenose yet!' and all that carry-on.

I can, I will, be King of My Own World.

'For Belinda!' Dolby toasts, and we each raise our cans – Sprite, Irn-Bru, Cherry-Coke – meeting with a metallic chink and a ripple of laughter in the middle and it's a great moment, and already I envisage us leaning back by the fire in Smith's, like captains of industry, puffing cigar-smoke and reminiscing about the time the bold Alvino won the hand of Falkirk's fairest. Brian will arrest my shoulder with a huge palm and boom, 'Bloody good show, old chap!' like in *Titanic*

and they will
     boot me from the car and drive off.

     Oh.

     Fuck.

     I look up and down the road. Inhale fumes of wealth. Occasionally,
when the wind is blowing in the right direction, these fumes waft
through Hallglen like royalty. Peasants standing on their tiptoes at the
front door and sniffing it, dreaming. Then going off and building
patios, installing satellite-dishes, in imitation of the gods.
     Here we have the original, the transcendental blueprint for every
working-class dream. Even the grass is different, the blades singular,
defined, stretching upwards on toned green bodies.
     The grass in Hallglen looks like it's stoned.
     Windows clean and lemon-fresh. Cars smooth and sleek and
parked even as place-mats. I feel like a monkey at a Darwin lecture.
     My fellow primates, in a car that looks like it's slept with half the
town. They make intercourse gestures at me through a fly-encrusted
window. Before me, the house of Tyra Mary-Louise (I saw the
register) Mackenzie. A place that has cultivated beauty. *Top Gun*
taking off in my head again, the Lads watching me from the sidelines,
Goose, Ice-Man, '*Okay Mav, let's turn and burn!*' I
     open the gate. It doesn't even squeak. Climb
     the steps, firm and deliberate, trying desperately to imagine I am
Very Very Sexy. The front door. Her second name: romantic handwriting on a gold plate. The way she runs her fingers through her hair,
her arm linked with mine, and everyone in the school watching us
kiss, stars touching, envious, my exaltation to the Michael Hutchence
of Falkirk High, the Lads applauding, hang
ing on my every description of her light bob

bing breasts, and from Belinda parked
at the end of the street I hear Sha
nia Twain moan man I feel like
a woman and as The Cruiser
smirks in my head and
the door opens I
get sudden insp
iration and
sing:

   'You've lost that lov-in feeling! *Who-oah that*

The old woman's mouth purses into an odd shape. Her ivory-white
knuckles press the head of her walking-stick and she stares.

   I just stutter, shutting down like machinery
and say
and say
'Um . . .
'I'm . . .
'from the . . .
'Save the Kids . . .
'Trust.'

She smiles toothily, her eyes shiny and white as pearls. Her lips go
'Ooooh!' and her fingers make a pincer-shape, scrabbling at the coins
in her purse. I glance round, desperate for an escape route, refusing to
believe I let Ally McCoist's shirt-number talk me into this. 'So *nice* of
young men to be involved with charity,' she's saying. 'Not like those
louts that tear up and down this street blasting that awful *music*.'

   At the end of the street the Lads start flicking me the tongue,
making me think

       what an excellent day for an exorcism

39

'Indeed,' I croak, holding out my hand to accept her change, 'It's thoroughly . . . um, *rewarding.*' I say 'rewarding' like it should have a question-mark on the end. The old lady's nodding thoughtfully, but I'm trying to see beyond her into Tyra's house. 'I hope to go to Sudesh . . . er, Saddam . . . to, um . . .' The hallway has a lovely terracotta floor. The names DUKE ELLINGTON and CHARLIE 'THE BIRD' PARKER are in framed glass. Tyra's Dad must be a boxing fan. Saxophone music floats with the motes of dust in the soft light and I can see plants. There have been no plants in my house since

'To what?'

'Sorry?'

The grandmother is smiling beatifically at me. I keep expecting her to say *c'mere an gie yer aul Gran a kiss*! the way mine does, but she chimes instead, 'You're going to Sudan to what, may I ask?'

'To feed . . . um,' I fluster, '. . . the world.'

She starts making more 'ooh!' noises, doing strange things with her cheeks, and though she reminds me of something horrible from a Roald Dahl story, it's not this that suddenly makes me stiffen, makes my arse-cheeks clench.

Tyra's Gucci shoes have stepped into view.

'Who is it, Gran?' she calls lightly, from the top of the stairs, and as I grasp at her change, the old bag

draws her hand back.

She switches, at the most inopportune time, from middle-class do-gooder helping out the needy, to middle-class miser being ripped off by scum.

'Sorry, I forgot to ask,' she grimaces, ice forming in her expression, 'You *do* have a form of identification?'

A sick feeling expands in my stomach as Tyra descends the stairs, poised and glamorous ('Whit'd ye say, sorry?'). The sheer of her ankle. The brief, hesitant stem of her leg. 'Gran?' she calls again, a film heroine rising from bed, 'Who is it?'

'You see it *has* been known for bogus operators to prey on areas of this sort,' the woman laughs patiently, not patiently at all. 'You *do* have identification, young man?'

(I fumble numbly in my pocket) Tyra's

waist! her

silken torso! Oh shit.

sashaying down the stairs like a phantom, her Basingeresque softness, her hand smoothing the blonde wood of the banister, my eyes sliding up her arm, her neck, her

'Alvin?'

'Tyra!'

'What are you doing here?' Tyra raises a quizzical eyebrow.

Her Gran turns to her, appalled. 'Do you know this young man?'

Tyra nods. She nods the way she writes, blinks, breathes, walks the corridor. Every movement is like the page of a magazine being turned by a breeze.

'Of course I know him. Alvin's in my English class.' The way she says *English*: like clear, clean glass. Oh! But the Gran turns to me. This news is grim. I am no longer some passing urchin. My germs and I are in daily proximity to her grand-daughter. She glares, like Brian spotting a Tim standing near the European Cup. I offer a cute expression that tries to say '*lil ole me*?' or something, but I'd be as well chatting up a squaddie with my what's-your-favourite-Narnia-book? line. No money so far, and certainly no grand-daughter.

'So what are you up to?' says Tyra (I can't look at her without thinking of the word Timotei), 'Are you collecting for charity?'

'Yes!' I beam, frozen, 'The Save the Kids Foundation!'

'Trust,' her Gran corrects me.

'Trust,' I smile. 'I'm going to Saddam.'

'Sudan?'

'Sudan.'

41

'That's good.'

We all nod. Tyra's eyebrows go up, then down. The absence of sudden killer meteorites in Central Scotland is a fresh concern to me. It's definitely *Sorceror's Stone,* is all I can think, and I repeat it, desperate. It's definitely *Sorceror's Stone.*

'I'm still waiting for identification, young man.'

'Oh Gran,' Tyra moans, 'It's just Alvin. Isn't it, Alvin? Isn't it just you?'

I smile, aiming for *Cosmopolitan, coming across more like Razzle.* But the *just* has done things to me. I am not Alvin; I am *just* Alvin. Threatless. Mystery-less. My manhood severed with one quick *just.*

'I can vouch for him.' She turns to me. 'It's *great* what you're doing for charity. Not many of the boys at our school have that much heart.'

If only you knew . . .

'Look.' The Gran is regretting her harshness. 'I *am* sorry. It's just that one has to be careful. I've seen people casing this property. There was an odd young man here two nights ago, staring at—'

'Yes!' I change the subject at the speed of light, '*Really* must go, Tyra! You know how it is. Lots of disadvantaged babies to feed!'

> she's show-showing it off then
> the glitter in her lovely

and as I clamber back into Belinda, Frannie and Dolby are having a sigh-filled chat about Frannie's parents splitting up, their frowns eradicated once gear is shifted and Belinda is coaxed away towards a nearby Chinky. We buy Sweet and Sour Pork with the money Tyra's gran gave me. I feel a bit guilty that she thinks it's going to starving babies in Sudan. I'm trying to justify standing on Tyra's street corner for half an hour in the pouring rain the other night. I wasn't 'casing the property'. My personal stereo was broken and I was trying to fix it. Not *my* fault it happened to break down in front of

show-show-showing it off then!
and all the people shake their money in

her house. Frannie and Dolby making contented eating sounds. Frannie pausing to stare through the steamy windows. His Mum and Dad have been married for twenty years. The first Suede album is playing. Too young to remember the first Suede album coming out. 'Bloody poofs,' everyone said at the time (according to Brian, who thinks anyone with a lisp or a limp is a poof).

What I tell the Lads about Tyra isn't necessarily what happened. That's why they're quietly eating instead of driving me to a tattoo parlour to have me branded with a picture of Orville. I tell them that I asked Tyra to come to the pictures with me. They said, 'Which film?' 'Um, *American Psycho*,' I said. 'Romantic,' Dolby comments. 'Anyway, whit did she say?' I tell them she was obviously flattered to be asked, that it was a big decision, and that she was going to have think about it. Frannie put his hand on my shoulder, nodded his pride and said:

'Alvin, son, you are almost a Lad.'

I wish now I had asked her.

Anyway, it got them off my case, I was not called poof, and give me a few days and I'll even believe I've performed some feat of derring-do.

In reality, after I realised Tyra's Gran had seen me watching Tyra's window, I was in no state to ask anybody to the pictures. I asked Tyra if she'd read Stephen King's *Night Shift* collection. She looked at me oddly and said, no, she hadn't had that particular pleasure. I scanned about for something else to keep the moment from ending. Um, did she want to borrow *Dark Side of the Moon* at all? No. Well. Could she tell me if it's, um, if it's *Harry Potter and the Philosopher's Stone* or *Harry Potter and the Sorceror's Stone*?

In America it's *Sorceror's Stone*, she said blankly.

Oh, I said.

Our reporter made his excuses and left.

> oh dad
> she's
> driving me mad!
> come see

I once thought I'd do the son-ly thing and ask my Dad's advice about women.

'Dinnae worry,' he told me, 'Ye've plenty time tae play the field. Ah didnae meet yer Mum till Ah wis, oh, about sixteen.'

I'm fifteen.

The sun is going down and tomorrow it will come up.

I study the Lads, wondering how my life/opinions/hair will have changed by the time I reach the chronically knackered age of eighteen. Dolby's mobile beeps. The theme tune to *Close Encounters of the Third Kind*. He answers it – 'hmp?' – and talks to someone called Darren about whirlpool fittings. The cape of night begins smothering the town. Dolby snaps shut his mobile, restlessly engages Belinda's engine (because Dolby, unlike the other two, has *never* liked talking about work) (outside of work), pulls away from the lay-by where my Sudan/Sudesh/Saddam trip has been devoured and we debate which members of Queen we would be if we were Queen (Frannie is Freddie Mercury, Brian is Roger Taylor, Dolby is Brian May, I'm the one that nobody remembers) and

that night I dream I'm in *The Blair Witch Project*.

My vision is shaky, dark, low-budget. Me, Dolby, Fran, Brian Mann, camped in the Callendar Woods with bottles of Becks for rations. Frannie wielding his camera, going, 'Pout, baby, pout!' and we're having an outrageous laugh.

But then there's this awful moaning. And the wind rises. And the leaves start blinking across the forest floor. Dolby and Fran's eyes, clear, stark white in the dark. They point to the space behind my shoulder, and Fran drops the camera. It whirs in the still, damp leaves. I start to turn, the wind picking its claws clean on my skin, and see

her

dangling from a tree. Danc

ing like a doll on a child's mobile. Her bare feet flecked with mud. This is the Blair Witch – I know it's her. Except it's not. It's someone else. Someone terrorising me from the fringes of my mind. The creak of the rope taut on the tree as the body turns, slowly, terribly. The fear rising to my throat as I become powerless to scream against seeing her

and

we

're so pretty, oh so pretty
Va-cant!

'Dad!' I roar, turning over in bed and sealing the Sex Pistols from my ears, 'Keep it doon for fuck's sake!'

I fall from bed, thump uselessly onto the floor. Sleep deprivation. Didn't they use that to torture witches? The Blair Witch? The image from my dream shivers back, but now I am lying on a threadbare mat where the dog used to piss, when he was alive. When Mum used to feed him. My dream lingers, then fades, pulsing into the distance.

Downstairs I think I can hear Dad crying, but it could be the whine of the back door as he opens it, or the muted whistle of the kettle. If it's Dad, I am not going to him, not after his last performance, when a *Trisha* special – 'Women Who Leave' – had him rolling on the floor like a baby.

I pull open my eyes, trying to shake the Blair Witch from my head. Stuff accumulated on my bedside cabinet, like an EC trash mountain or an art-project. Darth Vader alarm-clock. A fossil shark's tooth, 30 million years old (from a vending machine in Burntisland). Change from the fags I bought Dad last night, which he smoked nervously all through *The Runaway Bride*. A copy of Stephen King's *Misery*, its spine cracked and veined and open at the bit with the axe and the blow-torch. The poems of W. B. Yeats, the margins unwritten in. Things fall apart, the centre does not hold, yeah yeah, whatever. A biography of Billy Connolly that Brian keeps demanding back, even though I borrowed it from Frannie. Dad still crying downstairs and *Scotland's brilllliant*! The Big Yin grins.

On the bus to school, I realise I haven't done my English essay (again), though there are reasons for this: mainly Frannie's birthday and Dolby paying for fish-suppers, which we sucked up greedily in Belinda, parked round the back of the Howgate Shopping Centre. Dek has sent another postcard from London, his handwriting shaky, which I am reading, listening to the soundtrack to *E.T.* on my personal stereo (really good and not as slushy as it sounds in the film) and a second-year at the back throws a ball of paper which bounces off my head and I turn and give my best Brian Mann glare, but the motley bunch of gremlins just laugh, all teeth and acne and exuding a sort of *Grange Hill*-style menace, so I move up to the top deck where Falkirk is flattened beneath my power.

We pass the infirmary where I was born. The school bus passes this infirmary every day. Every day I'm reminded of my own unremarkable position in the world. The building is green and white and doesn't look anything special either and nurses come and go, unaware that I was carried there fifteen years ago and surely (perhaps? possibly?) I am worth more than this? I must be. Does Dolby know

the release date for the *Lord of the Rings* movie, since this will
    Hospital. Mum being wheeled in. Blood.
  alleviate our disappointment that James Cameron never got round
to making *Spider-Man*, a disappointment which gets heavier
  and heavier.
  and heavier.
Kids on the bus are screaming, stamping, rioting – lacquered
gently by the music from *E.T.* Third-year boys throw punches to the
sound of Elliot's flying bike. Falkirk walking by on its way to work,
its pavements grey, its buildings sunless, but its air filled for the
moment with strings rising towards the sky, and I reckon the world
might be easy to put right. Can't we plug it into the soundtrack
of happy movies and the homeless will find homes, mad
gunmen will pause on triggers, warring spouses will hold hands
and go to the window and see the moon eclipsed by the silhouette of
a bicycle?

how i wish

how i wish you were

the squeak of magic-marker down the bus window (KEEBO IS
GAY). Joints lit on the back-seat. I am surrounded by bubbles in a
lava pool. They suppurate, burst, without saying anything and I want
to rise from the ashes of my own ordinariness, *do* something in this
world that creeps silently away either side of my vision, be alive,
vibrant, but
  I remember how huge that map looked. The one that Dad placed
in front of me when I was little. Those infinite roads. The size of all of
those countries with fantastical names compared to tiny, shitty

Scotland

and I am Magneto in the *X-Men* movie and I can make the bus levitate and I can freak everyone out: girls' mouths twisting out of pretty shape, boys' eyes frightened as mice in a storm, all of Falkirk trembling before me as I bombard Connor Livingstone with a hail of paper-clips and Tyra pleads for me to stop and I show mercy (which she thinks is totally cool, because I don't have to do anything of the sort) and we have a coffee back at her place, to show her I'm still just a man.

The bus passes a woman in a bus-shelter. She's staring emptily. The rain drizzles down the shelter and the graffiti and across her slack, bored eyes. From here she looks a bit like Mum, a bit like Sissy Spacek in *Carrie*, but the bus passes before I can

approach Mrs Gibson's desk. The walk of shame! Presently no excuses are forming for why my essay isn't in, since I'd hoped she wouldn't ask, wouldn't give us the speech about how important our Highers are, how crucial the results will be for university admission, etc. etc. I don't belong at university. Surrounded by fifteen hundred Connor Livingstones? Brian's voice growls in my head like a rip-cord, reminding me what he, Frannie and Dolby used to do instead of homework:

'Dog it an go fuckin fishin!'

The rest of the class file out. Essays being left on the corner of the table. Tyra places hers respectfully down, slings her Prada bag onto her shoulder, makes quick eye-contact with me before angels start singing 'With or Without You' (the Popmart remix). I follow her, desperate to explain my appearance at her door the other night, but Gibson's voice hauls me back.

'Alvin, where's your essay?'

'Miss?'

She is leafing through the manuscripts, secretary-cool.

'I don't see your homework here . . . have you handed it in?'

48

'Um . . .'

I drift to the desk and pretend to help her look for it (making silent Muttley noises), but when I see the essay on top – word-processed, headed ©**Connor J. Livingstone** – I step defiantly back, disassociating myself from the white-collarness of it all. It is time to make a stand against The System!

'Naw Miss, Ah huvnae done it!' I state proudly, raising myself to my full five-foot four, 'Ah think Ah left it in ma blazer, which ma Dad um . . . washed.'

Gibson shakes her head. Folds her arms. Looks at me like I'm a new puppy, and it's Christmas Day and everything, but I can't keep pissing on the kitchen floor like this. I know what she's going to say. Instead of listening, some part of me starts evaluating *The Silence of the Lambs* against *Se7en* (result: that head in the box wins it every time). Another part of me is thinking about the woman standing in the bus shelter this morning, lonely and cold. A bit like Carrie. A bit like Mum.

'I had this same trouble with your brother Derek,' Mrs Gibson says, then pauses, purely for dramatic effect . . .

'He told me about your family, Alvin.'

Mrs Gibson holds my eye the way a lioness carries one of her cubs. Sympathetic. Almost tender. But letting me know exactly who's in charge here.

'Do you want to tell me why your work is continually late?'
I sigh.

Things escape in the sigh, which I can't chase and put back in.

On the blackboard is written a quotation from T. S. Eliot:

HUMANKIND CANNOT BEAR VERY MUCH REALITY

'Is this when ye tell me Ah'm university material again?'
'Yes.'

I run my hand through my hair, but it gets caught in all the gel.
'Ah dinnae want tae go tae university.'

'Well, I'm sorry to hear that.' She is looking at the floor,
disappointed. 'Can I ask why?' Yeah, she can ask, but what do I
tell her? The Lads, and how they won't be there? Connor Livingstone,
and how he probably fucking will? Since the time that Dek would
have had this talk with Mrs Gibson, Dad has gotten a lot worse.

I drift to the window, lean my forehead against it so that a cold
glass circle forms. Outside in the quad, TIMBERLAND fights
VERSACE, leaving dirty marks, and TIMBERLAND laughs and
VERSACE rages at the sight of herself and Tyra walks between these
warring masses like a ghost. Mobile phones ring all over the quad, a
dreamy processional anthem for her, and her hand sweeps through
her blonde tresses.

i can't live

with or without

'Miss.' My breath mists up the window, obscuring Tyra and the
sweep of her world in a single desolate puff. The words will not come.
I clench my fist and close my eyes but the pain does not go away. And
never will.

'Miss, I'm finding things . . . difficult . . .'

as Belinda's brakes squeal across the gravel, then silence.

Reedy crickets. The whole of Falkirk lit up in the valley below like
something from a Spielberg movie. Dolby going off on some theory
about the way the four of us, Lads, fit together, what we're doing here
on Planet Earth, all that post-laugh stuff. He's playing The Eagles,
with their tequila sunrises and hotel californias and tourist-trap
American shit that dull punters like us just lap up.

Central Scotland is glittering. A black sea filled with phosphorescent fish. The densest shoal is Grangemouth Oil Refinery. My Dad used to work in Grangemouth (when he could find work) and I probably will too, trudging through every shift, twelve hours a day, seven days a week, but tonight it looks like a constellation, a shimmering barrier reef. The mood in the car glides like a ray, but the sky is black and gaping as the mouth of a prehistoric shark, waiting to consume us all, Falkirk, Belinda, *The Very Best of The Eagles*. Me and Dolby covering all the subjects we can't when Frannie and Brian are there (who usually hijack the conversation back to Ibrox):

'Is there anything bigger than infinity?'

'Are mobile phones a government conspiracy?'

'Are the aliens in *Invasion of the Body Snatchers* really so evil?'

'I read somewhere that the aliens are supposed to, like, symbolise The Communards.'

'The Commun*ists*!'

Dolby's a closet philosopher. And very good at Physics. A clever guy. He's the only person I know who reads page two of the *Daily Record*, the bit with all the politics on it. He'll say things that make the other two snigger, glance at each other, go back to discussing the Old Firm semi-final (so long as Celtic didn't win it) but sometimes he stops me in my tracks, translating Discovery Channel documentaries into my language and crystallising a moment with the philosophical words of Jean-Luc Picard from the Starship Enterprise.

Frannie told me once that Dolby had the chance to go to Stirling Uni after school, but never took it. I ask him why.

Dolby shrugs, looks out the window, fiddles absently with the graphic-equaliser when 'Hotel California' starts.

But Frannie told me the answer. Dolby had dogged school whenever Frannie and Brian had dogged it, forgot his homework when Frannie and Brian forgot theirs, and said:

'Ye dinnae dump yer mates.'

End of argument. He opens another can of Diet Irn-Bru and chugs sugar-free girders. 'Jesus,' he gasps, 'Ah wish The Eagles wid go back on tour.'

And this is the sound of Dolby handing in his permanent registration for the University of Life.

'Anyway, better this than studyin,' he intones. Slurps. Stares at the black maw of the Central Scotland sky.

'Yup.'

'Only tossers an posh fuckers at university.'

'Yup.'

Frannie joined Tesco, became cock-of-the-walk in Stock Control. Brian worked behind the bar in Smith's, between filling in forms for his dream emigration to California. Dolby took the job in Whirlpools Direct, installing jacuzzis in homes he'll never get close to owning and

Now he has to know about shower-heads and delivery dates.

Not Physics.

Or *Star Trek*.

'But yer only nineteen,' I point out, 'Ye can still go tae college.'

He just looks at me. As if I'm offering cash to betray a close family member.

'Ye dinnae. Dump. Yer mates.'

And I don't like the way he says 'mates'. As if it's some kind of accusation.

So I divert him back to the old debate about the Irn-Bru can on the dashboard and Dolby patiently takes me through it again and his *Ghost Rider* t-shirt glows on his chest like E.T. when he's hurt or

. . . Ell-i-ot

'The Irn-Bru is in the car,' he explains, Open University-toned, juxtaposing fizzy juice with distance over time or something. 'An if the car's daein sixty-six miles per hour, that means the Irn-Bru must be daein sixty-six miles per hour. Agreed?'

'Agreed,' I mumble, scrutinising the outside of the can. I am going to understand the mystery of its descent. I am going to *know* how an object can drop in the front seat of a moving car and not land in the back seat but like the crap bit in every episode of *Friends*, soon I'm saying:

'You three are all Ah've got, man.'

Actually I try to say this, but I can't. These things dare not speak their name in Scotland. Dolby talks rationally about Einstein and how juvenile Ibiza is (he was supposed to go last year, but couldn't afford it), but I can see something in him too, trying to wrench its way out, like an alien in a sci-fi movie taking over the host. He eyeballs the landscape in front of us, pretty and glittering tonight but which tomorrow will look just like Falkirk again (like shagging Liz Hurley and waking up with Margaret Thatcher) and the Irn-Bru can still sits there, still unexplained, still haunting me with its physics and my place in the grand scheme of the Falkirk boyracer circuit.

'See . . .' he tries to explain, 'It's like . . . each ae us can be seen, right, in the sort ae movies we like.'

'How?'

'Think aboot whit happens when we hire a video.'

'Fuck aye.' There was one night when Frannie and Brian had a Mexican stand-off about whether we should rent *Armageddon* or *There's Something About Mary*. Neither of them would budge. 'Frannie eywis wants a comedy,' I grumble, 'And Brian eywis wants an action movie.'

'They want tae see themselves reflected in the world.'

'But you like sci-fi movies,' I point out. 'Does that no make you a bit ae a nerd?'

'A dreamer,' he corrects me. 'Aw in the terminology.'

'So if ma favourite movie's *Jaws*, whit does that make me?'

'A nerd. But the point is . . .'

53

And though he tells me what the point is, I can't quite grasp it. It's something to do with how a good video-shop should have comedy, action, sci-fi **and** *Jaws*, and that's why we work, and he elaborates this whole Stephen Hawking-style formula of group dynamics and opposing forces and the structure of friendships (yet still based, I think, on the video-shop analogy), and though I try to follow it, it just seems to come down to the fact that we're good as a foursome. We're right. We're fucking going places with *Going Places*. Palm Springs circa 2010: the four Lads in bermuda-shorts and girls in hula-skirts bringing phone calls from James Cameron, apologising for not doing the *Spider-Man* movie. So while Frannie sees himself unfolding in the strike-rate and punch-lines of Super Ally, Brian in the cigar and grimace of Clint Eastwood, and Dolby, watching the skies, I see myself in them.

and all of those roads, all of those futures, and this one useless, wafer-thin present which zips past fast blasting tunes uncool to the Connor Livingstones of this world, as we make the nights *ours*, every day wiping tables, stacking shelves, fitting whirlpools, studying for Higher exams worthwhile for the few desperate moments of escape at high-speed, the faster, the further away we drive, the more that parents, shite jobs, self-loathing, uneven Oasis albums recede into specks in the rear-view, meaning we can do anything, go anywhere, see anyone, *be* anyone in this pathetic little Scotland-or-something country. Like characters in a plotless novel, we race through night after night, story after story, film quote after film quote, eternity stretching before us like an open road, and *this* is the reason I gave Gibson for why my essays are late, cos you can check out any time you like but you can never leave.

'Whit d'ye suppose that song's aboot?' Dolby asks, finishing his Irn-Bru and starting to shift Belinda into gear.

'A hotel?' I shrug. 'In California?'

'Dick.'

We drive home. Back to Falkirk. Where Frannie and Brian are watching the World Cup qualifier in Smith's, their hands flailing at a near-miss. Elvis Presley singing, '*Oh I wish I was / In a land of cotton . . .*' and everyone in a huddle, joining in, delirious at Scotland managing to draw, a swelling shout, and it's a great feeling, and I spill my Cherry-Coke over Brian's new shirt and he doesn't even care but

Still.

It was the least exciting of all the roads we could have taken that night.

and Camelon, as anyone will tell you, is the Bosnia of Falkirk. Streets like grey labour. Chewing-gum accents and Danielles with their boyfriends and babies. The thousand-yard stares. Camelon's Hollywood Bowl, however, is the Narnia of Falkirk. Lights. Magic. Sound. Vision. U2 blasting out from all sides, and we four walk onstage – Bono, The Edge, Adam Clayton, Larry Mullen Jnr. – imagining women screaming and the stadium lights going down and a huge swell of sound charging towards us and

it's a beautiful day!

Dolby pays for the lanes. We scatter over to the pool-hall like pool balls, Brian trying to interrupt Frannie trying to interrupt him: 'Listen boys,' he warns, 'Ah'm no wantin nae carry-on the night. Ho! Yese listenin? We'll play a couple ae games ae pool, then Ah'll thrash San Fran on the lanes, then we'll go hame. That's it.' When there's money involved, which there is this evening, Brian takes things seriously seriously. 'Money won,' he reminds us, going all Paul Newman on our ass, 'is twice as sweet as money earned.' He and Frannie have a bet on tonight's bowling square-off. Brian reckons he's Champions League (even though the last time they played, Frannie beat him five games to three, then spent the rest of the evening singing Elton John songs at him for no other reason than the fact that Brian hates Elton John. The Mann was pissed then, of course. Which is why he was beaten. Of course.)

'Nae boozin this time,' he demands, the spirit of Elton creeping up on him, camply tinkling piano keys, 'Nae chattin up birds. An nae,' he repeats, '*Nae* fuckin film quotes!'

The minute 'Layla' comes on the jukebox, though, Dolby and Frannie start pinching each other's cheeks, hugging like the mob:

> we was wiseguys, goodfellas, like you'd say
> to someone: *you'll like this guy, he's one of us,*
> *he's a good fella* . . .

Brian slamming three balls in quick succession, aware of the attention we're drawing from Camelon weapons. He warns Frannie and Dolby to quit their Joe Pesci 'funny how?' routine, nodding to the glaring baseball-caps across the hall.

'Dose fucks?' Frannie dismisses them, 'Fuhget about it! Whatsamattawitchoo? Whatthefucksthemattawitchoo?'

'Quit it,' Brian mutters darkly, as if the raft of neon lights are hurting his eyes or he's fearing another night in the back-seat of Belinda, ground down by Frannie's a capella 'Rocket Man'. 'Ye playin this game or no?'

'Muddafuckin jew prick cocksucka . . .' Frannie lines up his shot in the style of Joe Pesci, swear-words tripping from his tongue. Frannie should really be an adjective. *Like you'd say to someone, you'll like this guy, he's one of us, he's Frannie.* We should all be adjectives. Film-critics should be able to discuss the new *X-Men* movie by musing, 'Well, it's very *Dolby*, isn't it?' Or Dougie Donnelly comment on the Old Firm game, 'It was a *Brian Mann* match for most of the first half.' Or U2 describe their new album as, 'Really, the

56

Franniest thing we've ever done.' And every living-room in every household in the land should know exactly what they mean. Otherwise, what's the point?

'Ball-bustin elephant-dicked asshole mutt!'

'Very good, Fran.' (growl)

'Who da fuck is dis prick!'

'Ah said gie it a rest.' (snarl)

'I oughta have ya whacked!'

Brian uncages himself on a line of balls; they ricochet with his business, and Frannie, here at his Franniest, leans to the girl sitting at the milk-shake counter. Weapon's-bird perm and tracksuit and trainers. 'Bet ye dinnae hear patter like oors very often,' he smooths.

'Naw,' she agrees. 'There's no that many dickheads come in here.'

Frannie laughs. And leaves her well alone. And we move over to the lanes: four adjectives with milkshakes and a gaggle of gangsters. Is this because Brian specified No Film Quotes? Bluenose-tight they may be, but Frannie can still wind Brian up like nobody else, like every time he's about to release the ball, Frannie goes: '*Muddafuckin asshole jerk*!' making it spin out of control towards the gutter. Brian can't retaliate when Frannie steps up because Brian can't impersonate worth a fuck (except Clint Eastwood, but that's only because he's silent and moody).

The-girl-who-called-Frannie-a-knob keeps drifting backwards and forwards, a phantom in Fila, glancing flirtatiously. Even with a bad, blonde dye-job, she's attractive in a skanky sort of way.

But then, here's me in a Meat Loaf t-shirt. Hardly Jean-Paul Gaultier.

Dolby rests his chin in his hand, tracking her with the precision of a rifle-ranger.

'Think she's interested?' I ask hopefully.

'Hmmmm,' he muses, narrowing his eyes suspiciously.

'Ball-bustin prick!' Frannie yells as Brian veers off again into the gutter (might as well be the next galaxy, considering how far he is from beating the Franman now, evidenced by his bullish neck filling with crimson, his fingers flexing, as Frannie coaxes more pins to the floor). Frannie grins smugly (this being a standing joke, in that Brian has the smuggest grin in Falkirk, but)

I feel damn fine tonight! Watching Frannie and Brian joust is like watching Little Richard fight Lennox Lewis. And I've barely thought about the shit going on at home, Dad's depression, Connor, Tyra, Dek, or F(uck) Scott Fitzgerald and my still-late essay, my Higher results, my future disappearing before me. But I am a long way from caring about those things. Why would I *possibly* want to stay in with the sound of sobbing from downstairs, a heart being continually broken, when I've got here my best mates, U2, Belinda parked outside and a road leading anywhere/everywhere/nowhere? Under a coruscation of neon tubes and MTV ads (how many kids in Scotland actually snowboard?) and the sound of bowling-balls hitting wood, teenage squealing, techno-techno-techno-techno, and Frannie doing DeNiro/Pacino/Brando, getting on everybody's nerves, I slink to the toilet. Halfway back, I realise I am walking behind the Fila girl. I would very much like to fila girl.

(pick a part that's new)

'Scuse me,' I cough, tapping her on the shoulder. She turns and frowns and is a meaner-looking chick than I first thought. Sort of like a female vampire in those old Hammer movies. In a track-suit.

'What?' she says, like the bottom note on a piano being struck.

'See ma mate ower there?'

(think of something cool, funny, Hollywood, Bono)

'He fancies you.'

She looks over. With all the interest of a cold plate of spaghetti watching an Open University lecture, she says:

'The knob?'

'Eh, naw. That's Frannie.'

58

She spies Brian and her face lights up. 'That good-lookin wan?'

'Naw. No him either.' (cold spaghetti again) 'The one sittin down.'

'Wi the *Riverdance* t-shirt on?'

'Aye.'

'An the Spider-Man badge?'

'He's got a Spider-Man badge!' I tut. 'Bastard.'

She extracts a long piece of gum from her mouth and snaps at it, like the crap shark in *Jaws IV*. 'Listen, Ah'm no meanin tae be cheeky or nuthin . . . But wan ae yese is wearing a *Riverdance* t-shirt, wan ae yese thinks he's Robbie Williams. An wan ae yese is, eh . . . *you*.'

I look at her.

I shrug.

'So ye comin over or not?'

Brian snorts (and I get the impression his game hasn't improved since I've gone. Frannie performing graceful pirouettes that culminate in a delicate smash of pins). 'That wis an awfy long pish for somebody wi such a wee dick.'

I grin his smug grin back at him.

'I – Mr Brian Mann – have been chatting up a *woman*.' I say the word *woman* as if it is the code-word which will reveal a cave-worth's of Ali Baba's treasure to them, but

'Whit's the score now?' Dolby asks. 'Five-one to the Franman,' Brian mutters, sending his ball on another lost cause. 'Heddy-*haw*!' Frannie roars, punching the air.

'Did naebody hear me?' I squeak. 'I've been . . . um . . . her . . . ken . . .'

There is a tap on my shoulder. I turn slowly. Facing me is a mug I recognise from the *Falkirk Herald*. The 'Round the Courts' section. His name is James Kotter – 'Kottsy' to his enemies (and beyond Camelon there are many) – and he has just tapped my shoulder. And his head resembles a bowling-ball. And he looks like a sports-shop doomed to walk the earth, brand names plastering his body like tattoos.

'Ken wha Ah'm ur?'

I nod like someone with a gun at their head.

'Well, see that lassie ower there?'

And I look over the simian rise of his shoulder to the track-suited hasper. Glaring malevolently. Returned to her village to alert the menfolk.

This is starting to remind me of a ritual very particular to Hallglen which starts, '*You swear at ma laddie . . . ?*'

'Aye.'

Kottsy unfolds his basketball-shaped arms and Olympic committees everywhere feel a tremor in the Force.

'That's ma burd.'

I nod again. And smile sort of weakly. And wonder if I should say something like, 'And, eh, a fine *burd* she is too.'

(Behind me I hear, 'Ah've won the bet, man, pay up.' 'Like fuck ye won the bet! You let Dolby take your third shot, which means ye *didnae* beat me on yer ain.' 'But Dolby didnae *hit* anythin, ya cheatin–')

(I *cannot* hear: 'Look! Alvin's in trouble! We must intervene!')

Kottsy gives me the once-over and I actually shiver. His last appearance in 'Round the Courts' was for an attack in a bowling-alley in Stirling.

With a bowling-ball.

'Cos she says ye tried tae feel her up, ya wee bastard.'

A reply which would be very *Frannie* would be, 'Aye, Ah was measuring her for a spare-tyre oan ma jeep.' A reply which would be very *Brian* would be a smack straight to his *Planet of the Apes*-type puss. But I have almost no Brian-esque or Frannerian qualities. And so the response is:

'Is that right?'

60

'Aye, that's fuckin right.'

'Is that right?'

The steel in Kottsy's eyes and the threat, taking off its jacket, in his voice, and the way he's positioning himself, shoulders thrust back, like Kong about to tackle the Empire State Building, tell me he hasn't come over to give me a warning. Inwardly, I throw a hand over my mouth and scream *Oh my God*!

While outwardly, I just keep saying:

'Is that right?'

'Yer a fuckin cunty-bawed wee snivellin knob, by the way.'

'Is that right?'

I have ice threading through my veins, and visions of Dad and my brother and the Lads weeping over my grave and swearing a pact that *Alvin's death must be avenged*! and so I keep saying

'Is that right?'

'Is that right?'

'Is that right?'

to everything, until he grabs me by the Meat Loaf t-shirt and roars, '*Aye it is fucking right!*' and when next I open my eyes I see:

1. Brian Mann and Kottsy in a whirlwind of fists and
2. A demonic host of Camelon weapons, leaping barriers and reaching into pockets and
3. Dolby gasping, stunned: '*Whit the fuck is this?*' and
4. The track-suited hasper screeching, '*You'll git kilt! You'll git kilt! You'll git fackin kiiiiiilt*!!!' and
5. A fist heading straight for my face and

in the car afterwards, we're fleeing! Frannie on the mobile, raving to some unseen pal while Bono goes, '*The real thing*! *The real thing*! *Even better than the real thing*!' the streetlights sliding up towards the top of the windscreen and away like plucked petals, and Dolby's hands locked on the steering-wheel, as he laughs, glances in the rear-view mirror at Brian and Frannie, their Rangers tops drenched in blood, Frannie's nose looking alien on his face, Brian with a cut on his forehead and blood running down in rivulets, soaking his clothes and making him look like the cover of *American Psycho*.

He is grinning wildly.

'Christ, we got hammered . . .' Dolby sniggers, and Brian stares at the char-black streets, lights, a *Falkirk Herald* board with something about a car-crash on the Braes.

'It's no so bad,' he murmurs.

He sounds almost wistful, as if inhaling the scent of a window-box in Kensington. His tongue licks blood from his upper lip, and an image flashes back to me of Brian and Kottsy locked in warfare, a storm erupting around them like Gandalf and Balrog in *Lord of the Rings*. The car-tyres screaming as we turn corners, waving at student nurses and Dolby plays the *Jurassic Park* soundtrack to calm us and described on the sheer glass of the windscreen Falkirk geometries turn, sharpen, the night receding to a pinpoint down the road, dinosaurs clothed in orchestral music, Rangers shirts made bloody, our guardian angels crowding the car pleading '*For God's sake, don't do this again*,' two refugees from *Reservoir Dogs* bleeding in the back seat, and like Lady Macbeth Brian keeps turning and re-turning his hands. Fascinated by how red they are.

'It's really no so bad . . .' he whispers, into the passing night, staring at that cooling red on his fingers. As if he's just played a concerto on a piano drenched in blood.

on the way to the hospital

we stop and talk to a hen-party. They are dolled up, vinyl-looking, hunting aimlessly for a party. Everyone, hunting aimlessly for a party. One of the girls leans in the window and whistles at Brian's crimson visage.

'Jesus Christ, whit happened tae you?'

62

'Painting,' he mutters, still delirious with adrenaline, 'Now fuck off.'

The least damaged of the four of us (me) arranges to meet the girls after we finish up at the infirmary. But they don't show, and we're not really bothered. Instead we take hold of the roads like Vikings taking England, singing 'Eye of the Tiger' as the fight becomes fabricated into mythical status, retold with ever-more incredible details. Brian emerges from the story with Kottsy, two of his mates, and three security-guards trying to wrestle his heaving form to the floor, and we convince ourselves that the wandering hen-party was attracted to our car by the masculine glamour we exude. I'm pretty sure we actually fought like water-balloons but when we start singing

> i love rock 'n'roll!
> so put another dime in the jukebox baby!

I realise this is the best time of my life.

'Thing is,' queries Frannie, 'How the fuck did it start?'

But nobody knows. And I'm not going to say anything. And in Belinda we zap through Falkirk and the sheer car-park spaces of our lives like a laser beam, listening to Guns n' Roses and *Tubular Bells*, the dimly-lit streets reeling and shifting with ballet-dancer grace to the sound of LA metal and the music to *The Exorcist* and so on and fantastic constantly-changing images appear (in that empty air that hangs above the road) then disperse like a burst soap-bubble, as Frannie and Dolby argue whether B&Q is a better shop than Texas, until Brian kicks sand on their fire, describing the recent Rangers win over Hibs in a voice that excludes all others, but planet earth is blue and there's nothing I can do, as Dolby's Adidas-clad toe stabs Belinda's accelerator and a mountainous rumble shudders up from her bonnet and Falkirk town centre swoops away behind us, the Global video-shop window screaming and the faces of Denzel

Washington, Madonna, Kate Winslet, like fly-posters whipped from walls by our passing and that feeling hits the four of us in the shoulder-blades as Guns n' Roses sing take me down to the paradise city where the grass is green and the girls are pretty and Frannie suddenly yelps

Heddy-haw!

and it doesn't get any better than this. Life as one fast rush of *Top of the Pops*, shops, the beep of Dolby's mobile that zips in thin lines back from the front seat where he is sifting through the CDs looking for a map for somewhere, anywhere we have the power to go tonight and the cells of my body are animal alive, singing, sharp as blades of

fourth gear

grass as Frannie goes, 'The Cruiser's best movie?' and titles bat about the car like dragonflies: *AFewGoodMenJerryMaguireCocktailBornOn TheFourthOfJuly InterviewWithTheVampireJerryMaguire* again but nobody says *Top*

fifth gear

Gun, until Brian says, 'Nobody said *Top Gun*!' and Frannie starts to tell us about

every

single

girl

on the check-outs he ever dreamed about sha

The pauses are fleeting.

Life lived at a breathless jet-pace, only for the moment/a split-second.

But then

You get older.

The rests are more frequent. Longer. The wallpaper fading,

64

becoming achingly bearable, until you

Come back from the fridge.

Sit down in front of the TV.

And realise your day is one long continuous pause. The world sounds like the hiss of television interference. The air has been exhausted by being breathed too often.

You've either forgotten how to move, or you can't be bothered, and so you just stay there. Hunting for your life down the back of the couch. Not sure when you last saw it, if you ever had it. One time

I found a photograph of my parents up the loft. Sometime before Dek left/after Mum. What was I looking for? Old *Spider-Man* annuals? Doesn't matter. The torch sweeping the ghost-crowded air. That thick pile-smell, like breaking into an Egyptian tomb. Dust passing into my lungs, settling in a sediment in my bloodstream. Teddy-bears and an old VHS and cookery books and battery-less cars and car-less batteries and sealed shoe-boxes and veteran one-eyed Action Men.

Amazing how one small shoe-box can hold so much history, can be grave-robbed with so little fuss.

Me and Dek in *Ninja Turtles* t-shirts, grinning at the spectacle of a Scottish summer. Mum comforting Dek, a squealing piglet in her arms. What is she wearing? Dad watching me crawl awkwardly across a sheepskin rug, which is still in our living-room to this day. But they didn't/couldn't/I wouldn't let them seem real, those people, trapped in the flash of the past. They were too innocent and had far too much hope welling in their eyes for me to admit them to this cut-and-thrust present. They had to have (surely? please?) become extinct somewhere between now and then, with their crawling babies and butterfly smiles and what-is-she-wearing summer's days dissolved to dust, floating like tiny astronauts in the loft. Ground control to Major Tom.

It was a lost time. It taught me something, that photograph. It made memory seem useless and sentimental, a thing which evolution has failed to breed from us.

Then I found a picture of Mum and Dad before we were born, and (jesus)

when Dad lists the roll-call of bands he saw at the Maniqui in his computer-printer way, revives the glory of punk in the voice of Stephen Hawking, somehow . . . I don't know . . . I always imagine him then the way he is now. I see him bearded, in his slippers, nodding appreciatively along with The Jam, while a thousand punks erupt all around. But

There he was. Caught in the stark blink of the camera. A can of lager, spiked red hair, a sneer worthy of Johnny Rotten and a ripped t-shirt that snarled I HATE PINK FLOYD and he had

Mum.

Pert in her *Star Wars* t-shirt. A low-rent Debbie Harry. Eyes piercing out like blue daggers. Danger and glamour flicked in a middle-finger. The next year they had Dek, four years later they had me, and somewhere along the path Mum lost her mind and stumbled into the fog to find it, and I sprang

down from the loft. Padded into a simmering living-room. Dek was swearing to Dad he was going, he was sick of this house, he would go as far as London if he fucking had to. Dad, growing roots into that armchair of his. Gazing pitifully at his rebellious son. His frown hung heavy at each corner, laden with toast crumbs, and he groaned like a coffin closing.

Dek made some last retort, stabbed the TV off with the same spite that had just spat at me from Dad's own teenage face in the photo. He whirled his jacket onto his shoulders and stamped towards the front door, where a car filled with booze and Nirvana waited to spring him to town. Door slammed. Photographs rocking gently on the walls. Smiles like boats on a choppy sea.

Resting.

The dust settled on the mantelpiece.

Dad stroked his beard thoughtfully.

And I sat down.

Was there any residue of energy left in him? Could I geiger-counter check for it crackling round his body? Where was the young punk? Where was the older man who'd roamed the country like a tireless lion, looking for work to fund the patios and satellite dishes and double-glazing which Thatcher had generously sprinkled on the working-classes? It was only then I realised how much he looked like Dek, if my brother was a man in his forties whose wife had left him with two hungry sons.

'Alvin?' Dad said eventually, as if someone had had to wind a key on his back for him to do it.

'Aye?'

I waited.

'Put the TV back on, wid ye?'

I stood, trekking the icy wastes of the living-room. And just as I bent to touch the button of the television, Dad's slump reflected in the black face of the screen, there was a quick crackle of electricity and

the cover of the new U2 album looms like the mothership at the end of *Close Encounters* and me and Frannie rush to the window of Virgin, pressing our faces against it, toddler-amazed, and everyone in Falkirk High Street stares, *One-Flew-Over-The-Cuckoo's-Nest*-concerned, like we're a couple of escaped Jack Nicholsons and somebody really should call Nurse Ratchet, but they don't understand! The world is about to be put right! All hatred, famine, war, sorrow, eradicated from the Earth in one interstellar burst.

ALL THAT YOU CAN'T LEAVE BEHIND.

'Ye ken whit this means?' Frannie grins, turning to me.

'Whit?'

'There's a new U2 album coming out!'

'So there is!'

67

There's an Asian man in the High Street, strolling despondently with a sandwich board which says LOOKING FOR ANSWERS? but Frannie and me are too excited to pay him much attention. We nod at each other, satisfied, workers just completed construction of the Forth Bridge, the sweat and the grime soaking our blue collars, God smiling down at our protestant work-ethic and delivering this boon, this glinting jewel on a velvet cushion.

COMING – it says – OCTOBER 30th.

But it feels as distant as a retirement home.

The amount of living we compress into these year-long days before the new U2 album. The way time seems elasticated, stretched by desire, snapped by disappointment, like a bendy-toy. *Saving Private Ryan* that night seems to last for six hours, not three, and all the way through, instead of feeling thoroughly ashamed of myself for not dying a horrible death in the war, I can only picture me and Fran with big seventies headphones clamped to our ears, chilling to the new U2 like superstar DJs and . . .

'Fuck's sake,' Brian sighs, shaking his head at the TV. His own Dad is in the army, serving Her Majesty's. Brian barely sees him. This is why he has the house to himself, with all its lonely, family-less spaces. On screen, a soldier hunts for his missing arm on the grey Omaha beach. A wall of rain on the horizon, sweeping closer. The soft fall of pain. Bullets, blood. Someone shot through the skull and

. . . me and the Franman pogo-ing with forty thousand nutters to 'Sunday Bloody Sunday', Frannie ignoring the Irish Tricolour flags, Dolby's there! He's pretending that he doesn't think Bono's a knob and has even learned the words to everything on *Achtung Baby* and and and . . .

'Aw thae lives lost.' Brian's eyes are becoming misty. He wipes at them, manfully, dignified. I wonder when he did last see his father. Bodies littering the beach, the surf a light crimson colour, lapping like a stray dog at a scrap of bare meat and

. . . soon Bono calls me up onstage during 'With Or Without You' for a slow-dance and I'm cuddled into him and even though he's been performing for two hours he's not sweaty or nothing and over his shoulder I see Frannie and Dolby sick as dogs and I smirk and give them the finger . . .

'If Ah wis a religious man, Ah'd say a prayer for thae boys.' Brian switches off the video, disturbed, sort of talking to himself, like a dick, distant, humbled, and later that night we

slide towards the derelict car-park like sharks.

Across the horizon, lights in a row signify parents with young children, watching television, maybe *Who Wants To Be A Millionaire?* The Middlefield Industrial Park has concrete walls spidery with lichen, vacant, dusty windows, chains hanging sullen over gates (except this one, which an underpaid security guard has 'overlooked'). Idlewild are singing 'Actually It's Darkness' on Radio One, but Dolby cuts them off as we turn the corner. Makes Belinda a vacuum. Makes the noise from the car-park bubble and spit to life.

Laughter, young and male. Honed on oil-refineries, garage fore-courts, shop-floors. Motors revving like dogs on a leash. Music, dance mostly, but bursts here and there of Shania Twain (from a pink Fiat Punto), Fatboy Slim, Limp Bizkit. My blood drums along.

Brian going, '. . . so ma Uncle Tam in California says Ah can come out there any time Ah like. Ah'll be workin behind the bar in his pub, like, but California boys eh?'

'California girls!' Frannie nyuk-nyuks.

Light sluicing from the cars up one side. Silver metalwork with a flip of rainbow. A girl answering a mobile-phone, her silhouette knife-thin against the blaze. A tower of Reebok checking his text-messages. Mobile-phones ringing everywhere for a few seconds, a seizure of bleeping. Drug deals spiralling into the air above us.

As we cruise up the line, Brian points at the boys: 'Ford Fiesta . . .

Fiat Uno . . . Golf . . .'

Frannie points at the girls: 'Yoda . . . Snaggletooth . . . Hammerhead . . .'

I watch two Fila-monsters place loose change on the roof of a Vauxhall Corsa. The bass throbs and the coins dance, a miniature rave.

'The guy's name was Shiney,' Dolby's muttering, as we smooth past a gang of girls. Their eyes like lions spotting a wildlife photographer. 'Met him on a chat-room last night.'

'Shiney?' Frannie asks, 'Whit sort ae fuckin nickname's that?'

'Whit sort ae fuckin nickname's Frannie?'

Chat-room, I'm thinking. *Internet*, I'm thinking. '*First Killings By Internet Cult*', I'm thinking.

Tyra Mackenzie was wearing a salmon-pink blouse today, with a silver chain. And she's had her hair tinted auburn. And her top three buttons were undone, her skin lightly freckled like eggshell.

There's a tap at the window. Some dude gestures for us to roll it down. He casts an eye over our dashboard – looking for woofer speakers? strobe-lights? – and snorts to see it bare.

'Are you Shiney?' Dolby asks him, guarded.

The guy doesn't say anything. But when he smiles his front teeth jut out like a rodent's. 'Why?' he yips. 'Whit d'ye want?'

'Just telt Ah should ask for Shiney . . .'

The weapon seems to realise something. His teeth nibble excitedly at his bottom lip. 'Aw, you the chat-room boy? Uriel?'

Frannie glances at me, smirking.

'Nae bother, pal.' Our host breaks into a grin. 'Ah'm Shiney! Just makin sure yer no the pigs, ken?'

'Of course,' Dolby manages nervously. 'Em . . . where dae we go then?'

Shiney's grin is bringing on nightmares. It seems to eat into the sides of his face. He's dressed head-to-toe in Adidas, his hair slicked back as if he's just climbed from a toilet. He catches my eye, sees my discomfort, and his grin burrows further into his cheeks. Then he's rubbing his hands. 'Well . . . Got yer reddies, gents?'

We fish in our pockets for a couple of quid (Brian grumbling like a old war colonel) which we hand to Dolby, which he hands to Shiney, which Shiney pockets greedily in one of those bags that hang at your belly, the kind used by those guys at the Waltzers that shout '*scream if you wanna go faster* . . .'

'Just drive up there, mate. Watch the races if ye want. Wait yer turn for the Burnout.'

Dolby nods.

'Burnout?' says Frannie, as we are coralled to the head of the car-park past – I can't believe it – a van selling Mr Whippy ice-cream, 'Whit the fuck's a Burnout?'

'Suppose we'll see,' Dolby mumbles, turning the wheel smoothly, treating Belinda tonight like she's a girl he wants to keep sweet. As if their relationship hangs in the balance.

We park behind a purple Mazda, two noddies dropping bottles and chart-hits from the half-open window, elbows (NIKE) leaning non-chalantly. There we wait, listening to Primal Scream, not talking, watching the cars purr in and out, creating a secret language with their engine sounds, windows rolled down, banter, fags ignited, a sudden laugh like a Guy Fawkes banger. Someone boasting, not caring who hears him: '*last December*! *Aye*! *Wrote-aff three fuckin motors an a mountain-bike*!' as a girl with a clipboard (neat hair, like a student or a secretary) asks if we want to put our names down for a race.

'Um . . .' I mutter, confused, 'Ah've no brought ma trainers.'

'Shut-up, dickhead!' she tuts savagely.

'It's awright hen,' Dolby answers. 'We'll just watch.'

They all glare at me, mortified.

After a while (in which Frannie bores us with another Ace of Spads story; he has, supposedly, one of the largest pornography collections

71

in Scotland), motors start gathering in the middle of the car-park and the air tightens. There are whistles and cat-calls. Expectation.

'So this guy on the Net was telling me the things they get up tae,' Dolby's saying, 'like recreatin the Grand Prix course every year roon Fawkurt . . .'

Shiney with three fingers in the air.

'But maistly they jist meet in places like this and . . . um . . .'

The crowd clears. Shiney picks up a flag, holds it aloft, stretching his arm so high his back becomes a poised, drawn bow.

'. . . race,' Dolby says then

two cars appear in a burst, their tyres screeching. They jostle, neck and neck, fumes billowing. Everyone cheering. They accelerate towards the wall at the far end of the car-park, but the crowd converges behind them, blocking our view. The sound of squealing brakes.

We crane our necks.

Confusion settles to the ground like dust. Girlfriends' anxious hands fluttering at their throats but then

Two figures stumble out from the cars.

Spontaneous applause. Arms wave in the headlights like a strobe show. Friends grabbing the victor, shaking his hand, patting his back, telling him he's *mad, mad*, he's a *mad cunt*, but he doesn't seem quite there for a second. He smiles, vaguely, his face incandescent with triumph, then he takes a long, unbroken gulp from a can of Miller, throwing back his head, beer pissing from his lips, and something animal is roared at the black black sky.

'Fucksake . . .' the four of us gasp and

the Burnout goes like this.

A gang of people stand in front of a car with their hands on the bonnet. The driver pulls the handbrake, starts revving up the engine, gradually increasing pressure on the accelerator. When it hits the floor, they drop the clutch, and the wheels spin madly on the spot. Then they release the handbrake. The crowd screams and scatters like a shoal of fish and everyone laughs.

Three of these break up the races. One car sacrifices its handbrake. The second rears forward like a tiger, noddies laughing and slapping the bonnet as it escapes. The third car collapses, the engine surrendering, a genie of smoke hissing from the grille. All of the other cars honk horns and flash lights at this and we watch. The dangerous allure of it. The way girls drift towards the drivers and hang at their sides like ornaments. Low-grade electricity buzzes between us. 'This is the shout!' Brian proclaims, charged, excited, sweating, and then we're leaping out the car to join the crowd, wringing each other's shoulders, yelping like children and it's

Monday morning.

Still shaky.

Two smashed bonnets, two burned-out clutches and Frannie copping off with a skank in the back seat of Belinda while we stood out in the night air, freezing, but full of wonder. The dazed shouts. The way the drivers stop expertly before the wall. Someday, surely, they all know, one of them won't stop in time. And that's what makes it so cool.

Anyway, I'm standing here with the hash-heads at the back of the History huts, pinballed from the prefect room, which they wouldn't let me into again.

Not that I partake, mind. Just that Muzz, Doc and Walenzic – the Cheech, Cheech and Chong of Falkirk High – have between them the Floyd's entire back-catalogue on CD. Today it's my copy of *The Wall* for Doc's *Delicate Sound of Thunder*, Walenzic's *Piper at the Gates of Dawn* for Muzz's *Animals*. Hands appear from the reef of smoke then withdraw covertly.

'Sure ye dinnae want a draw?' Walenzic offers, squinting through the grey fronds, 'Just one for Syd Barrett?'

'Quite sure,' I cough self-consciously.

Muzz and Doc laugh explosively (at?) before degenerating into a whispered exchange and small, brief paroxysms of giggles. It's guys like these who are responsible for our scheme's nickname 'Hash-Glen': sniggering, slack-eyed Syd Barrett/Jim Morrison acolytes that have a thousand potholes scattered round Falkirk High. Harmless. Sometimes even good for patter. And they definitely know their Floyd. But when I'm with them, I feel funky, unfunny, on the edge of things. This is what I do: float from group to group, liked by all, accepted by none. Like Icarus, I soar against the underbelly of the Livingstone Set, then descend, wings fluttering, to the level of the grasshoppers.

Each thinks I surely belong with the other lot.

Not sure where I belong.

Maybe in that Floyd song, 'Mother Do You Think They'll Drop The Bomb'.

'This is cheap shite, Muzz,' Walenzic splutters. 'You been buyin aff that guy doon the Boag again?'

There is a famous story of Muzz when he was twelve, buying off Mark Nightingale from the Boag. Muzz boasting to everyone at Doc's house that he had the shit, that he was *well-in* with the FEAR crew, not knowing that Marky had sold him two Oxo cubes.

'Ha-fuckin-ha,' Muzz tuts.

Doc is the rumour-conduit of Falkirk High School. An oracle in Nikes. He hears things vibrating across the floor, or spoken to him in a dream. You can see Doc lounged in some doorway at break-time, a pale wraith in a shroud of ganja, murmuring, 'New Chemistry teacher's a dyke, gen up' or 'Kurt Cobain faked his ain death'. He knows where every boyracer in Falkirk has been in the last month, who they saw there, what they were listening to, probably knows where they're going next. We could consult him, cross-legged before a poster of Bob Marley, for Kottsy Reports, if we fancy a cruise round Camelon. We could leave Rizlas at his door by way of thanks. He knows all about Brian's tête-à-tête with Kottsy and he knows where all the races are happening and he knows about the party coming up in Tyra Mackenzie's.

'Should be a classy do,' he muses, then takes a long, cheek-filling toke. 'Nae skanks like us there.'

'Fuck that, man,' Muzz shaking his head, unimpressed. 'Be full ae fuckin snobs. David Easton, Gordon French, Louisa Wainwright, Jennifer Haslom, Connor Livingstone . . .'

'I hate that cunt,' Walenzic tuts sourly, 'Fuckin cokeheid. Rich, junkie scum.'

He offers me his roach, which I refuse.

I ask Doc what chance there is of Tyra – hmm, I dunno – making herself available that night? and the three of them glance at each other, sensing my agenda with some opened third-eye or shit. Their three heads shake in unison, and they adopt the tone of the drunken Irishmen in *Titanic*

yer as likely as have angels fly out of yer arse as get close to the likes of her, boyo!

and then start a raunchy conversation about Tyra in various states of undress, positions, Hendrix songs playing in the background, which makes me quite uncomfortable, so I distract them:

Do they reckon we'll get an invite?

Loud, cackling laughter from the witches three.

'Us?' 'Ye fuckin jokin?' 'Sure yer no wantin some ae this?'

'Anyway, Alvin,' says Walenzie, 'you'll be awright. Tyra's keen on you.'

'Is she?' I reply too quickly, and they collapse again into an ecstasy of giggles.

75

I sigh, turn, see first-years hurrying back before bell-time, staring at these fifth-years and their funny cigarettes. They peek at us and scuttle on. Their shoes are gleaming black. Their hair is cut straight. Their eyes are alive with zest for life. They are wondering how it all becomes a sad toke behind the History huts.

'Naw, seriously,' Doc remarks, sticking the spliff behind his ear, 'You're brainy. You'll end up invited.'

'Ah will not!' I tut (secretly thrilled that he thinks so), 'Ah'm no like them!'

Walenzic shrugs, gazing melancholy into the distance. 'Might no have their money, mate, but Ah dinnae see ye fillin yer brain full ae this shit either.'

They all stare down at their joints, suddenly glum. Smoke hangs around their heads like gaseous lead. Their eyes are downcast. Dismal with hash. The school bell rings in the distance, and they look up, slowly, as if God has whispered to them. And so I leave them there, standing dumb as drugged rabbits, revelation floating between their fingers. My copy of *Delicate Sound of Thunder* in hand, I head for class and Tyra? a party invite? one foot in the camp of Cleopatra? I picture myself in Tyra's front room, surrounded by Jennifer Haslom, Louisa Wainwright and Tyra in silken garments, all dancing seductively to the second side of *Delicate Sound of Thunder* (Dave Gilmour's solo at the end of 'Comfortably Numb') and I am not coping. Today someone stopped to speak to me in the hall ('Heard your mate kicked Kotty's heid in') and I stood there, listening, restraining a deep need to run away, far away from him. But I did nothing. Except stared. Nodded. Snarled convincingly, 'Aye, an Ah helped him! That cunt'll no mess wi the H-Glen Crew again!' and later, in the toilets, I wrote feverishly on the back of a door

THIS WORLD IS KILLING ME

and so we're in Brian's living-room, right, and the film *Batman* is on TV (the good one, the one before Arnie and Kilmer and Clooney came along and ruined it for everyone) and we're swapping a single can of Irn-Bru since none of the Lads has been paid from work yet. Brian makes a steaming plate of *toast à la margarine* while we watch King Keaton at work, munch, snigger at the seventies décor of Brian's living-room while he goes and makes more toast on the grill.

'Who lives in a house like this?' Frannie intones, sweeping a finger along a shelf like that nancy-boy from *Through the Keyhole*.

'Shaft!' Dolby laughs.

Soon we're slouched like collapsed deck-chairs. Homer-bellies on show. Only vaguely registering the film. Frannie and Brian moaning at the length of their shifts (they do look tired) and when they ask about Tyra, I shrug, then tell them that, like Juliet, she is the sun. No, I definitely don't. They lapse into a brief self-pity at the approaching age of nineteen, until Frannie, quite unexpectedly, leaps from his chair and shouts 'It's him!'

'Who?'

Frannie stabs at the rewind button. The screen whizzes back to a scene with a reporter walking into his office. All of his colleagues are mocking his interest in the story of a caped vigilante stalking Gotham City. One of them says, '*Hey, I got something for ya!*' and hands him a cartoon of a guy dressed as a bat. Frannie continually replays

'*Hey, I got something for ya!*'

'*Hey, I got somethi –*'

'*Hey, I got –*'

this scene, mesmerised, freezing on the frame of the sarcastic colleague. 'It *is* him!' he gestures, 'Look.'

'*Who?*'

'Ye ken Rodney in *Only Fools and Horses*?'

'That's no him.'

'Obviously. Ye ken his girlfriend Cassandra?'

'Em . . . aye.'

'Ye ken Cassandra's Dad?'

'Frannie, are you alrig–'

'That's the guy that plays Cassandra's Dad!'

'Oh fuck off.'

'It is, look at him!'

'Frannie, aye, Tim Burton's putting together the cast for *Batman*, and he's like, "*Hey, any of you guys seen* Only Fools and Horses? *We gotta get Cassandra's Dad.*" '

'Ya bastards, Ah'll prove it!'

Frannie forwards the film to the credits, his face scrunched determinedly. He traces his finger down the cast-list until, right at the bottom, appears:

Bob The Cartoonist **Denis Lill**

'How much?' he demands, palm open.

'Frannie, come ontae–'

'How much?'

Brian responds firmly. His eyes narrow on an irresistible bet. 'Ah'll bet ye the bottle ae Macallan sittin in that cabinet. There is *nae way* Cassandra's Dad fae *Only Fools and Horses* is in *Batman*.'

'Bottle ae Macallan?' Frannie's eyebrow raises, challenged to a duel. 'Nice whisky that.' Straight away he's cracking open an *Only Fools and Horses* tape, forwarding Rodney and Del Boy and Grandad and Cassandra and Cassandra's Dad, who jerk about like androids, until the credits roll up, and he stands poised at the video.

Cassandra's Dad **Denis Lill**

then he's whooping and leaping about the room, punching his fist in the air. I have never seen him so happy (which is some feat, since

Frannie is not known for his sullen approach to life) and me, Brian and Dolby just look at each other, shaking our heads.

'That has made ma year!' Frannie gasps, wiping at his eyes and plucking the Macallan from Brian's fist. 'Denis Lill. That has made ma year . . .'

They pour the whisky. I decline a glass, content to watch rolling hills and heather and ancient claymores strike victory round their mouths. Frannie closes his eyes, blissful. Dolby has a look on his face like he wants to kill someone. Why? Whirlpools Direct is laying off workers. Maybe it's this. Maybe it's something else. Maybe he

has a new mobile-phone which plays 'Never Had a Dream Come True' by S Club 7 and the first time he gets a text we're in the middle of the Howgate Centre, just outside Argos (which has two *gorgeous* lawnmowers in the window) and Dolby's jacket beeps. We pause our argument over which lawnmower is the sexiest (surely the Flymo?), Dolby taking the phone from his pocket, his eyes wide, excited, as if about to discover the location of the Soviet microfiche. Heavenly-white tiles surrounding us, reflecting the light which shafts like white knives from the glass ceiling, and shops, and shoppers, roaming, dazed as lab-rats, the four of us crowding round this minuscule machine to read the words

HOPE U GET THIS

then gasping like infants being brought a cake crowned with tiny, flickering lights. 'Wow.' 'That's cool.' We watch this message glow submarine green, each impish pixel one small step for technology, one giant leap in the lives of four piss-poor Playstation players and (grannies, who probably marvelled at the invention of tin-openers, staring mutely at our celebration and) thereafter the Lads go text-message crazy.

With Frannie, on the way to watch the Rangers game in Smith's:

U STINK

With Brian, selecting a birthday card for his Gran:

U R A JOBBY

With Dolby, browsing for comics in Forbidden Planet in Glasgow:

SPDERMAN IS A POOF

until it gets to the stage that when we're in Belinda, they're actually sending messages from the front seat to the back! I see Brian smirk like a kid setting off a stink-bomb, punching secretively at his mobile and then Frannie's says

FRANNIE MORE LK FANNY

to which Frannie replies, chuckling, and before long Belinda is a roving arena of techno-warriors (sponsored by Siemens/Nokia/Cellnet) and Brian is moaning at me to

'Put a fuckin smile on yer face, Alvin.'

He fingers the new tattoo on his bicep, of an American flag, which beams his Californian dream like some transatlantic beacon. If any of us should have been born Yank, it's Brian. Tom Cruise capitalist barman bastard. He'll fit right in over there. 'Just havin a wee laugh, eh?'

'Hilarious,' I brood. Frannie, beside himself with glee, starts typing out another text, realising that 'Brian Mann' rhymes with 'frying pan'.

'Get yersel a mobile and join in then, ya miserable–'

'An get that fuckin baseball cap *aff*!' Dolby interrupts, furious.

'Giein us some bad name, you!'

'Aye, whatever.'

'Ah'll whatever ye! Ah'm in the hairdresser's hearin them gawin on aboot these "boyracers" that are menacin Falkirk! Ah dinnae want lumped in wi scum like that. Aw cos ae your fuckin baseball cap!'

'Nothin tae dae wi the speed yer daein?' I reply.

'Shut it, Runt.'

Frannie presses 'Send', sniggering mischievously. Brian watches the message invade his phone, grinning, and I don't want to spoil their fun or shit, I mean I'm glad they're enjoying themselves, but come on

'Is this no just a case ae wee boys an their wee toys?'

The question hangs unanswered, creating rage in the front-seat. Grim heads

shaken, despairing of this sole commie in their redwhiteandblue utopia. Did Dolby really hear somebody in the hairdresser's say that? Have to get rid of these zits if we're heading for fame, likes, dodging

down into Princes Street, ABC cinema showing Another Big American Film (the poster has an explosion on it), Rosie O'Grady's devouring an endless line of teens, Pinocchios waiting to be made into humans, The Lads quietly resenting the fact that, because of me, they're not in that queue, wishing they could scoot me to the pier in the Tom Hanks film *Big* and be back in time for last orders.

in the window of a bridal shop for a brief second I see

'Mum?' Frannie yabbers earnestly into his phone, 'Ye tape *The Fast Show* repeats for me? Whit? *The Fast Show*, no *The Antiques Roadshow.*' Outside the sky is lemonade and middle-aged women (the kind we like best) are in tops, shorts ('a flash ae bra-strap on an aulder woman,' Brian muses, wistfully, like a Yorkshireman petting his whippet and praising fond mornings on the moors). The soundtrack to *Bram Stoker's Dracula* on the stereo, a track called 'Vampire Hunters Prelude'. It builds with a slow menace, conjuring mist and sharp-eyed evil and dark Transylvanian hills. Totally ruined by Frannie yelping *Fast Show* quotes at his Mum.

'Suits you!' he gesticulates into the phone, 'Dis ma bum look big in this?'

I wish Brian was inviting us over to his ranch in California, cold beers in the fridge and cowboy boots hardening in the noonday sun. I wish it wasn't so long to the next Clive Barker novel coming out. Dolby eje

cts *Dracula* and replaces it with Radiohead, plaintively crooning to 'Exit Music (For A Film)' like a minstrel in an old medieval play (the ones with the funny-shaped guitars). Thom Yorke's sorrow crackling and fizzing with technology as we slide from the town-centre down, down, up, across, like computer-game characters, towards middle-class suburbia in Carronshore while Frannie's phone-chatter twists and rises into the desolate space above Central Scotland.

There's just too much, I can't help but think. Just too much.

'Mobile phones are essential purchases, Alvin,' Brian turns to me, still simmering at my boys-with-toys comment, the bare-faced cheek of it.

'Aye Mum,' Fran's yabbering at his mobile, 'The guy that used tae be on Harry Enfield . . . the wee ferrety-lookin fella.'

'For emergencies an that.'

'No Lily Savage! *Is Lily Savage ferrety-lookin?*'

I take a deep breath and uncage Mrs Costa's Modern Studies lesson from this morning, which takes even me by surprise and goes something like: 'Mobilephonesaretheproductofaconsumeristculture-whichpropagatesthemyththatluxuryitemsare'essential'purchasesinor-dertokeeptheeconomybuoyantandthusensuringthesurvivalofthecapit-alistorganism . . .' even making the inverted commas on the word 'essential' with my fingers but

'Fuckin Radiohead,' Brian tuts, ejecting *OK Computer*. 'Just aboot fuckin greetin here.'

He replaces it with *The Best Eighties Album in the World Ever*, starts humming (droning) along with Kim Wilde. Songs-from-before-I-was-born and mobiles chirping like bio-mechanical birds and text-messages sprinting to the surface of phone-screens everywhere and Dolby veering us onto a long, cool, Eagles-album-cover stretch of Scotla

> we're the kids in america!
> (whoa-oh)
> we're the kids in america!

nd, as the past, present, future slide, merge, exist simultaneously in the furry-dice ambience of this car, these *Back to the Future*-like lives. The sound of the summer revving up and waiting to be measured out in the quick increments of mobile-phone technology while in the years between U2 releases we grow older, and don't even notice.

just too mu

A mother with two children strolls past, her bra-strap showing.

'Phwoar!' goes Brian, 'Look at the experience on that!'

'Ken,' Dolby murmurs, the only one who was paying attention to my brave (I thought) anti-mobile-phone stance. 'Alvin's got a point.'

'On tap ae his heid.'

'Next summer,' he muses, an opera-critic frown, 'When we're drivin about here, text-messagin's gonnay be totally auld-fashioned . . .'

'Fucksake!' Brian moans, 'Yer takin the Runt's side? Ye'll be listenin tae fuckin Suede next!'

accelerating so fast it's like erasing Scotland from the

smoothing Belinda in, out, streams of traffic, never leaving seventy, the sun making a spider's web of light on the windscreen, turning/dancing/sucked away. We overtake a fellow shitty-in-the-city Belinda which flashes its lights and we flash ours back and the driver, a young guy like us, grins. A connection.

'Just,' Dolby explains, a laugh breaking across his face. 'Ah wis readin an article in *The Guardi* . . . em, *The Sun*. An it wis sayin that in a few years we'll have mobile phones, like, *embedded in oor skulls* . . .'

'Cool!'

'–an microchips in oor eyes that kin make us see in the dark-'

'Duh! Is that no whit light-bulbs are for?'

'–an televisions that know the things ye watch an record them for ye.'

'Ma Mum does that.'

'Your Mum does *everythin*!' Brian quips filthily.

'Shut it, skank!'

'Ah mean, the world's goin by so fast we kin hardly see it . . .' Dolby keeps checking his rear-view mirror, Keanu-refusing to drop below seventy. 'Sonly a few year ago that fax-machines, the Internet and *Jurassic Park* were a big deal. Think aboot this: oor grandchildren are gonnae look at us like we're a fuckin joke.'

The laughter stops.

The excitement irrigated from Dolby's voice.

He looks like the Vatican have released the date the world will end. To him only. And he cannot tell a soul. And he has to encode it for us like this. And the road becomes a conveyor belt, rolling a million souls to the void, and Dolby is dumb with the fear of being obsolete in a matter of several short years. His hands on the wheel. Curved. Tight. Hard. A sort of look in his eyes that reminds me of the sky as the night lays its arm across the day and things grow cold and sluggish.

The four of us here, now, present, correct, as real and vital as the first flash of a mobile-phone screen as it's switched on but

One day we'll be De Niro at the end of *Raging Bull*. Fat. Fucked. Perched on the end of the bar in Smith's mumbling Brando's '*I coulda been a contender*' speech and as the implications of this start to roll like a boulder through our brains, none of us catch each other's eye. Lest we see ourselves old and cough-ridden.

We avert our gazes to the window, where magic is thinned into a straight line by the endless course of tyres on tarmac, rushing, montonous. The new U2 album ever-retreating on the horizon, like an illusion of the sun. Billowing air that falls behind us then becomes flat again. Empty.

I think about my Dad's face when Mum left. The wrinkles a tiny fan at the corners of his eyes. How small he looked, in his old chair in the corner of the living-room. Everything he'd done with his life converging in that instant, destroyed in that instant, but then

Brian farts

'Aw, you're *stinkin*!'

and we piss ourselves laughing.

> we're the kids in america!
> (whoa-oh)
> we're the kids in

a white Fiat Punto, the word *GIRLZ* printed on the back, draws up alongside us. Dolby beeps the horn once, twice. Frannie up at the window like a dog when the door goes. A parallel female universe of our own car: four girls giggling behind glass. At the next set of traffic-lights, he rolls down his window, gestures for them to do the same. Their Brian Mann complies. Frannie hands her a card with his mobile-phone number on it and as Dolby burns away and their car drops

back

the girls laugh mutely. Passing the card round. 'Now *you*, Runt,' Brian points out, Clint-anxious, 'should be able tae pull at least *wan* ae them babes.'

'Or?'

'Cut yer dick aff an stick it behind yer ear.'

85

'Fuck you.'

'Fuck *you*.'

'Fuck her in the front-seat . . .' Frannie murmurs, uses his fingers to spell out his mobile number, then mouths

> you talkin to me?
> you talkin to *me*?
> i'm the only one here
> you talkin to me?

and his phone rings.

He answers, quick, beaming like a game-show host, 'Chris Tarrant here from *Who Wants To Be A Millionaire?* The next voice you hear will be my own, saying . . . some shite.' The girls in the Punto behind us, filling the glass case with their mirth. They look just like The Corrs. Frannie nodding, 'aye?aye?aye?' then spluttering

'Heddy-*haw*!'

as Front-Seat Corr looks through her ringlets

at

me.

'She wants tae talk tae Alvin!'

'Whit should Ah . . . um . . .' I stutter, Frannie's mobile landing in my lap like a grenade and I stare at it, terrified, and

hello . . . ? hello . . . ? hello . . . ?

Dolby explodes.

'Fuckin talk tae her then, dick!'

'Whit dae Ah say?'

'Tell her ye play for Rangers, Ah dunno.'

I pick up the mobile, cautiously. Place it to my ear like it's about to bite me (which, if you've ever seen *Nightmare on Elm Street*, you'll know it might).

'Hello?' I try to control the rise and fall of my chest.

'Turn around,' the voice on the phone purrs.

Bobbing behind us, girls exist. They are all older than me – about the same age as the Lads – no bra-straps visible, but stun-ning. Front-Seat Corr opens her kisser and we talk awhile, Frannie, Brian, watching me take this penalty kick. European Cup final. This is what happens when one of us is with a chick: he is himself, at that moment, The Lads, the essence of Lad, and I'm so swept away by this that when she asks what I do for a living, I can't help but grin

'Ah play for Rangers.'

When next the Punto skids back into view, all four of them are staring wide-eyed.

'Rangers?' Front-Seat Corr peers, unconvinced. 'Are ye no a wee bit young?'

I feel my pupils glint; hers glint back.

'If yer good enough,' I smirk, 'yer auld enough.'

She scrunches her mouth gamely, drawing nearer Planet Impressed but still not sure she wants to land. 'Put yer mate back on.'

> you talkin to *me*?
> you talkin to

the Franman, haggling, loving the fact that a car-full of girls is following like he's one of The Beatles. Brian telling Dolby about serious Falkirk weapon-boys he has to turf out from Smith's (plus actions). Kottsy has been sending boys in to noise Brian up, sound out how quickly he can respond to an invasion. One night we're going to get the call for back-up. This is Dolby's worry. He and Brian go back the longest of the four of us. Think they met in Primary Four, after Brian nicked Dolby's Action Man or something naff like that. These days, half the fights Brian gets into are because Gentleman

Dolby, the People's Friend, will offer to hold the door open for the girlfriend of the wrong guy, or cheerily ask some Barlinnie turk what his favourite Queen song is. And it's like that bit in *Casino*, when Joe Pesci wades in to defend De Niro

> *while I was wondering why the guy was saying what he was saying, nicky just hit him. no matter how big the other guy is, nicky'll take him on*

and I know Dolby could never have fucked off to college and left Brian. Even though, if Brian goes to California, it might be the end of the four of us. So if I win the lottery I'll buy Dolby a big widescreen telly and a DVD player and he can watch *Gladiator* and *The X-Men* and *Star Trek* movies all day, and I'll get Frannie a seat in the director's box at Ibrox and phone them up from the States, where I'm chilling with Brian and young, blonde American bra-straps.

Frannie snaps closed the phone. The Punto veers away towards Grangemouth.

'Fucksake!' I complain, 'What did ye say tae them?'

He rubs his chin, measuring me the way a scientist measures rainwater. 'Ah hope ye've brought yer shaggin shoes, wee man.'

'Why?'

'Cos they want tae meet ye at Cally Park. Ten minutes.'

The door swings open like a pod in a sci-fi movie.

Dolby steps out intrepidly first. Looks at Callendar Park like it's undiscovered country. Holsters the mobile-phone. The sky lowering itself onto the ground awkwardly, like a fat man going to bed.

My heart is making the sound of a rabbit calling for help

> *theywantmetheywantmetheywantmethey*

but not the Me in the mirror, with hair that looks like a squirrel's slept in it and a dick that could be used for fish-bait. No. They want the Me that plays for Rangers.

I don't have hair that plays for Rangers. I certainly don't have a dick that plays for Rangers.

Dolby sits on the grass and plucks a flower and places it over his face and lies back. The sun flicks red and yellow paint at the skyline. The air cooling. Dolby blows and the flower spins into the air gracefully and he says

I have given a name to my pain . . .

'. . . it is Batman!' Frannie finishes, and they both cackle, as if this is The Funniest Joke In The World Ever. 'Good auld Denis Lill.'

Brian the Mann gazing round Cally Park, restless. What's on that craggy mind of his? The trimmed tourist-brochure grass? The big high-rises, where his Dad used to stay before he joined the Forces, before he left him on his own in Falkirk, alone save for us? The laughing, colourful mouths of the flowers? Cally is Falkirk's very own itsy-bitsy Central Park and Brian strides across it like he's in the wild wild west. If he smoked, I'm sure, Martin Scorsese would use him in films. If Martin Scorsese was in Baxter's Wynd and fancied a pint or the racing-results, that is.

Brian hurls a five-pence piece at a nearby tree. It hits without leaving a mark and falls. Frannie starts doing his hair in Belinda's wing mirror, saying

I ask you to kill Superman, and you can't
even do that one, simple thing?

before lulling into silence again. There is an unspoken sense of girls about to be on the scene. Dolby picking flowers, Brian gazing into the

Sergio Leone distance. Frannie tries flexing his repertoire until Brian growls:

'Fuck off with the impressions, dick.'

I do my hair in the car window, mimicking Frannie's movements. My slightly bovine face peers up at me, awkward, as if I'm somehow not who my reflection expected. Sometimes, way across the horizon of a decade or so, I imagine myself a phoenix. Risen. A film-star at parties, working the room, slipping tenners into the hands of waiters, my movements smooth as if in a dream or on camera, immaculate female hands reaching out to touch me but

No mistake. Right now I'm the ashes.

'Sure they said Callendar Park?' I ask Frannie across the roof of the car.

'Sure.' He wets his fingers and flattens a bit of his Coisty-cut, squinting.

'No Dollar Park?'

'Naw.'

'Or Callendar Square?'

'Stop shitein yersel,' Brian humphs, reaching into the pocket of his jeans and tossing me a small packet. 'Here. Just in case.'

My first thought is it's drugs.

Drugs! Brian? Drugs? The man who threw six Boag wide-os out of Dolby's sister's seventeenth for smoking hash and sneaking Bob Marley's Greatest Hits onto the stereo? But the word DUREX speckling the packet confuses me for a second.

'Whit the fuck's this for?' I query.

They look at me, sharply.

'Whit the fuck ye think it's for?' Brian laughs, 'Skimmin?'

'Ah'm no gonnae need this!'

'Ridin bare-back?'

'Ah'm no *shaggin* any of them!'

Brian strides over, puts his hand on my shoulder. 'Wee man. Ah *know* yer no shaggin any of them. But there is that tiny, million-tae-one chance that wan ae them might fancy yer miniscule tadger . . .'

I repeat something they've all heard before, tapping the condom back into his pocket. 'Sorry, Brian, Ah'm saving masel.'

'Who for?'

In my mind she's a belly-dancer, shimmying up to me in her Falkirk High School blazer, a veil, and nothing else. One of her breasts peeks out from behind a prefect stripe.

'Tyra,' I reply defiantly. 'Ah'm savin masel for Tyra Mackenzie.'

Brian covers his face with his hands. 'Alvin!' he implores, exasperated, 'If a girl asks ye tae shag her, it's considered *extremely impolite tae say no!*'

'Peer pressure!'

'Alvin, son, you are the only virgin we know . . .'

'Nae mingers for me,' I emote, waving a Shakespearean finger. 'When this shagger starts, it will be with the finest creation on God's earth.'

'Tyra's probably gettin a ride at the back of the Maniqui right now,' Frannie mutters, 'Brian's probably fuckin shagged her already!'

Brian turns to him, snappily. 'Whit ye tryin tae say?'

'Brian, you cannae get it *up* unless yer surrounded by bin-bags.'

'Ha! Listen tae Mister While-U-Wait! *Just up against the Persil boxes, Elaine, ma shift starts in five minutes . . .*'

I sit down on the grass next to Dolby. He is tinkering delicately with his daisy-chain. Someone has turned the thermostat on the day down without telling the sun, and birds everywhere frantically clipe.

We look out at the swing-park, where weans climb things and throw balls and there is laughter, light as party balloons. All of this ahead of them. Children's mothers scattered across the tarmac, the useless flapping of their skirts, the opaque tragedy of their eyes. Something wells up inside me at the sight. I want to tell Dolby everything. Right now. I want to take my pain and terror in a lump sum and dump it here on the grass so we can poke it with a stick and humiliate it. Instead I say:

'Ye read that last Clive Barker book?'

'Aye,' he replies. 'Shite.'

Dolby shrugs and starts to chew the end of the daisy-chain, making it ragged.

'Brian, ye shagged Snaggletooth at the back ae *Laurie's*. Ye shagged Chewbacca at the back ae the *Martell* . . .'

'Ya liar! Ah never went near Chewbacca! *You* shagged Chewbacca!'

'Right enough,' muses Dolby, 'Ah didnae see any ae oor books sittin next tae Clive Barker's when Ah wis in WH Smiths.'

Me and Dolby put our hands behind our heads. In the sky, a cloud shaped like an angel glides past in slow-motion. Parts of its wings detach and drift away. The angel becomes the colour of a strawberry. What does it mean? Who knows. Who the fucking fuck knows.

'Chewbacca? She the wan fae Shieldhill? Wore boxer-shorts?'

The angel fragments into smaller versions of itself. A mouth forms in its head and it screams at being ripped to pieces. There is a vast, vague terror in the sky. I can't get out of my mind that night I sat in front of the police – one bar of the fire on – and they asked if my Mum had anywhere to go, anywhere she might want to run to. The policeman leaning in close. The smell of Grown-Up. Coffee and leather. *Now tell me, honestly. Yer Daddy doesnae need to know. Did yer Daddy ever hit yer Mammy? Did he? Cos hittin yer Mammy's what might have made her run away* . . .

The sound of Brian and Frannie arguing is almost as calming, reassuring, as the singing of the birds, and I can't imagine not being with them. They are as intrinsic to life as fresh air, pollen, chlorophyll.

My sullen, slow rot. My running to stand still. My causal/casual slide into freakishness.

'Should you no be studyin for yer exams?' Dolby asks.

'Aye,' I shrug. 'But fuck it, eh?'

Dolby does not respond. Not with the *Aye, fuck it! Live it up while yer young*! that I'm expecting. I hear him grunt despondently, our strawberry angel blown to bits, its mouth expanding, corrupted by sky, until its face is filled with a single, silent wail.

'D'ye think Brian'll really go tae America?' I ask him, but he doesn't answer. He's glancing up, listening. Getting to his feet like Hooper spotting the shark in *Jaws*.

'Oh boys?' he interrupts Brian and Frannie, who're disputing which of them has slept with the most Catholics. 'Oh *boys*!? Looks like they've come for their noon feeding . . .'

The Punto raises clouds of gravel. The girls in the front clearly do not resemble anything from *Star Wars*. At all. We watch them like castaways seeing a ship approach. Numbed by its strangeness. Frannie starts singing under his breath

fun
girls
wanna have
fun
girls

Slam. Slam. Slam. Slam. Brunette. Blonde. Redhead. Brunette. One of them lands two six-packs of Hooch on the top of the Punto. Another adjusts her socks, draws on her fag like a pretty inmate. Another sits on the bonnet, arms folded, sizing us up. The Lads stand and watch dumbly.

'Awright?' says the one on the bonnet.

'Awright.'

'Hiya.'

'Hello.'

I don't say anything.

'Youse boyracers then?' one of them asks.

'No,' Dolby growls, whipping the baseball cap from my head. 'We are not.'

Her eyes flick between us, as if selecting a victim, the whole thing like a re-enactment of the cellar scene from *Pulp Fiction*. I keep waiting for one of the Lads to say something, anything, Brian to ask where their brothers drink, Frannie to do his Ali G impression, Dolby to say, 'It's *Trekker*, not Trekkie!'

But they just stare. Arms stiff by their sides. Three Gregorys on a planet of Girls.

'Whit wan ae yese plays for Rangers?'

'Him!' they all shout, their arms swinging round to me, and I am thrust forwards, looked up and down, summed up and chewed over with bubble-gum.

'He disnae play for Rangers!' one hoots, breaking into the six-pack. 'Ho! Son! Whit's yer name?'

I scramble my mind for the most Hun-like name I can think of. 'Ally . . .' I stutter, '. . . Ferguson.'

'Ally Ferguson? Wendy! You ever heard ae an Ally Ferguson?'

Wendy steps out from the car. Rangers shirt. Rangers scarf. She can see the lie go up and down and round my body like a barium meal. 'Ally Ferguson . . .' she muses. 'Whit position ye play?'

'Centre-right, em, forward.'

'He's in the reserves,' Brian adds hurriedly, and doesn't need to groan for me to know that he's groaning.

'Aw aye,' Wendy smiles. 'Ally Ferguson? Ah mind. You no come on as a sub against Motherwell last season?'

'Aye, em. That's me.'

'Scored two goals?'

'Probably.'

Wendy nods, amused. 'Well. Pleased tae meet ye, Super-Sub.'

We spread into the park, the girls clinking Hooch and blowing smoke-genies. We trade lives with them for a while, as the water from the loch laps against the banks, as the trees rustle and hiss, as the world revolves through space in slow-motion and I think:

(Girls!)

Halfway round the loch I tire. Or pretend to. Wendy drops back with me. 'It's quite tiring this,' she pants unconvincingly.

She offers a Vodka Hooch, but I shake my head firmly.

'Don't drink.'

She offers a fag.

'Sorry. Don't smoke.'

Wendy tuts, 'You don't drink, you don't smoke. What *do* you do?' and winks secretively.

'Ah, but–'

'Ah but!' she interrupts, 'Ah but! Abbot and Costello!'

We laugh. Sweet. Jesus.

'Look at your mates,' she gestures. The Hooch has relaxed them from their C3-PO stiffness. Slaggings bat back and forth. Anecdotes. The night Dolby, pissed, climbed the ivy at the side of Frannie's house, crash-landing in the bushes. A sprinkling of Heddy-haws. Nothing is forced about it. The girls (Rachel, Shona, Caroline) look on, amused, infusing the banter with stories of their own ('Rachel, mind that time you snogged the drummer fae the Stone Roses?').

Sometimes we think we're the only group of mates in existence. Hermetically sealed in the world of Belinda, breathing an atmosphere of in-jokes. Then we meet these

> fun
> girls
> wanna have
> fun

girls, with their own Frannie, their own Dolby, their own Brian, their own Belinda, their own running arguments, their own movies, albums, books, parking-places, seats in McDonalds, mobile-phone brands, an unuttered history that we've crashed against by accident, and this is how it works, and it's easier than I thought it would be.

'Lassies are just like guys aren't they?' I ask Wendy, this revelation sudden, 'Except they're, like, lassies.'

Wendy shrugs, spinning crisps towards a rugby-scrum of ducks. 'Um . . . well, Ah've got bigger tits than you.'

'Aye . . . em . . .' I cough, trying not to look at them, 'How did you four meet then?'

Wendy folds her hands behind her back. She has a gorgeous chest. Really suits that Rangers top. I like the way a little twist of her hair keeps escaping her ear, the way she keeps folding it back, keeps forcing me to conjure Tyra's image.

'Um . . . well, me and Caroline used tae hang about at Graham High. Eywis been pals. Caroline knew Shona through the Judo and Shona met Rachel eftir shaggin her boyfriend. They had a bit fight aboot it, like, but baith realised it wis the boyfriend that wis the dick, ken?'

'Em. Aye.'

'Wan night, for some reason, we aw endit up at the same hen-party. Crap night tae. The four eh us jist sat at a table an bitched aboot the bride.'

'An here ye are now.'

'An here we are now.'

'Heddy-haw.'

'Heddy whit?'

That Frannie laugh up ahead. Like Bucks fizz over a barbecue at a mate's house. One of the girls – Caroline? – creasing herself. Dolby covering his face, mock-embarrassed. Brian has heard it all before. We've all heard it all before, but Frannie has that infectious laugh. None of the four of us, I recognise, are bad people. A wave of affection for them rolls across me and I push it away, starting to fade, viewing the scene from a distance. My own mouth moving, undirected by me. I have sent someone out to speak on my behalf. A better person than me. I do not exist, cannot, not really, not fully. Oh God.

there's too much

Now tell me, honestly. Yer Daddy doesnae need to know. Did yer Daddy ever hit yer Mammy? Did he? Cos hittin yer Mammy's what might have made her run away . . .

'So when did ye join Rangers?'

'Whit? Oh! Em. Last season. Aye, last season. That's a funny lookin duck that wan, look!'

'Have ye ever met Coisty?'

'Em. Aye. Sure have. It wis me introduced him tae Frannie. Want his autograph?'

'Coisty's a prick.'

'So he is,' I hurriedly backpedal, 'Annoyin as fuck. Aw that "Coisty the dressin-room joker" 's a lot ae pish.'

'Gies a drink ae yer Coke.'

I pass it and she slurps, thirstily. A single bead of Cherry-Coke trickles a path through her freckles. My eyes drop straight to her chest.

'Cheers,' she gasps, her forearm raking across her mouth. 'You lookin at ma tits there?'

'Naw.'

'Just as well.'

She holds my gaze.

We've reached the other side of the loch, where it's still, and you could believe for one cool second that Callendar Park has been plucked from a holiday brochure. At the other side are the swing-park, the boating shed, the vandalised climbing-frames, the places you make for as a bairn. Over here is a different realm entirely. An Eden with a bitten apple. Purring with sex.

'I am Brian Mann and I don't care/I love the Rangers and I've got big hair!'

'Frannie, you are one Tesco-loving, scumbag Hun.'

'Hiy! Ah do not love Tesco!'

'Your pals are funny,' Wendy smiles. 'Must get loads ae lassies.'

'Tons,' I cough.

'Yese just oot for a shag the night then?'

Wendy on guard with an arched eyebrow. Carefully gauging my reaction.

'We certainly are not,' I protest. 'You've got us aw wrong.'

'No Ah huvnae,' she grins. 'Come on. Why did yese bother tae meet us here?'

She has the accuracy of Zorro. Her accusation quivers against my abs.

'Ah'll tell ye why. Deep down, right, aw we want . . . aw we've ever wanted . . . is just tae wake up wi some nice girl on our chest, right, an hear thae three special words.'

'Which are?'

'*You're so cool.*'

'Aw right.' She nods, pressing the blade of her gaze further in. 'Ah can see Ah've got yese aw wrong.'

'Listen,' I appeal, sweating, 'This is what women dinnae understand aboot men. *Other guys*, right, are mair important tae a guy than women. It's no aw aboot the shaggin! We're cultured! Me and Dolby have read *Lord of the Rings*! Brian doesnae let anybody deal drugs in his pub. Frannie's met Rodney fae *Only Fools and Horses*!'

'So?' she urges, pushing in the blade-point, 'Whit makes you so special?'

Good question.

Horribly good question.

What makes me so special?

I'm on the verge of answering *I am human and I need to be loved* but instead I consider it, truthfully, then say:

'Someday Ah'll write a thesis on Clive Barker and Stephen King.

Exploring their craft and bringing the two ae them to the, um, critical fraternity.'

'You stand for . . . Clive Barker and . . . Stephen King?' she asks uncertainly.

'Uh-huh,' I nod, 'They're easily the best authors in the world today. Ah cannae decide which ae them is actually the better. King has the common touch, as shown by *Stand By Me* and *The Shawshank Redemption*–'

'He wrote *The Shawshank Redemption*?'

'–and is probably scarier. Ah mean, Jesus! That bath scene in *The Shining*! But Barker has the better imagination and tackles much more philosophical issues than King. Ah'd recommend–'

'Yer cute, Super-Sub,' Wendy grins, pulling me after the others. 'God knows ye cannae relate tae women, but cute aw the same.'

'–*Imajica* by Barker, and probably the *Different Seasons* collection by King–'

'Take mah arm again.'

'–which is better than any ae his other–'

'Take ma fuckin arm!'

'Um . . . okay.'

The wind lifts leaves into the air and back down again. The sun brushes the trees with golden fingers and at last I feel a calm. Optimism creeping up on me. The Lads and Lassies still making whoopee up ahead and I'm walking arm in arm with A Girl, and U2 have a new album coming out, and everything feels vibrant and alive and young and exact and Wendy, sighing, leans close into me so that the others can't hear and says:

'Ah bet you've got a tiny dick.'

The Cherry-Coke catches in my throat.

'*Cough*! Whit did you just say?'

She's allowing the Lads to drift further in front of us, her hand snaking round my waist. 'Goan – let me see it.'

'I will not!'

'Why no?' she smiles. 'Must be tiny . . .'

'No it's no!'

'Well . . .' Her hand touches my crotch, her breath on my cheek and something

stirs.

'Let's hae a look then.'

'In the middle ae Callendar Park?'

'There's naebody about.'

I glance round. The Lads, oblivious. The wide-open space filled with leaves, branches, empty spray-cans, a squirrel which is surely not much concerned with seeing my willy.

It is suddenly a turn-on.

'Go on,' she urges. 'I'll show you mine if you show me yours . . .'

My gaze falls to her chest. She almost pushes my eyes down to them. Hurriedly, I fumble with my zip, feel the cold air on my exposed knob and exclaim:

'There!'

She peers down. Nods approvingly. Then gives a sharp whistle and everyone turns to see me standing in the middle of Cally Park, my willy hanging out like a tiddler.

One of the girls puts her hands to her mouth.

And Wendy, triumphantly:

'Ally Ferguson! Like *you* play for Rangers, ya–'

Free periods this morning. The sun has me rolled up in bed. The world the colour of umber, the dull sound of the ticking clock at the start of 'Time' on *Dark Side of the Moon* seems far, far away. Don't have to be at school until assembly, just before lunch-time. Don't want to move from here ever though, it's so warm and lovely and dark-side-of-the-moony and nothing can harm me, nothing to fear.

She didn't even mind that I want to take Clive Barker to the critical

100

fraternity.

I smile against the warm covers.

I go to the bathroom and make an incision to my face. It bleeds for a while and I dab at it until it clears.

Downstairs, Dad looks in good form.

'Ye missed it!' he's guffawing, 'Richard an Judy. This wee lassie agein prematurely. This wee toddler wi a sixteen-year-old body. By the time she's sixteen she'll hae the body ae an eighty-two year old.'

'That's a sin, man.'

'Naw, it's funny!'

'Naw, it's no fuckin funny!' I shout at him, suddenly scathing. I hate it when he does this. Laughs at dying puppies on *Animal Hospital* and the greety expressions on the kids' faces. 'It's a tragedy! That could have just as easily have been me or Derek, so dinnae come it!'

He mutters under his breath, slamming toast into his mouth.

'Whit!'

'Nothin.'

Stroppily, I roam the kitchen for mail. Hospital appointment card for Dad. Probably to blame for his mood this morning. No fucking bread left either. When Mum was here there was always bread in the bread bin. Usually a few other things, right enough. Vodka. Pills.

Coco-Pops. King of Cereals. I set them down on the table.

'Dad?'

'Hmm?' he munches, non-committal. Doesn't like it when I argue back. Retreats like a puppy with its arse skelpt, in fact.

'Ah minded somethin the other day.'

'Hmm.'

'See when Mum disappeared . . . the policeman who came roon . . . asked me if you'd ever hit her . . .'

Dad's eyes, calm, still tuned to the telly. He picks up the remote-control and changes the channel, muttering. 'Cannae stand that bloody Richard Madeley–'

'He said that might have been why Mum left.'

'–him and that Finnegan woman. Obnoxious pair.'

There's a stain under my school photo on the wall there. In my memory, the coffee is unfolding mid-air from the cup. The orchestral smash against the wall, and the brown seeping

slowly

down.

Their shouts meshing and Dek trying to separate the pair of them and maybe this is just an implanted memory like in *Blade Runner* but if it was how would I know?

too much

'Was it, Dad? Was that why she left?'

'How should Ah ken?' he shrugs. 'Pass us up the *Daily Record*, will ye. See whit's on telly.'

I pass it to him and wait while his eyes travel the first couple of pages.

'Did you ever hit her?'

'Look!' he snaps, crumpling the paper. 'Did *you* ever huv tae restrain a drunk woman wavin a knife in yer face and callin ye the Antichrist?'

'Aye, Ah did actually.'

'Did ye ever huv tae share a hoose wi somebody who hadnae been sober for a week, who nearly burnt the hoose doon four times because she'd left the grill on?' Darkness ringing his eyes.

'Ye ken Ah did.'

'Did ye ever go intae yer room and find everythin ae value missin, but three bottles ae whisky under the bed?'

'Aye, Dad, Ah did that too.'

I'm trying to work out if that single droplet of salt-water in my cereal will affect the taste. He better not have ruined my Coco-Pops (King of Cereals) cos there's none left in the packet, just a wee plastic figure from a new Disney film.

'Well then!' Dad throws the *Daily Record* onto the couch. The air catches it the wrong way and its pages scatter. 'If you ken so much aboot it, why are ye fuckin askin?!'

The stairs creaking and his bedroom door slamming and Bob Geldof rumbling, muffled, asking why he doesn't like Mondays. Like, how are we supposed to know?

This didn't end when she left, the bitch.

I hate her.

Dek's latest postcard, lying on the breakfast bar, has a picture of a sunbathing woman carefully combing her pubic hair. On the back he has written

From one fanny to another!

and it makes me head out to school in a better mood than I should be. But I still miss him. Miss that monkey-face he used to make to cheer me up, the rubbery bottom-lip and the ears sticking out.

The incision I made on my cheek still stings.

When Mum and Dad used to take us on walks in the woods, me and Dek would always be mad-charging round the next bend, desperate to see what lay ahead. Mum warning us not to run off, keeping us tight by her side, and the anticipation so great it was painful, we just *had* to see, we could not stay still, anything could've been waiting for us. A fire-breathing dragon? A lagoon? Or if we were on a drive, and we saw the lights of a town far in the distance, we'd always think it was the shows. *Dad, Dad, it's the shows! Can we go ower there tae the shows?*

Then we'd get there. And realise it was just another shitty scheme like Hallglen.

There were never any dragons or lagoons either.

The sunlight taunts, light without heat. As I wind my way through the stark seventies labyrinth of Hallglen, past the primary school where my childhood was spent in a warm haze of Barrs limeade and football, some of the school weans follow me shouting, 'Awright big man! Like yer PVC jaiket, ya mad jester, ye!' and I slip my earphones on and the Velvet Underground drones them away.

Onto the Glen Brae, underneath the high-tension towers, across the cold-blasted space of the ash-park at Lochgreen. The Falkirkscape wide and still below, God's dust-jacket for his crappiest book. Grangemouth oil-complex unfurling pollution against the sky. I am tired. I am weary. And I barely make it into assembly before they close the doors.

Mr Melville strides up to the podium. His red hair seems to burn with an Old Testament authority. Connor Livingstone follows him with immaculate panther movements. Hair slicked and flicked into place. Sees me standing dishevelled at the back of the assembly hall, shakes his head, and then

Tyra!

Her name is like chamber music. Murmurs of approval as she steps onto the stage. Her face cool and smooth. Her skirt keeping her tantalising thighs out of sight. She sits, hands flat on her knees, looking into the middle distance, goddess-like. Connor smiles at her and she smiles at him, like they're Bucks Fizz about to perform at Eurovision, and when she looks out at the assembly, I try to catch her attention the same way, nodding away like some TV magician whose tricks are failing, but she doesn't see me.

Melville gives one last sweep round the hall for late-comers and I merge nervously into the curtain.

'We have!' Melville booms, like a big mad Welsh vocalist, his eyes bulging, 'A special guest for today's assembly . . .'

Two Tammyhill neds in front of me fizz with sarcasm.

(*'Britney Spears?' 'Kelly Brook? In the scud*!')

104

'Now, most of you are coming up to an age when those privileges which you have been hitherto denied will be made available . . .'

(*'he means shaggin!' 'look at Melville shitein himsel tae say it!'*)

'. . . the consumption of alcohol and tobacco . . .'

(*'shaggin!' 'gon, say it.' 'shaggin!'*)

'. . . the right to vote . . .'

(*'shaggin! Gon!' 'Ah bet he disnae say it!'*)

'. . . and, of course, intercourse with members of the opposite sex. Or in these post-Clause 28 days, members of your own sex . . .'

(   )

'These are not privileges which are given lightly!' His eyes are bulging and veined. 'As you pass into adulthood, you will be accorded even greater responsibility. An occupation. A family. A home.'

Brian watching *Saving Private Ryan* with moist eyes. The young hurled, flailing, into the fray.

'This responsibility must be used wisely and with proper consideration for the society which has conferred it upon you.'

Gunshots. Bullets. Blood.

'. . . and so we have here Mr John Johnson of the Automobile Association, who is going to speak to you about the issue of safe driving.'

If Ah wis a religious man, Ah'd say a prayer for thae young boys. Ah'd say a fuckin

I am instantly bored, even though Mr John Johnson does his best to scare the shite out of us. Slides of car wrecks and high-speed collisions and burning motorbikes and dolls flung to the side of the road flash past. He thunders, 'And the driver of *this* car was only twenty-one!' at the appropriate points. But his presence here has the opposite effect. Cars? Driving? Freedom! I gaze round at these hopeful faces, thrust from blazers. Bright, young, arrogant eyes, glinting at the highway of the future through an imagined windscreen, feet pressing invisible accelerators, dying to be let loose on the world, then

The assembly mutates. Like in a horror film.

Every one of us old and bent in the year 2070, staring vacantly at a giant TV screen in an Old Folk's Home. The sixteen-year-old kitchen-boy mocking us over bowls of gelatinous soup, dying to get out from work and into his hover-car with his mates, to attack the highways that float eerily in the night above Scotland.

'Auld bastards,' he smirks, turning the key in the ignition, taking off with the rest of the boyracers towards the ozone layer. Or what's left of it.

Tyra shines amid this apocalyptic ruin. Perpetually young. My angel of the motorway. I catch her eye. She smiles as if to say: '*Boring or what.*' Or maybe: '*Kiss me/Out in the milky twilight.*' But it's all I need. Something has possessed me. The spirit of all of those dying cars? The nightmare prospect of myself trapped in an Old-Biddy's Home in the future with a silver-haired Connor Livingstone and his golf buddies? I have a few thousand days in which to live, and I will not be mute, because when I am jammed in that armchair near the end of my life, the decades having spilt like coins between the cushions, I want to know that I did what I could to have the woman I loved.

Carpe Diem (and all that shite from films that Dolby likes). I'm going to fucking ask her. Right now. Straight after this assembly!

she is

the

106

most

beautiful

On the screen above her, a twisted Ford and a wrecked Cortina embrace in a metal union, their fenders locked, their smashed windows touching lips, the love leaking from the radiator down, down, towards the drains.

'Tyra!'

I try to push through the throng, but she's being led away towards the Rector's office with Melville and Mr John Johnson. Connor at her back, musing falsely: 'Well, yes, I thought there was quite an *impact* to the presentation. If you'll pardon my pun!'

'Tyra!'

My heart going at it like a Motorhead album. The fear and the defeat of fear. Three bints reading an exam timetable in my way and Tyra almost disappearing from sight into the admin corridor. I slam against the double-doors, shout

'Tyra!'

like a shot prisoner. But Livingstone is holding them closed.

Appealing sweetly.

'Sorry, Alvin,' he frowns, 'Tyra's busy with her prefect duties at the moment. We have to lunch with Mr Johnson to thank him for his informative talk.'

The veneer slides from him, slick, onto my hands, making me feel like I need to wash.

'It's just for a second, Connor! Ah want tae–'

'Not *now*, Alvin,' he commands, like I'm a collie-dog (half-expecting him to shout '*Stay!*' and throw me a rubber bone). 'It's really very important you don't interrupt. You might get her in the prefects' hut at the end of the lunch-break.'

'Connor,' I mutter, exasperated. 'As you well know, I am not a prefect. I'm not allowed into the prefects' hut.'

107

The Brian Mann creeping out from under my clothes. This must be how the Incredible Hulk feels (or would do if he had to contend every day with Pulp-song-made-flesh Livingstone). Connor closing the double-doors on me, officiously. 'Sorry. No non-prefects allowed in the admin corridor. You *might* see her in English class after lunch . . .'

His Head-Boy badge gleams victoriously.

'Connor!'

I start banging on the glass. But Livingstone is retreating further up his own privilege, his last look towards me a handsome shrug. 'Is she havin a party soon? Ih? Is she havin a party? Ah'm Ah invited? Ih? Ah'm Ah invited?

'Ah bet *you're* invited ya fuckin–'

She isn't in English class after lunch.

Still ladying it with Lord Livingstone and Mr Melville and John Johnson. John Johnson. Sounds like a name you'd give your tadger. Mrs Gibson is reading a solemn passage from *The Great Gatsby*, shuttering the blinds, making the classroom dark with terrifying speed and I am trying to conceive various strategies for getting into Rosie's.

'*The music had died down as the ceremony began and now a long cheer floated in at the window, followed by intermittent cries of "Yea-ea-ea!" and finally by a burst of jazz as the dancing began . . .*'

Tyra's vacant seat. I will the emptiness to take on her shape. She appears, in a special-effect, morphing out of thin air. Her whole body is the colour of iced-water. Her voice the sound of classical music.

When the bell goes for the end of period, she explodes like a shot aquarium, and I push my fingers to my temples and rub at a sudden, whining pain.

'*"We're getting old," said Daisy, "If we were young we'd rise and dance . . ."* '

Despite the randomness of events in my life, despite the speed at which it all crashes past, despite the Lads, Belinda, the colour, the laughter, a new and grown-up world opening about me, the big bursting choruses followed by inventive guitar-solos, despite friendship, family, education, the welfare state, the abolishment of the nuclear threat, I still sense horror lurking. At the end of the road. Something dark, unformed, mysterious, waiting for me to hit it like in the prologue to a werewolf story, the Lads all hanging around for something to happen, for the alarm bell of their thirties to go off maybe.

If being a teenager was a job, you wouldn't apply for it. 'Enterprising youths wanted for angst-filled soul-searching. Seven-year contract. Bathroom breaks. Will affect your sex-life.'

Dolby's mad-keen on going back onto the cruising circuit, been bugging us about it for weeks, since he's found 'Shiney' in another chat-room, going on about 'the buzz you get, better than drgs' [sic] like one of the Hash-Heads from Falkirk High, puffing and spluttering and whining on about 'freeing the weed, *maaaan*'. So we give Belinda the old spit and polish – don't want them thinking we're boyracers – and head to another 'secret location' in Grangemouth and it's all covert and mad, like being in *Donnie Brasco*.

On the way there, Frannie tells us about a group of ducks he saw on his way to work this morning, 'Obviously lost like, cos fuck knows whit they were daein ootside Tesco.'

'They'll be fae Cally Park,' Brian suggests, scratching his stubble, reading an article in *Maxim* about a bottomless bar in Texas, which I glance at over his shoulder.

'But Tesco is, like, a *mile* fae Cally Park.'

'Aye,' Brian tuts. 'Hence bein fuckin *lost*.'

'Anyway,' Frannie continues, '*Dick!* It's a mammy duck and her wee chicks, and one of the chicks is laggin behind in the car-park–'

'They were in the car-park?'

'Aye,' Frannie seethes, impatient, 'As ye just pointed oot, they were fuckin *lost*, weren't they!'

'Go on.'

'So this wee chick's laggin–'

'Duckling.'

'Whit?'

'Duckling, no chick. Chicks are baby hens.'

'Aw, right, so this wee *duckling's* laggin behind, and Ah'm watchin it squeakin away, tryin tae keep up like. Wee shame for it. Ah wis gonnae go ower an gie it a hand, but then somebody shouts on me – ken Big Maxie? – an when Ah look ower again it's disappeared.'

'Disappeared? The duckling? Are ye sure it didnae just catch up?'

'*Will ye listen tae the fuckin story?*'

'Ah'm listenin! It's just takin too fuckin long!'

'It's takin too fuckin long because you keep fuckin interruptin!'

'It's just dull, Frannie. It's just a dull story. Chicks in a car-park. So whit?'

'Oh, Ah thought ye said they were *ducklings*!'

I pick up the copy of *Maxim* which Brian has disregarded in favour of refining Frannie's storytelling, to read an interview with some girls on a night out in Glasgow:

MAXIM: Are Scots lassies up for it, then?

Heather: We're quite forward if that's what you mean.

Lisa: Aye, I mean if we see something we want, we just go and get it. Life's too short to be a wallflower, intit?

MAXIM: How far would you go in bed?

Karen: Threesomes. Foursomes. I've even dressed up in my school uniform once.

MAXIM: Who was that for?

Karen: My science teacher.

Lisa: Truth is, I'd love to get off with another woman while a man watched!

Heather: Yeah! But that's like giving him his fantasy on a plate. You have to make him work for it.

MAXIM: What do you look for in a man?

Lisa: I love it when a rough man just takes me, and he's all sweaty from a day at work and we have really filthy sex all over the house!

Frannie and Brian have resolved the issue of whether a duckling can be called a chick: 'So the *chickling's* disappeared, right, an Ah'm a wee bit concerned for it, eh? Cos it's a wee shame bein lost like that, an the mammy duck's noticed, an she's gettin aw frantic, lookin for it, so Ah starts lookin for it. And then Ah realise where it's gone . . .'

p.12 VIRTUAL MAXIM: Score with Courtney online! Can you get to first base with our cyber-babe? (www.maxim-magazine.co.uk).

p.22 YASMIN BLEETH: '*In Baywatch*, I didn't play a model or a bimbo, I played a responsible role. It just so happens lifeguards wear bikinis . . .'

p.16 LADS NIGHT: We take you to Sheffield, for the ultimate night out with the boys!

'It had fallen doon the drain.'

Frannie pauses, to deliver the emotional punch of this. We're trying not to piss ourselves at the image of this duck floundering in the fag-ends, quacking helplessly.

'So Ah lifted up the grille, an Ah'm just about greetin by now, like, cos the thing's so panicked, an its fur's aw dirty an its wee heart's beatin like a drum an Ah haud it in ma hauns an carry it ower tae the mammy duck, really feelin like Ah'd achieved somethin, ken?'

111

. . . page after page of Porsche Turbos, Gent USA gear, Nokia ('Fun Outside, Serious Inside'), Ralph Lauren shaving products, Jimmy Bee shoes ('Jimmy's Gonna Sort You Out!'), Pierre Cardin t-shirts ('Label Envy!'), the 'twenty most wanted stereo systems in the world' ('I prefer large knobs') . . .

'But the mother had been killed,' Frannie concludes, mournfully. 'Run ower by a car. An aw the ducklings were hoppin and flappin round her body, splashin aboot in the blood.'

There is a space in which no-one says anything. Frannie gazes towards the window.

We drive on.

The races are busier than last time. There's about eighty motors, and puffa jackets dash across the car-park, leaning into windows, making preparations, revving engines, comparing sound-systems, wheel-trims, while Grangemouth Oil Refinery looms above us, sooty smoke spewing. A sticker saying MAD MALC. Neon tubes and dry ice and a *Blade Runner* effect glows on the sprayed shells of the cars. Alloy wheels gleam futuristically. The words BORN TO CRUISE. A repetitive whump of bass.

The guy called Shiney is here, even recognises us. 'Just watchin again, gents?' he grins, making us sound like perverts at some strip-show, and as we cruise past, Brian mentions a rumour that Kottsy, the weapon from the Hollywood Bowl, might be sending a squad into Smith's to turn the place over.

We watch the races: the pod-race in *The Phantom Menace* with Falkirk scenery. A Renault Megane and a Clio neck and neck and I notice one of them has an Irn-Bru can on the dash and I ask Dolby again why this can wouldn't land in the back-seat if dropped in the front but he

          can't always get what you want
          no you can't always get what you

shushes me. Three noddies are heading our way. Dolby rolls down the
window. They glower at us like plumbers faced with a continual leak.
'Can we *help* youse chaps?' one of them (sort of) growls.

'Just here tae watch the races,' Dolby answers, shrugging, 'Cleared
it wi Shiney on the chat-room likes.'

The noddies frown. 'But yese are no . . . eh . . . racin yersels?'

'Be a funny thing tae race yersel!' Frannie laughs, and they look at
him, and he shuts up.

'No,' Dolby says, clutching Belinda's wheel protectively, 'We're no
up for that.'

'An yese arenae daein the Burnout?'

One of them has walked to the rear of the car and is checking the
licence-plate, and it occurs to me that if we just come along here and
watch every time – spare pricks that we are – they might actually
think we're

'Polis,' one of them, a guy called Swaz, says to the other.

'Fuck off!' Brian splutters, 'Look at the age ae this wan! He look
like polis?'

The three noddies turn their attention to me, sitting hunched in
the back seat as if on a potty.

'Runt's no even auld enough tae vote!' Brian laughs, 'Eh no?'

'No even old enough tae vote,' I repeat.

The noddies nod, still checking for a hidden blue light or the letters
POLIS scratched away from Belinda's bonnet.

'Well if yese arenae polis,' Swaz requests calmly, 'ye'll no mind if
we use yer car for the Burnout?'

'Course no,' Dolby replies, powerless.

We wheel Belinda over to a corner, where boyracers surround an

113

XR3i some weapon has 'come across'. The car is being re-decorated with dance music against its will, its features tested by cackling youths (electric sunroof, voice that intones 'rear door not shut' like the background to a Radiohead track). As they notice our arrival – haircuts, label-less gear – I feel the part of the castaway walking into the tribe. Without a gun.

'Ye sure Belinda can take this?' Brian whispers to Dolby. His large hands cover his knees, flexing.

'Ye sure *Ah* can fuckin take it?' Dolby replies, with a deep breath, as we get out of the car, leaving him in the front seat like a Lego test-pilot. 'Just make sure ye get oot the fuckin way in time!'

We gather round the bonnet.

Me, Brian and Frannie are in central position. Our hands splay, our shoulders tense. Three noddies (Adidas, Nike, Fila) jostle and grin and I swallow what feels like a ball of paper in my throat and just before Dolby, staring blankly through the windscreen, turns the key, one of them turns, shouts

'This is what it's fuckin aw *aboot*!'

and Belinda roars, a waking dragon. We take the strain, our heels digging against the tarmac. The car makes a noise like a rottweiler on its leash, the tyres screaming as the six of us push against it. Frannie looks like a rock-singer midway through a ballad, and just as I start to laugh,

our ground slips.

Belinda inches forwards. Someone shouts, 'Clear!' and we leap away as Belinda accelerates, Dolby hard at the wheel, the adrenaline shooting into a five-point star inside me; I whoop, delirious, slap hands with Brian then hear a

crack.

Someone screams.

The sound of splintering bone. A tyre bumping back to the ground.

A long, uncontrolled wailing.

'Chas? Chas? Ye awright? Ye awright, man?' Me and Brian glance at each other. My lungs suddenly feel like lead. Dolby, pale, behind the wheel. The weapons all surround Chas, who is howling like the war wounded. The surface of the world ripped open; something ugly yawns beneath. Frannie whispers: '*We should mibbe get ootae here . . .*' but Dolby is a salt-pillar, mouth hanging open as if he's killed someone, so we just stand there, useless as grandparents at a rave, watching

eShiningTheGoodtheBadandtheUglyRagingBullDirtyHarry-
PredatorCarrieJawsForaFewDollarsMoreJerryMaguireArma-
geddonTradingPlacesCasinoTheBreakfastClubBornonthe-
FourthofJulyEntertheDragonBoogieNightsLAConfidential-
DieHardTheExorcistFullMetalJacketIntheLineofFireTheGod-
fathertwOneandTwo(noThree)SavingPrivateRyanScreamA-
liensTrainspottingTheXMenTheTerminatorTheUsualSus-
pectsAFewGoodMenBatmanLockStockand

the same argument erupting as we retire to Global Video: Brian a bulldog, objecting to every suggestion. Dolby usually mediates, but nobody has seen him all day (probably out with Prontaprint Lisa, latest Lassie Pal, for whom neither Brian nor Frannie has given approval).

Frannie has demanded Eddie Murphy's 1983 classic *Trading Places* ('An listen tae you *quote* it aw night?'), while I've opted for a film starring Katie Holmes from *Dawson's Creek*, but Saving Private Brian gets his own smug way as usual, and we're forced to suffer another three maudlin hours in the trenches with men. With men! Without Katie Holmes! When he sneaks to the toilet Frannie grumbles it's as well we never fought in the war beside Brian Mann: '*Cover ye, ya cunt? Who's been coverin ye the hale war! Cover yersel, ya lazy bastard, Ah've a*

115

pub tae run.'

Outside, the day and night have appeared at once like a tragi-comic mask, and the three of us are yakking about Brian's new barmaid (not only a visible bra-strap, but panty-line) when

Dolby comes in.

His face is heavy.

He looks round the room, his tongue running over his top lip, quick.

'Where've *you* been?' Brian grunts, pausing the video on Tom Hanks' grime-covered face.

'Something tae tell yese,' Dolby mutters, ashen.

I turn the sound down on the stereo. Radiohead raising only a quiet racket. Dolby pacing up and down in front of the drinks-cabinet.

'Whit? If it's aboot that guy's broken leg–'

'It's no aboot naebody's broken leg!' he retorts, defensively. 'Things just huvtae change! Awright?'

'Aye okay,' Frannie placates him, stunned, 'Whit's the problem?'

'Ah'm . . .' He breaks off, wipes his hands across his face. There's a hole in his *Ghost Rider* t-shirt, just above the eye-socket of the Spirit of Vengeance, and I'm sure it's nothing to do with his news but it terrifies me all the same, like a hole in the universe. Dolby adores that t-shirt.

'Hurry up!' demands Brian, 'Whit is it?'

'Ah'm no afraid tae admit it anymair . . .'

'Admit whit?!' A shard of panic in Frannie's voice. Each of us suddenly reassessing all the times we've been alone with Dolby (did he say anything? make any untoward physical gestures?), our mental picture of him shifting. Brian's face avalanches with terror.

'Tell us!'

'Yer no . . . ?' Frannie can't even bring himself to say it.

'Ah'm . . .' Dolby stands erect, holds up his head. '*Uriel*!'

The room resounds with the note of a piano falling from a van.

For one brilliant second I imagine Dolby is going to open his jacket and unfold a pair of wings. In an interstellar burst, back to save the universe.

'Whit d'ye mean yer *Uriel*?' Brian sneers, 'Is that some sort ae *code*?'

'Ah've changed ma name,' he nods defiantly. 'Deed poll. It's done. Nae mair Martin Dolby.'

My head is roving from Brian to Frannie to Dolby and back like Regan from *The Exorcist* and I laugh out loud. The three of them stare at me.

'Uriel . . .' Brian groans, hiding his face with his hands, thinking, no doubt, about the first punter in Smith's he has to introduce to Dolby.

Frannie looks almost betrayed, as if Dolby has kept a lottery-win quiet or something. 'Let me get this straight,' he snaps, 'You want us, yer best mates, tae call ye *Uriel*?'

'Or Uri,' Dolby nods, 'For short.'

'Uri?'

His hand shaking, Dolby whips the *TV Times* out from under Brian's coffee-table, where it lies with the *Rangers News* and all the books on undercover agents in the IRA. 'Ooh,' he goes, totally without conviction, '*Buffy*'s on . . .'

'Uri?'

Dolby flicking through, rapid, searching for exciting television, preferably on now, right now. 'And *Live and Let Die*. Dunno but youse, but Ah always preferred Roger Moore like. The actin eyebrow.'

'Uri?'

'Fuckin Uriel?'

'Uriel, man, ye cannae be serious!'

'Look Lads . . .' Dolby collapses into the settee. His eyes roll up, corpse-like. 'Ah'm nineteen. Ah've been fittin bloody whirlpools the last three years ae ma life . . .'

'So?' tuts Frannie, 'Ah stack shelves for a livin! Dinnae see me

117

changin ma name tae Frodo!'

'Alvin – you've read *1984*? At the school, eh? Ah tell ye, Ah'm sick ae bein a fuckin *prole*.'

He leans back, hands behind his head, his weary gaze unravelling the patterns on Brian's cornices as if they are an escape map to a battlefield of orcs and elves, gladiators and wizards, dragons rearing from the mist of his imagination and flashing the undersides of their gilded bodies. 'I'm sick ae bein Mar-tin-fuck-in-Dol-by,' he seethes, 'Whirpool fitter.'

(Frannie mouths at me: '*Whit the fuck's a prole?*')

'But Uriel, man?' says Brian, fraught, as if by changing his name, Dolby is telling Brian to quietly go fuck himself. 'Ye cannae seriously expect–'

'*Listen!*' Dolby snaps, scissoring upright, 'If you're aw ma mates . . .'

He glances at me.

Help us out, Alvin. Please.

'. . . ye'll be happy fur me.'

But the only thing I can think to do – what can *I* do – is, uselessly, stand up and cross to the drinks-cabinet, pick up a bottle of peach-schnapps, watch the clear liquid slosh and sway seductively and

you ever huv tae restrain a drunk woman wavin a knife in your face

unscrew the top before my conscience can stop me.

The awful sound of it gurgling. My knees pressed together at the top of the stair, listening to the cap unscrewed in the kitchen. The hurried gulp and gasp. And though I couldn't sleep, I would not go to her.

'Since, fellas, we're aw forgettin that Ah'm sixteen tomorrow . . .'

I hand one of the glasses to Dolby.

'And tae celebrate oor mate's, em, news . . .'

I swallow the schnapps.

Feel it burn down my throat. Hot. Irrevocable.

118

'Let's get pished!'

so Brian cracks opens the Glenfiddich he's been saving for Judgement Day – 'Heddy-haw!' – *The Best Rock Album in the World* . . . *Ever* turned up, up, way up, Frannie hollering 'Follow, Follow! We Will Follow Rangers!' and though I try a sip of the whisky it makes me feel sick so I stick to the peach-schnapps, my stomach fluttering and the Lads raising Holy Hell and I smile weakly, drain the dregs which are turning, slid

ing, snidily, like poi

Ur-*i*!
Ur-*i*!
Ur-*i*!

son. Dolby slugging the Glenfiddich, shaking his head, dazed, while outside the clouds unburden themselves, unforgivingly, washing the scum from the streets and Led Zeppelin allowing No Quarter inside and the next-door neighbours starting to bang and Brian banging back, laughing – 'Fuck youse! Ma mate's an angel!'

Dolby and Fran flick through Brian's CDs – *The Wall*, Motorhead, the soundtrack to *The Beach*, Craig David, Motorhead again, sudden up–

mother, do you think they'll drop the bomb?

surge of schapps in my gut, and I burp, and as Brian absorbs the sight of me skating towards drunkenness, he beams, arm trapping my neck, whispering something buddy I don't quite catch for Dolby and Fran raking through drawers for the photos from our first fishing trip (the one where I fell in), laughing fraternally – 'Am Ah right? *Am Ah right?* Aye, yer a good wee cunt, Alvin! Number One Runt!' – and round about here without me even noticing the decision is made to go to the

'Toon Centre!'

Brian slams us into the taxi, falsetto Blondie-singing (not 'Atomic'), the driver, amused, another squad of Lads at large, an average night, until Dolby leans forward, puts his hand on the cabbie's shoulder and goes:

'Ah'm so happy, mate . . . This is the maist important day ae ma life . . .'

'Wettin the baby's heid?'

'Naw. Ah've changed ma name tae Uriel.'

'. . .'

We pass Belinda, waiting cold and patient outside Dolby's house, lonely as a whale calling for a mate in the ocean, but tonight the Brae is a magic-carpet ride into a town of riches, excess. Daylight disappearing rapid-style, covering its own ass, because the town is alive, and Chris Moyles is on Radio One doing a feature called *The Top Ten Restaurant Arguments* while we yabber about

Where to sit.
('. . . headin straight tae Rosies or . . .')
9. Complaints about the food.
('. . . *is high, but I'm holdin on* . . .')
8. Speaking too loudly–
('. . . Alvin, we're gonnae get you *so* pished . . .')
7. Rudeness to staff.
('. . . shame for lassies wi wee tits when ye think about . . .')
6. Who pays the bill.
('. . . *wanna be your number one* . . .')
5. Loud or messy eating.
('. . . but the Runt's no gonnae get . . .')
4. Spillages.

('. . . *nuuuuumber onnne* . . .')

3. **Eyeing up other diners.**

('. . . shame for guys wi wee dicks when ye . . .')

2. **Pinching partners' chips.**

('Sorry, mate, did you say *Uriel* . . .')

1. **People getting extremely dru**

into Smith's first, Brian commanding his lassie staff – 'Get ma guests here a round ae Aftershocks' – while me, Frannie and Dolby gridlock the jukebox. Brian's is a proper pub: off the High Street, cobbled lane, everything made from wood, real fire crackling in the grate, real horse-racing on the telly. Real auld geezer to hassle you like fuck at the jukebox. Scrooge they call this annoying bugger. 'Pit Sinatra oan,' he croaks, like a wean pleading for a Christmas present. 'Sinatra . . . everybody likes Sinatra . . .'

Dolby cares not. 'Sorry, mate, we're payin for it, eh?'

101/4 Wam Du Project – *King of my Castle*
120/6 Oasis – *Rock 'n' Roll Star*

> 'Fuckin Sinatra, boys, eh? Nane ae that modern stuff . . .'
>> 'Look, pal. It's oor money, we'll pit oan whit we want!'

'Shelley! *Ho*! *Shelley*! Round ae Aftershocks? The laddie's sixteenth . . .'

098/13 Radiohead – *Paranoid Android*

'Naebody likes that garbage . . . Got tae play stuff

everybody likes!'

'Naw ye dinnae! It's ma pound coin, ma choice!'

Sinatra! . . . 0 . . . 6 . . . 7 . . .'

067/01 Frank Sinatra – *My Way*

'Hoi! Did you just type that in there?'

'Boys!' Brian calls, 'Haw! *Uriel's Angels*! Leave that fuckin jukebox, here's yer Aftershocks. Sawright, Shelley hen, Ah'll ring it through the till later.'

151/12 Bruce Springsteen – *Born to*

'Runt!' Brian toasts, raising his little beaker of Aftershock, gentlemanly, 'Here's tae yer sixteenth! First night pished!'

'The Runt!'

'Runt!'

'Runt,' I manage, staring at the tiny red abyss at the bottom of the glass (medicine? mouthwash?) before I throw it (blood?) into my throat and screw shut my

'AAAaaaaaGGHHHH . . .'

'Eeeecchhhhh . . .'

'UH. UH. UH.'

Brian swallows, calmly, then places the empty beaker onto the bar. 'Right, Shelley, another round ae Aftershocks.'

The taste of washing-up liquid and nitrogen and aniseed in an illicit rave on my tongue (at *no point* did I grant them a licence), Frannie, Dolby, hunched, deformed with the awfulness of it. Frannie moans:

'. . . EEooooAAgggggg . . .'

and I shake my head. Buffalo charging from one side of it to the other. Shoogle my

arms like

      plasticky

               glasses lined back up on the bar, filled with, filled with. Scrooge wandering up to the jukebox, fumbling through the discs and wincing as

   tonight . . .

         I'm a rock 'n' roll star!

Oasis churn up the pub. 'Hey, wee man!' Scrooge calls to me, 'Borrow a pound for the jukebox, pit some Neil Diamond oan?' 'Borrow?' I blink at him, 'You'll give me it back?' 'Aye!' His lip raises, showing a rusty car grille of teeth. 'How cheap d'ye hink Ah'm are? Just tae pit "Love On The Rocks" on!' I flick a pound coin at him, and Brian's new barmaid Shelley is

   totally un-ugly! As she leans, chestily, to pour the Aftershock, her cleavage looms, but she catches my gaze, pushing it away from her breasts.

   'Right!' Brian lifts his beaker, 'To Good Man Ur-i-el. The artist formerly known as Dolby!'

   'Uri!'

   'Uriel!'

   'Hmp,' I gulp, knocking it back and when my head revolves back to planet earth I see Shelley sort of frowning, her brittle whisper to Brian – '*You watch that laddie tonight*' – while I just grin at her, foxily, glowing.

   'She is *so* cool,' Dolby mutters, wistful, 'A cool girl with cleavage.'

   '. . . who kens how tae mix cocktails.'

   'Oot ae oor league, boys.'

   'Never!' I proclaim, slamming my plastic beaker onto the bar with manly conviciton, startling even myself.

Brian laughs. 'You, Runt? Every punter *in* here's tried tae pull her!'

I glint drunkenly, watching the expert way she whips a packet of Ready Salted from the box, her arse rolling in her regulation skirt, and almost tell her I am human and I need to be loved but I'm just one of many bodies crushed in a cluster round the bar, waving empty glasses at her, yet it's me she responds to, promptly, maternally, and soon I'm trying to get my pound coin back from Scrooge and his ugly-puppet features are outraged.

'Ye want it back, wee man!' he seethes. 'There it's back then! Ah'll gie ye yer measly one pound back! Ken how? Cos Ah'm no a cheap cunt like you!'

Scrooge totters to his warren by the fireside, muttering, and in the mirror that hangs solemnly above the bar I see myself lacquered on the surface. A hunched, lonely figure in Shipyard Scotland, hands curled round a drink as if trying to keep warm and I am suddenly a young version of my own Dad. The hair swept back from a worried forehead. The gormless frown. Life minus four decades.

   sledgehammer break from the pool-table shatters

   and Frannie groans as Shelley passes, her twenty-six womanly years moving sensuously.

'Shelley! Psst?' I gesture her over like a bairn who wants the teacher to see his best work. 'Shelley, tell us. Ah'm dyin tae know. Whit's yer favourite Narnia book?'

Shelley frowns at me, washing a glass.

'What?'

'Your favourite Narnia book,' Frannie translates wearily. 'It's his chat-up line.'

'Oh. I'd say . . . um . . . Probably *The Lion, the Witch and the Wardrobe*.'

'Wrong!' I make a noise like a buzzer on TV. 'Everybody says that!' I can tell she's impressed by the subtlety of this sociological experiment, and Frannie is hunkered right up to me on the bar stool and Brian and Dolby are taunting each other across the pool-table like Apollo Creed from the *Rocky* films: '*When I first met you, Stallion, you had the eye of the tiger, man! The eye of the tiger . . .*'

[fog outside the house]
[schoolbag on the kitchen floor]
[mum? what's for dinner?]
[mum?]
[mum, are you]

'Long have Ah known you?' I ask Frannie, remembering fine games at the Hallglen ash-park when I was twelve and Frannie was about fifteen. Matches that would last till the sun dripped away behind the roofs of the scheme and we couldn't see anything and we were thirty-four bairns playing spot-the-ball in the dark, kicking clods of ash and falling in, falling out, falling about. Everything simple. Dolly dimple.

'Dunno?' shrugs Frannie, 'Five years?'

'Man,' I marvel, 'Ah've always admired your attitude to life. Ken? Always a smile on yer face. Always tellin jokes, nae matter whit. You're the Man!'

'Naw,' Frannie mutters. His face darkening. Pushing his drink away down the bar. 'Ah'm no the Man, Alvin.' His voice is ironed out. Insistent. 'Ah work in Tesco, that disnae make me the Man.'

'It does!' I protest. This is suddenly the most important thing in the world, that I make him see this. 'You, Dolby, Brian – youse are aw ma heroes! Ah owe youse everythin.'

'Alvin, yer no listenin tae me . . .'

'Naw, you're no listenin, Fran! You're the Man. Fran the Man! You're, like, Bill Murray in *Ghostbusters*! You're Coisty!'

The shutters are coming up on Frannie's eyes, revealing someone quietly loading a shotgun. Someone surprised to be interrupted. He

125

talks quietly. Firm. As if aware there are lawyers present. 'Now listen . . .

> finally you're paranoid
> but not an
> android

. . . Ah'm no Coisty. Coisty lives in a big hoose in Bearsden. Coisty's scored mair goals than anybody in the Scottish league. Ye listenin? Ah'm the guy that cleans Coisty's windaes.'

'. . . the Man, ken? . . .' I say sort of pitifully, watching a dribble of schnapps balance and fall from the rim of my glass.

'Ah dinnae lord it about at university. Ah dinnae even run a bar like that big-nippled prick ower there . . .'

Brian cannons a ball into a pocket and smugly sips his pint. Pretending it wasn't that great a shot.

> [mum? ye upstairs?]
> [mum what's for]

'. . . aw ma heroes, ken . . .'

'Ah work,' Frannie raises his eyebrows, as if to make me see the simplicity of this, 'In Tesco.'

'But you fuckin love it there, man!'

He sighs and shakes his head. 'Ah love it cos Ah'm eighteen an Ah've nothin tae spend ma money on but petrol and U2 CDs!'

'. . . always gawin on about how much ye love it in Tesco . . .'

'No sure Ah'll love it when Ah'm fuckin thirty-nine though! Get me?' Brian's barmaid patrols the counter like an amazon, pausing to wipe a spillage just in front of us. Catching my eye again. She has a smile like the actress Kirsten Dunst. Man I'd love to

'Get me?'

126

'Aye, man.' Frannie is not angry. But he's that way someone goes when they're suspecting an argument about music is a veiled attack on their beliefs. 'Ah get ye,' I mumble. Knowing my compliment has shot past him and into waste, into the cold of outer space, into

the queue for Rosie's, here, suddenly, before I even notice. The wind whipping bits of paper across the neon sky. Cosmetic faces creased against the cold and I feel lost, orphaned, fighting to be awake to the evening's possibilities, then I am, I'm into it/up for it, wahey! A storm rumbles out from the doors of the nightclub and I *will* get in this time, even though I haven't thought of a date of birth or nothing. Dolby and Frannie arguing about petrol-money owed from last week and the Aftershock is at the piano in the front cortex of my brain, taking requests, and the cinema is showing MISSIN IMPASSIBLE 2 and a girl from Woodlands High School pretends to be with me and the bouncer doesn't even

'Heddy-haw!' Frannie roars. They slap my back, making me cough, laugh, splutter all at once. 'The Runt's made it in! How does it feel?'
 Brian gesturing to a barman he knows, who serves him before a wall of pissed-off clubbers. Dolby waves to a girl on the stairs. 'Wee man!' Frannie beams proudly, 'Ye made it. Whit d'ye think?' well I think

[dad, where's mum?]
[ah've just got in from school and she's no]

Rosie O'Grady's is rising around me, a temple of hedonism. I drink it in, the Aftershock and the schnapps swilling between my ears in a miniature wave-machine. My head buzzing. Young boys/girls darting behind the bar, shaking drinks, lifting drinks, pouring smiles. The dance-floor filled with prettiness. A staircase rising in the centre of everything, girls lounging on its celestial steps, as if in a colour remake of some classic black-and-white movie. They release smoke into the strobe-lit air, turn, slowly, posingly, as muscled shirts appear by magic and hover at their sides. Gyr

> if you buy this record your life will be better
> your life will be better
> your life will be

ating hips, kiss-tinged schoolgirl lips, locked in an ecstatic jam, waves of pink, violet, red smashing and rippling against a shore of heads.

!This is it!

Dolby shouts something as we're contracted into the crush of bodies. Two women, breast to breast, blocking my path – 'Whoa hen,' – I laugh, unsteady on my feet, and they chuck me a dirty look, as I am forced to the stairs, sole oasis in this coruscating beauty, reach the

front step.

Gasping. Sitting down. Laughing. Sweat beginning to rise and coat my skin and I scan round. Brian caught in the faux-lesbo snare. He raises a sly eyebrow at their jiggling bodies. Frannie frantically tapping his mobile –

is

it

ringing?

Dolby says, his facial movements seeming to down-gear as if on slow film-stock. 'Hoi,' the bouncer commands, looming above, and I don't believe it. It's THE OUTLAW JOSEY WALES. 'Need tae move. Cannae sit here, mate.'

I look further up the stairs, where three gorgeous girls are sharing a Smirnoff Ice and office-stories, arranged like empty wedding dresses.

'Whit aboot them?' I nod. 'Are they movin?'

The bouncer's lips lift, like the thing in *Alien*. A row of rock-hard teeth. 'Are you givin me hassle?'

'Ah'm . . . just . . . ken . . .'

I stutter my way back to the dance-floor, terrified, retreating from the xenomorph in the bomber-jacket who stares after me, mad, death-filled.

'Alvino!'

Dolby/Uriel grabbing my shirt, pointing towards a (young) Lulu lookalike and her mate, 'Two reds up ahead. Ah dare ye!' I grin and saunter towards them, a superb chat-up line forming. I am confident of this. I am King Alvin of the Allison clan. I am young and I am alive. 'Watch this,' I nod to Dolby.

There's a flicker of life from the girls as I approach, but their posture is locked. Wary. I am not wearing Ben Sherman and my hair is not cut in any sort of fashionable style. I am a threat. I must be opposed.

'Evening,' I smile Fonzily.

'Hello.'

'Hiya.'

One of them scratches the bridge of her nose. It is slim and faultless.

'My mate over there . . .' I gesture to Brian, formally slugging his Becks. This is a cracking chat-up line. 'Do you reckon he's gay?'

'What?'

One of them blinks. The other one – who is nothing like Lulu close up – stares away, distracted.

'I said my mate over there-'

'I heard you.'

'Well . . .' I try to connect with her large, dull-blue eyes, though this is like trying to shake hands with smoke. 'I was watching Ricki Lake, and *she* said that you can't tell if someone's gay or straight just by appearances so . . .'

The girl stares at me over the rim of her Smirnoff; looks across at the queue for the toilets, perhaps needing to go. No, I refuse to believe this princess has a bladder or bowels. But she's not getting the subtlety of this chat-up line at all.

'Sorry, what did you say?'

'Well I was just wondering if . . . it's possible . . . if you can tell . . .'

'Tell what?'

'Um . . .' I say, '. . . if he's, um, gay or, um, not . . .'

My God, what am I talking about?

What the fuck am I doing here?

Her friend – non-Lulu – picks lint from the front of her dress carefully. 'What does it matter if he's gay or not?'

'Uh, that's not what I'm getting at,' I point out, 'Do you think you can *tell* if–'

'It's what's inside that counts,' she shrugs, devoid of empathy with me, 'You shouldn't judge people by whether they're straight or gay. That's haemophobia.'

Both girls are looking away now. One up at the stairs. The other smiling flirtatiously at someone in the bar queue. Both of these girls are achingly beautiful, as if they've just stepped through a curtain of rain from another dimension, not seeming to know, or care, that I've read, like, a whole Thomas Hardy novel, seen *Citizen Kane* twice, maybe three times!

One says blankly: 'That's just haemophobia.'

The other one blinks.

'Sorry. What are you talking about?'

so I buy myself a double peach-schnapps, having lost the Lads somewhere in the dry ice, and down the drink, and thin figures are rising from the mist as I punt myself away from the bar into the dancefloor into dazzling eyes. Slim cheekbones. Soft cleavages. I am in the final reel of *Apocalypse Now* with all its gorgeous sounds, portentous imagery, Brando mumbling

i watched a snail crawl along the edge of a straight razor. and that's my dream. that's my nightmare.

as the DJ, one of those wannabe Fatboy Slims, does theatrical turns on the deck and shouts, 'Lemme hear ya say yeaaaaahh!' in the style of a fire alarm sending terror through an orphanage – 'Falkirk! The weekend has landed!' – and tanned legs and the smooth smalls of backs and fingers circling glass rims become unf

ixed the more I stare, dissolving into a chaos of loveliness, the floor tipping like in a disaster movie. Tyra isn't anywhere here. Disappeared into the mist like the Blair Witch. I search out her milk-white form, try to find her outline through the spectrum of lights that blink and swan-dive and rise, then I see

[long has your mum been gone?]
[son, this is important]
[this morning?]
[she sent you out to school and you haven't]

the Lads like a cluster of barnacles in the far corner. I stagger into their communal space, shared with a couple of chicks Frannie went to school with. Their mascara-ed eyes bear down on me like sharks and I feel a dull lifeless pain at my heart and pick up a drink someone else has left and down it greedily.

'Where d'ye go tae, ya wee rodent ye?' Brian asks, patting my ba

ck! 'Ye find any Babeular action on the floor there?' 'Naw!' I bray, my voice like Pinocchio's turned into a donkey. A churning pressure in my gut. I slug another double and Dolby and Fran are telling the school-bints about how we ran up Brian's mobile-bill by calling the

Chris Moyles show every weekend for six months and as Brian, horrified, learns this news, his

[she'll come back]
[don't you boys worry okay]
[if your mum was drunk she won't have an]

arm locked round my neck, his fist gnashing my hair. I am released to breathe smoky air. Ceiling the colour of fireworks. The world seeming to explode with lustful glances, glinting earrings, remixed house-tracks. Tongues darting from lipsticked lips. Happiness spreading like a disease across the dance-floor. My mouth tastes sickly, I feel ill, unravelled, oddly depressed. No-one can help me. I realise this. Things only end badly, otherwise they don't end. The Cruiser said that in *Cocktail*, you know. Frannie and Brian fight for first slaggings of Dolby's new name. 'Thing is, right . . .' Brian whispers to him, grinning, 'We were *sure* ye were gonnae tell us ye were a poof.'

'A poof!' The school-girls have faded like lions into the black, afraid of our Lad-light. The four of us embrace, sloppy, pished. True love amidst all this

record your life will be better
your life will be better
your life will be life will be

decadence, and Brian going: 'Dolby, man, nane ae us wid mind if you were a poof.'

'Ah wid!' says Frannie.

'Dinnae listen tae him. Nane ae us wid mind. No me. No wee Alvin there. No that Orange cunt either . . .'

'Aye Ah wid!' Frannie repeats.

Brian and Dolby lean boozily, pressing their foreheads together.

'Disnae matter if yer bent, straight, black, white, Chinky, reptilian, or had yer arms and legs cut aff . . .'

Brian pauses. The music seems to fade. Their eyes locked, a meaning almost biblical transmitted between them.

'You. Will always be. Ma best—'

whoooa

Dolby holds me up, leading me to a free table, my hand stretching for the unattended drinks, Dolby (Uriel!) slapping it away. *Alvin, ya skank! They're no yours!* Fran and Bri start dancing with a girl who resembles Uma Thurman in *Pulp Fiction* but I'm sure comes from Reddingmuirhead (or Bonnybridge), Brian stiff and robotic, as if on old, flickering footage. He dances like someone is threatening him with a knife. The music shuddering and a billion girls silhouetted against the party, against the world, but Tyra's absence walks the room like a spectre. My stomach weeps, the booze staggering through empty capillaries to my head and Dolby (Uriel!) is saying *Listen!* His eyes bright. His tone demanding. I am dying, convinced of it.

'Yrr ma fckin best pal,' I interrupt, 'Aw yese. Fckin lve yse gyys . . .'

Alvin . . . he's barking, though the bass blasts most of his words away *. . . talent, wee man, ken what Ah'm . . .*

'Ken whit yer sayin,' I reply, a (Becks? Miller?) stain seeping into my shirt, which I *know* won't come out. 'Loads fckin talent in here!'

. . . Naw that's no whit Ah'm sayin . . . He slides his chair closer *. . . listen tae me . . . you've got brains, man . . . get tae fuck away fae Falkirk . . . It's deid! Ken whit Ah'm sayin? . . .*

'Naw man!' I protest, hugging him, 'Us frr will eywis be thegither! Meenyoun Briann Fran. We'll fckin eywis be thegither . . .' The love swelling beneath my shirt like a big cartoon heart, as I turn and see a

weapon at the summit of the stairs. Being told The News by his weapon mate. His face turns bad, like fruit in speeded-up film. His mouth hurling sounds into the thick air. Hair seeming to grow on his arms. Oh jesus, it's Kottsy and he's looking at us. The words 'kill that

133

cunt' stab from his mouth at

   . . . *no listenin tae me* . . . Dolby (Uriel!) carries on, insistent, *get
studyin for yer exams, man . . . go tae university an marry some wee
psychology student . . . want tae be a dick aw yer life? Ih? Is that what ye
want? . . .*

'Dolby if you'd been a poof, Ah widnae've minded. No wan bit.
Ah'm so happy, man! Ysss are ma best mayss. Owe mfuckin life t . . .'

I tail off.

There is a moment of clarity.

The dance-floor is spread beneath like a menagerie. The beaks of
vultures, dipping into Bacardi glasses. Squawking lies at the bar.
Everything is evil. One of the most gorgeous girls I've ever seen turns
to me and hisses, '*Whit the fuck ye lookin at, wide-o!*' Bodies,
germinating, mummified in a wrap of brand names and

the horror

the horror

this is what I've been inducted into. Adulthood. The parallel universe
beyond the glass. I tap a girl on the back and ask if she's read Clive
Barker's *Books of Blood* and she pushes me away, as if I've offered to
sever her limbs. You haven't seen the film *Carrie* either? No. Just
checking! Just checking!

   . . . remember reading somewhere how sleepwalking starts in
children as they become aware of their mortality and all the clubbers
here are shrunken and dressed in pyjamas dangling teddy-bears and
looking for mothers and padding single-file into a vast consuming
darkness . . .

   '*If we were young we'd rise and dance . . .*' said Gastby's love.

Everything dead. And lovely. And dead. Pre-programmed dance-
moves. Youth risen from the grave for one last, final, oh-fuck-it-then
rave, before the whole charade collapses and when I turn Kottsy has

Dolby down on the ground and is trying to kick the shit out of him but Brian and Frannie are racing from the dance-floor and everyone is staring, appalled, and I charge into the fray like a super-hero, like Spider-Man, grabbing Kottsy's arm, booting at his ankle, booting, biting his elbow, and then someone's hand closes on my shoulder and I'm

In the back of the taxi.

Headlights passing. Sullen shop windows, street names. Me slumped in the corner of the cab singing 'Animal Nitrate' to myself, which is on

(the first Suede album?)

(*Dog Man Star*?)

Anyway, the boy in the song, he's just an animal.

My black eye pulses and my back hurts. My Mum on the corner of Montgomery Street, waving fondly. I wave half-heartedly back (just *totally* can't be arsed with her right now). Shelley from Smith's in the back-seat next to me, stroking my hair, saying to someone, '*How did you let this boy get in such a state?*' and

Shelley from Brian's pub

likes

stuff from The Gadget Shop?

her flat crammed with toking aliens, bottle-openers in the shape of scarab-beetles, inflatable chairs, lava-lamps. She crosses the room, puts David Bowie's *Hunky Dory* on, laughs at me trying to remove my shoes, as a chess-set, with shot-glasses for pieces, is brought out from a side-cupboard, more Gadget Shop shite. Shelley filling one side with whisky, the other with vodka, and before I can protest I've lost a bishop and three of my pawns and Shelley has lost her blouse, her socks, her ear-rings, the lobes burning a sexy red. Her upper chest flushed with whisky. The CD jumping at 'Oh You Pret-Pret-Pretty Things!' The sound of a party from the next door room and her bookshelf filled with fat Marian Keyes paperbacks (*Rachel's Holiday*, *Watermelon*). 'You're next,' I try to warn her, like that guy at the end of *Invasion of the Body Snatchers*. 'The whole world's fucked,' I say, then '*I once had a girl/or should I say/she once had me*,' but she doesn't hear, drawing my zip down, down, without any fuss, the lava-lamp squirting plasma up into the purple liquid and Shelley's mouth touching the bruises on my neck and she's whispering 'shhhh . . .' and although I try to think of a *Top Gun* quote all I can remember is that line from *Robocop* which goes 'dead or alive you're coming with

I wake.

The morning light twists in smooth, slow curves.

A dream about the river Ganges fresh in my head. Me and Robert DeNiro in a canoe, the soft sound of paddles in water, lulling. Nice dream.

The first thing that seems out of place is the duvet.

Mine has blue flowers on it, but this one has yellow. A yellow flower crushed against my face, bits of lint in my nose. I sneeze, dislodging a dull lump of pain. The mucus particles fall through the sunlight and settle on the strange, yellow duvet.

My bed doesn't usually have a pair of naked shoulders in it either.

Shelley from Brian's pub is zonked out next to me. Her hair plasters her face with medusa-like curls.

I lift the duvet cautiously.

Look down the length of her body . . .

Making my way to the kitchen is like scaling the north face of the Eiger. With a head full of Nirvana b-sides. My whole body aches, especially the back of my neck, which feels as though it has been

136

clawed by something.

Christ.

The Lads ship-shape, in the kitchen. Folding toast into their mouths and flicking through the Sunday papers, various cuts and bruises on their faces, and I can just about read one of the headlines through the slats of my eyes (a Rangers win) as the Lads clock me and roar, as if I've knocked one in during the last minute of an Old Firm final.

I crumple, wincing. Posh and Becks loom apocalyptically in *The News of the World.*

'Well then?' Brian beams.

'Ye shag her?' Frannie beams.

'Long did ye last?' Dolby beams.

I cannot even swing my head round to look at them. TLC singing 'No Scrubs' on the radio and I feel yuk. 'Just think,' Brian seats himself next to me. 'Everyone in that pub has been *dyin* tae dae whit you did last night . . .'

'Look, Ah'm sure she's a very nice girl,' I protest, 'But–'

'Nice-girl schmice-girl! You shagged Shelley!'

and I can only groan at the stark sound of it. While they celebrate my virginity drying on the bedroom sheets, I press my face to the formica, where it's nice and cool and nothing is demanded of me and *Life's Little Instruction Book* lies innocuously open, saying

76. Remember, overnight success usually takes about five years.

77. Never indulge in lawsuits.

78. Keep warm blankets in the boot of your car.

79. Avoid sleeping with barmaids you hardly know.

80. Forget about Tyra Mackenzie now, knob-head!

and I catch sight of the date at the top of the paper, just above

Beckham's fringe.

Happy birthday to me.

We leave, with our grins, jackets, newspapers, hangovers, heading towards Belinda, and I can't even bear to go in and say goodbye to Shelley, thank-you, see you again, any of that shite, so instead I just leave a note telling her we've used her bread and milk, close the door quietly behind me, hear it click, sigh, gaze up at the sky but there's only

Richard and Judy featuring a slot called 'Back From The Brink?', about suicide. Linda from Sussex, Eloise from Maidstone-on-Kent, Susan from Peebles all call up with heart-wrenching tales of shaking in the doctor's surgery/being driven to drink/failed infertility treatment. I watch this, transfixed, the tea in my hand shedding heat from its surface until I look down and find it's grown a limpid skin.

Richard says, 'An hour at a time, a day at a time. And reach out to the ones who love you.'

Dolby is beeping the horn outside. But I am slack-jawed, struck dumb by the level of grief, particularly, in the voice of Susan from Peebles. I cannot move. Dolby continues to beep, the noise of a cartoon character opening and closing its mouth on the edge of the galaxy. I cannot face him. The possibility of movement. Richard and Judy are conducting a phone-in quiz.

Which planet is named after the goddess of love?

What nationality are Abba?

Who is married to Brad Pitt?

I creep to the window, kink the blinds and see Dolby looking at his watch, hear Belinda's engine chug. The caller has won a cash prize. A rebellion seems to be occurring deep within me, then fading, then re-surging again. I nearly run out into the street in my socks to tell Dolby to step on the gas, collect Brian and Frannie from work (like in *An Officer and a Gentleman*) and drive, drive, drive to Florence or

Reykjavik or the Côte d'Azur, where we four can live in illicit comfort like DiCaprio in *The Beach,* sinking pink drinks and summoning ladies to show us their tan lines and

the lack of love from Tyra Mackenzie, like cold light from a distant star. In its beam I am hunched, riddled with evil (Dolby is still beeping) and if you're going to *force* the issue – though please, for my sake, don't – I remember this:

It is the beginning of the nineties. Everything is black and white that year. The furniture is angular. That is what's in. I am seven years old, and Mum is about to burst with fury, and Dek, tearful, is trying to subdue her. I am watching *Children's BBC.* Mum has chain-smoked her way through a packet of Silk Cut, twitching bird-like with the effort of each sentence.

That day, she'd taken me and Derek down Falkirk to buy new clothes for school. When she'd bumped into a couple of old, now rich, friends – what they'd bought, where they'd moved to, where you should *really* go for your holidays – she'd been hesitant and clipped, her nerves sucked down to the filter. Me and Dek made faces at each other, monkeys and donkeys. Falkirk had newly opened the Howgate Centre, heralding a bright new dawn for the local retail economy. Mum dragged us in and out of Poundstretcher, What Everys, and (most embarrassingly) Leckies, the second-hand goods shop. She moved us with the agitation of a cat. Dek didn't like the Clarks shoes he was fitted with, couldn't he have Nikes or Adidas like everybody else at school? I'd whined at the scratchiness of the Leckies shirt, imagining who might have worn it before me, gripping onto the guard of an electric fire when Mum tried to pull me over to the trousers. Grey and flannel. Me and Dek stopping at the paradisal window-fronts of John Menzies, Woolworths, Toys R Us, awe-struck by towering blocks of Gameboys and Nintendos. *Can Ah get that, Mum? Mum, see when Dad gets his wages, can Ah get that?* 'Can Ah get! Can Ah get!' Mum repeated, trying to haul us onto the Hallglen

139

bus. *Aw Ah ever hear fae you pair is 'Can Ah get'*! Into the house and the TV switched on and Dek in a sulk and Mum's voice peppering the cartoon soundtrack, ordering me to *get it turned doon an stop diggin intae thae fuckin Coco-Pops, ye'll spoil yer tea. Whit is for tea, Mum? Ye'll get whit Ah fuckin make ye. Aye, but whit is it? Is it stovies, Mum? Mum, is it stovies? Is it, Mum? Ah hate stovies! Mum, Ah hate stovies! Tough, ye've ate them afore, ye'll eat them again! Weans these days huv goat awfy fancy stomachs! Mum, Ah've jist goat a normal stomach, but Ah still hate stovies. Ah'm no wantin stovies!* Mum clattering with pots and Dek with a petted lip in the corner and the *Teenage Mutant Ninja Turtles* blaring and I'm wailing about the unfairness of stovies, following Mum round the kitchen to tell her this. My bare feet cold on the black and white tiles, chipped from things being dropped, thrown. *Dek, tell her, eh, we're no wantin stovies? Mum, dinnae pit stovies on, Ah'll jist pit some Oven Chips oan for Alvin. Yese arnae gettin Oven Chips, yese are gettin fuckin stovies! Yer Dad wants stovies, so Ah'm makin fuckin stovies! Ah've no goat the time tae make four separate dinners, Derek, noo get oot the road tae Ah git the ironing-board doon.* The starved horse of the ironing-board clanks to the floor. Mum sweating, the dinner erupting in plumes from the hob behind her. She kneels to my level. I wish I could remember her eyes, even their colour. *Alvin, son, d'ye ken whaur Ah keep ma Crabbit Pills, upstairs at the side ae the bed? Can ye go up an bring me wan doon? Will ye dae that for me? Ah wid, Mum, but that wan Ah got for ye earlier wis the last yin. There's nane left.* Mum stands, sighs, runs a hand through her hair. Covers her eyes. Dek is peering over the top of the ironing-board at me, making more monkey faces. I laugh; Mum swats him away, lifting the iron, muttering. The water hisses a steamy tantrum. Me and Dek play furniture olympics, an assault course of coffee-table, sofa and drinks cabinet. Empty drinks-cabinet. *Will you pair fuckin shut up through there! Ah'm tryin tae make the dinner an iron yer Dad's shirts an ma period's due an Ah've nae Crabbit Pills till Ah can get tae the* doctor's the morn! *Mum, he kicked me! Shut up, ya wee clipe. Mum, Ah did not kick him. Mum, Derek kicked me! Will yese fuckin shut up the pair ae yese!* Mum stomps towards the drinks-cabinet, finds it empty, clutches at her own ears and squeezes closed her eyes. *Bastard never even left me a drink! Mum, Dad says ye've no tae hae any mair drink. He telt us it's bad for ye. Aye, well, yer faither disnae need tae pit up wi you pair aw day, wi yer fuckin 'Can Ah get' an yer 'Ah dinnae want that' an will you fuckin stop jumpin ower that couch, there no enough holes in it awready? Mum? Mum? Ye dinnae make holes in a couch by jumpin ower it. Aye, well just quit it. Aah! He's kickin me again! Mum, he's twistin ma arm! Mum! Aaah! Muuuum! Will yese fuckin shut up, Ah swear tae Chist yese are drivin me roon the bend, ye'll huv me in fuckin Bell's Dyke before the year's oot Ah'm tellin ye, if if wisnae for you pair an yer faither oot at work aw day an Ah've nae fags whaur's ma drink go an get ma Crabbit Pills the fuckin doctor's is shut Ah'll no be able tae get them tae Tuesday ma fuckin heid that's ma migraine startit and Ah've the claes tae finish an the dinner tae iron an the dishes tae buy an the messages tae be washed afore he gets in will yese fuckin just gies peace Bell's Dyke ya wee bastards that's whaur Ah'll end up will yese just sit doon an Ah cannae cope Ah cannae cope Ah cannae fuckin*

Dek puts her to bed before Dad gets in. He takes the stovies off the ring and makes me Oven Chips. And when I go up to see her, she is staring slackly into the middle of the room. And there is a beaded chain of saliva, like a dewy web, connecting her mouth to the pillow. And she doesn't seem to hear me when I try to say sorry. And everything is black and white and angular, because that's what's in that year, but I wish I could remember the colour of her eyes.

Dolby slams his hand onto the horn one last time, making me pull on my trainers, grab my bag, breathing hard, and run down to

The surf, and two men in waders trying to haul in a small boat.

It bobs and pulls against them, an unruly child that wants to stay out longer. The boat loses. Forcibly manacled to a tractor, it is dragged home, shame-faced, across the length of the beach.

Two girls carry surf-boards manfully towards the water, blonde hair waving in a salt breeze. They skim the boards nose-first onto the spume then charge into the cold like foals. In the foam and dip of the grey waves, they darken, wetten, shine. Their eyes press into saline creases, as they ride, and fall, and rise to ride again.

Small boys digging plots on the tide-line. The muscles of their faces are determined. They dig, flicking the sand behind them into the sea, which creeps silently and fills the hole again. The boys dig and flick, strenuous, the centre of the earth beckoning, the sea inching and swallowing their work, but they must keep at it. Keep it at bay. Further up the beach: the ritual of the upturned bucket. Others burying their mothers in a dress rehearsal of death. The old folks, nosing mournfully towards the real thing.

This isn't a holiday, I begin to think.

It's *Saving Private Ryan*.

Braw drive. Lovely wee beach. Plenty young yins! Nice pubs. Away doon! Enjoy yersels for god's sake, ya miserable

We've been lurching towards boredom in Falkirk. The same haunts. The same roads. The same conversations. There's only so many times you can snigger about the size of Brian's nipples. I've been unable to think about anything but the recent, tragic loss of my virginity to Shelley The Barmaid, the fact that when Tyra Mackenzie gets round to doing it with me, I'll already be spoiled goods. So me and Dolby chucked a couple of covers in the back of Belinda (as well as a pile of practice exam-papers, York Notes, Torrance's *Higher Biology*, just in case I get the inclination/fear) and after we drove by Tyra's house (so I could look, yearning, upon the light from her bedroom window), we took off to one of my Dad's old pit-stops, in the days before Mum.

Saltburn-by-the-sea. North-East England.

It was like running away from home. Putting the foot on the accelerator and following Belinda's nose and the spirit of adventure. The surging landscape, the pulse of road-signs past the window. The second we pulled away from Hallglen, the patter and the laughter jet-planed, the sun crashing against the windscreen, Dolby starting to insist that I call him Uriel (I can't believe he went through with it), and Scotland mutating into strange regions – every time we say the word 'Hawick' we pretend we're dragging phlegm – over the border to Angleterre and the window rolled down and *Bat out of Hell* roaring fantastically, triumphantly uncool and

> i'm gonna hit the highway like a batterin ram
> on a silver-black phantom bike!
> when the metal is hot
> and the engine is hungry and

we arrive to find this. Grim England.

The window-wipers sweedge wearily across the beach-scene.

'Whit d'ye want tae dae?'

'Dunno. Whatever.'

'Could go for a sally?'

'Heddy-haw.'

We exit the car and head along the promenade. The sand skitters across the shop-fronts like insects. We're both thinking the same thing: we could have been this bored just staying in Falkirk. We could have sat one more night in Brian's living-room, Frannie listing the minutiae of his daily routine in Tesco, Brian tour-guiding us through Clint Eastwood video terrain. We could have drunk the money we've forked out on petrol, or gambled it, Kenny Rogers warning *know when to fold, know when to hold em, know when to walk away, know when to run.*

143

The two surfers have tired of wrestling the elements, jogging to their car across the beach. The sand leaps up in flits from their toes. They begin to strip, chilly, behind the cover of a car door, and we both try to transmute the metal into glass.

Then, so suddenly it's funny, one of them hoists the leg of a shop-dummy onto her shoulder and carries it to the boot.

'Hey!' Dolby shouts, friendly, 'Sorry tae hear aboot the accident!'

'Up yours,' she replies.

as her friend wheels her chair out from behind the car.

'Aw, eh, Ah didnae mean . . .'

In the Ship Inn later, I'm still giggling.

Dolby moodily sucks his pint and frowns, that I'm-no-happy-with-you frown he could have copyrighted after Frannie snogged his sister at the Maniqui. 'Ah dinnae want the Lads hearin aboot that,' he warns, pointing. 'Ah mean it. It wisnae funny.'

'It wisnae funny wan bit,' I agree, trying to gag my splutters, knowing Brian and Frannie will think it's Christmas Day when I tell them.

Dolby, you see, until he changed his name to 'Uriel' (which the Lads have embraced with the same enthusiasm as Celtic's 3–1 defeat by Caley Thistle), was notoriously difficult to slag. I have acne. Frannie has a love of Tesco's bordering on the obsessive. Brian has nipples like satellite-dishes. Dolby? He has the same name as a sound-system. Hilarious.

But that *up yours* is going to stick to him like shit and he knows it.

'Mocking the afflicted's nae laughin matter, man.'

'Aye awright,' he mutters, ripping a beer-mat unhappily. 'Wide-o.'

Our accents have attracted attention. Beach-blonde weapons. Funny differences between the weapons here and the ones in Scotland; they're all blonde for a start (probably a remnant of a Nordic invasion they're looking to take out on somebody), and they don't have that French crew-cut so beloved of the Scottish ned. Don't growl either, or ask if you've 'goat a fuckin problem?' Just stare. Like menacing fish.

I ignore them, listening to some crap old nineties song on the jukebox, my gaze roaming the décor of the inn for distraction, learning that Saltburn used to be a – *fuck off*! – smuggling haven. Mock Wanted-posters and sepia newspaper cuttings warn us to be on the lookout for strangers. Well, we won't be smuggling anything in, me old mateys, but we might just leave with the hearts of some of your local wenches if you don't quit eyeballing. I'm even more ecstatic to learn that the King of the Smugglers, their own local hero, was a Scot. A poster recounts a pitched battle on this very beach-front between Scots bandits and King George's tax-men. Needless to say who won.

Heddy, and indeed, *haw*.

Dolby is off blethering again about Prontaprint Lisa, as he did the whole way down. We couldn't leave Falkirk until he'd cruised past her shop twice (once catching her – *gasp* – photocopying!). Plain-looking lassie if you ask me, but she's lit Dolby's fire. No doubt Brian the Mann's right in his prophecy that she'll join Dolby's bulging club of Lassie Pals, these being the ones he invites out to listen patiently to their problems, before dropping them off at their front door resolutely unkissed, untouched. 'Gettin a peck on the cheek an bein called a "nice guy" at the end ae the night?' Brian usually sneers, thumping his Rangers badge and slurping his McEwans Lager. True enough. The nicest thing any girl's ever called Brian was 'motherfucker' (but she was a Tim, he says, and doesn't count).

I have to interrupt this rhapsody to point out the impending weapon trouble we have, urging Dolby not to look round, which he does, then snorts with such Brian Mann contempt that I have to check I've come on holiday with the correct Lad.

145

'Them? Weapons? Wee fuckin laddies, Alvin!'

'They're the same age as me.'

'Like Ah say . . .' he laughs dryly. But indulges me. He drains his pint, I my peach-schnapps and lemonade, and we head out to judge the local talent contest. Mother Hubbard's cupboard is bare, however, and no *heddy-haws* are uttered the entire way to the chip-shop, where, unbeknown to Numeros Uno and Dos here, a third En-ger-land encounter awaits.

'Whatsit called, mate?' The guy sticking his hand behind his ear theatrically, leaning across the hiss and fizz of the batter.

'Irn-Bru,' Dolby repeats, keeping his annoyance in check, drumming his fingers on the sauce-stained counter and contemplating, I can see, the wisdom of the whole trip.

'Ivan Blue?' The guy shakes his head, his hasper assistant giggling behind her hand. 'Sorry, mate, don't know him. Live round here, does he?'

'Naw,' Dolby growls, '*Irn-Bru*. Ken? It's a drink.' Dolby does a 'drink' action, as if he's talking to a foreigner. 'I-R-N. B-R-U.'

The guy takes this in, wrinkling his face like a mole peering up at the light. '*Irrn Bruh*? No. Don't sell none of that in here, pal.'

Dolby mutters something I don't catch, running a harassed hand through his hair and probably, by now, regretting the 'drink' action.

'Gies a can ae fuckin Tango then.'

Outside, two girls sit hunched on a wall like frogs, straws jutting at odd angles from their mouths. About twelve years old. Thick jackets, thick stares. They look us over, snigger (sows), and in such a situation, Brian would be asking them what the fuck they're laughing at, Frannie would be dashing to offer them a chip; either way, problem nullified.

But me and Dolby trundle on, moodily picking at our soggy haddock as our enthusiasm for Saltburn, for life, for the space-time

146

continuum itself, unspools.

Their taunts follow us, like extras from one of Brian's Clint Eastwood movies, eyeing the new gunslingers in town. I'm half-expecting them to croak after us, 'Ay! Greengo!'

But they don't.

'*Wankers*!'

Dolby's fists clench the newsprint. It crackles like the batter behind the counter of the chip-shop. He turns, sees what I see: the animals that have lurked behind the façade of this seaside town have now reared out into the dusk. The genus that hunt in packs and use Childline as a defence policy.

I count – one, two, four, seven beady eyes blinking like Midwich Cuckoos. 'Whaur's Brian Mann when you need him?' Dolby mutters, retreating quietly as more emerge from the shadows, following, yelping – 'Hey, jocks! Och aye the noo, MacTavish! Where's yer haggis?' and we thrust our hands into our pockets, upping the tempo, no idea where we're going, ducking from street to side-street, each empty, dust-blown, papery, the way that every seaside town seems to be, come the end of the summer, a chill blustering off the sea and filling the streets and howling, and dropping, and the beach-blonde weapons laugh and close the distance.

'Belinda?' Dolby mutters, glancing back.

'Heddy,' I agree, 'Haw.' And we make for the beach-front, speeding up, ducking by, vaulting walls (cursing my Dad) but when I look back to see how close the raised knives are they've

Gone.

The street hangs, patient. Vacant. A shopkeeper pulls the grate down over his Ronnie Barker-type store. He stares warily. His quaint Saltburn-by-the-sea shop taunts us with granny-ornaments, when truncheons and black masks are more the sort of thing, I'm thinking, tourists are likely to need.

Seagulls wheel above us.

Slivers of adrenaline thread through my veins.

'Hey,' I whisper, 'Is this no like that scene in *Jaws*?'

'Whit?'

'Ken – when the shark disappears under the water . . . an everybody's holdin their breath, waitin for it tae smash oot fae the sea . . .'

Dolby stares at me.

'Whit the fuck are ye talkin about?'

'Ah dinnae ken. Ah feel a bit light-heided.'

I swallow.

'Are we gonnay get battered again?'

'Shut up.'

The beach-front is deserted. The Somme veterans who were trying to sunbathe in the rain have given up, or died, along with the one-legged scene of Dolby's shame.

Only ghosts are out now, writhing malevolently in the moonbeams.

'Beaches are terrifyin places at night, eh?'

Dolby doesn't reply.

I'm glancing at the brood of waves, which bring to mind another scene from *Jaws*, the one I remember being glued to, wide-eyed, in front of my Auntie Marlene's TV. The girl's nude, phosphorescent form enveloped by waves. She rubs the sea into her hair, smiles, calls:

Come on into the water!

'Hey. D'ye ken Bram Stoker wrote *Dracula* twenty miles fae here? Place called Whitby.'

'Aye,' Dolby grunts again, picking the cold fish from the newspaper then dumping it back in its puddle of vinegar.

'And Queen played one of their first gigs in that pub we were in earlier?' The sand hops across the salt-encrusted concrete, in and out the thin gaps. The sea whooses and hisses like one of the relaxation tapes my Mum was given by the AA.

Brian and Frannie in the back seat after our hammering at the Hollywood Bowl, their shirt-fronts draped in blood, grinning like skulls cos of the adrenaline . . .

'Aye.' Dolby scrunches the newspaper and boots it grimly over the car-park into an open goal, but doesn't celebrate. He's peering across the darkness, eyes pinched, troubled.

'An did ye ken Saltburn was where the vibrator was invented?'

'Aye.'

'Ya liar, Ah just made that up!'

'Shush the now, Alvin.'

I squint, trying to make sense of the grey shapes, blurry without my contact-lenses. Belinda still waiting at the far-end of the beach, coldly wondering when we're coming back

except

Perched on the bonnet, his fag-tip glowing like a fire-fly on a stalk, sits a local weapon. Arms folded. He sees us coming, and smiles, almost charming. Fuckin Les Dennis here, and I don't believe it, the stereo's playing, which means the little bastard has managed to get into the

'How ya doin, lads?' the cheeky fucker's beaming, off on some James Dean fantasy I'm looking forward to seeing Uriel, apocalyptic angel, end for him.

'Awright,' Dolby replies, gestures. 'Want to get off the car, mate?'

The weapon frowns and peers down at Belinda's scratch-work. Then shrugs, careless and free as a wean in a play-pen. 'Nah. Not really.'

Dolby nods pensively, checking automatically for the boy's back-up. We can see up the length of the beach, and like I say: just ghosts.

'Fuckin move it,' Dolby growls (my heart starting to pound with fight-nerves), 'We're wantin away fae this shit, hick town.'

The wee boy – about fourteen we're talking here – raises his eyebrows and places his palms on his cheeks.

149

'Oooooooh!' he says, like Dale Winton.

'Whit's your name, pal?'

The weapon explodes. 'Andy-fuckin-Pandy's my name! You keep your mouth shut, you jock bastard!'

Dolby retreats a step, wondering, as I am, what's making this underage knob so cocky. He soon supplies the answer, calmly taking his mobile from his puffa jacket. Punches numbers. The song playing inside the car says *the english motorway system is beautiful and strange* . . .

'Jez? Gaz? Yeah, they're back at the car . . . yeah, giving me plenty hassle . . . think they're sumfin from *Trainspotting* this pair, Scots gits . . . wanna send a squad round, sort em out . . . ?'

Dolby's calm, listening to this. But I know he's sweating. A small lump expands in his throat. Brian, Frannie, two hundred miles away and a platoon of Englishmen about to get us back for *Braveheart*.

Then Dolby surprises even me. He takes out his own mobile and starts dialling.

'Brian? Aye? Listen, how far away are ye? We'll we're just doon at the beach and there's a wee noddy sittin oan the bonnet, willnae move . . .'

He glances up at me, then away.

'Doon in a couple ae seconds? An ye'll bring the whole team? Cool.'

He snaps closed the phone. Turns round and gazes out to sea as if studying it for a photograph.

The weapon-boy looks at the back of Dolby's head. Then at me.

'You heard of the S-Burn Posse?' he asks. 'Craziest fuckin gang in North England!'

'Em . . . aye?' I nod, as if he was telling me about some mark he'd managed in a Science test at school.

'They'll be here any second! Any second now!'

Dolby leans over to me, speaking just loud enough for the boy to

150

hear.

'Brian bring that Stanley blade doon wi him?'

'Um . . . Ah think so,' I reply hesitantly.

Dolby nods. The weapon's hand strays to the phone inside his jacket. Dolby reaches for his, and the weapon draws his hand back, slow. The two of them stare at each other like gunslingers in a Western.

Headlights.

At the far end of the car-park a motor swings into view.

'You're dead now!' the weapon grins, 'S-Burn Posse!'

Dolby walks towards the car, raising his hand. It stops. Too dark to see in, but me and the weapon try anyway.

The far window is rolled down and Dolby leans in to speak to the driver. I can't hear what he's saying, but he points in our direction. Two silhouetted heads in the back seat turn towards the weapon.

But he's gone. A vacant space on Belinda's bonnet where his mardy-arse was.

The car pulls away, slipping out of the other side and onto the main-road. Dolby trots back towards Belinda and glances at me across the roof.

'Directions,' he says, and we
exhale.

On the pier, we breathe in the salt air and try to calm down.

Dolby grins/sighs/laughs.

The adrenaline has washed away. My insides are a desolate shore. The sky meeting the sea before me in a seamless accident and there are gunshot stars and lights from the boats and cold rolling off the sea in waves and the sound of slopping water and my virginity floats on the surface like a discarded polythene bag. Everything mesmerisingly bleak.

'How ye gettin on studyin for yer exams?'

'Shite.'

'Who's yer teachers?'

'Em . . . Harry Kari for Geography . . .'

'Ah had him. Mad bastard.'

'Deansy for French . . . Pitcairn for Biology . . . Gibson for English . . .'

'Gibson? There's a lassie who wants tae change the world.'

'Ye reckon?'

'Aye. Shame she'll wake up in twenty years an realise she made fuck-all difference.'

Dolby stops. Spits. Watches it fall spit-kilometres.

We stare down into the water, vast, black as dreams. His words ripple in the empty air

fuck

all

difference.

When I was little I was terrified of swimming, could always imagine this massive shark roaming the pool, waiting to swallow me whole, *What Everyone Wants* trunks and all.

That beast grins beneath the surface now. Its sail-like tail beats against the deep. Its mouth stretches wide as a cavern, my arms spread either side as I leap and fall, the wind clothing my face, the brittle sea collapsing under my weight, the waters, rolling over my head. Endless. Comforting as death . . .

'Alvin?'

'Whit?'

'You gettin a feelin like ye want tae jump in?'

'Aye.'

A beat.

'Want tae head ho–'

'Aye.'

And so we smuggle ourselves back to Scotland under cover of darkness. The lights of England shrink into the night. I think about the crap shark in *Jaws IV*, swimming in endless faulty circles, leaning its smooth mechanical head out of the water with its rubber mouth yawing up and down. The film crew have long since abandoned it, but it keeps swimming, round and round, in the huge Atlantic, round and round, until eventually it just splutters to a halt. Dies.

And I feel as though I've come close to some truth about being human, but that it sped from my mind as soon as entered it.

Dolby steps on the gas. He seems frustrated about something. Quiet. Above the sea, a lone gull rises against the backdrop of sky. The wind is its foe. The gull flaps uselessly, hovering, impotent of motion. It slips in and over the currents of air, searching for a corridor, before a huge head of wind rebuffs it and it descends sullenly, falls like a feather, or an angel kicked from heaven. Back to a perch on the pier with its grounded mates. The gull squawks, blinks, shuffles perturbed feathers. Watching Belinda dissolve into a paradise of black.

I remember reading once that if you travel at light-speed, or fast enough, then things become illusory. Ghosts are produced.

When I get back I find my brother in the living-room, talking to Dad.

I linger, dumb, by the door for a second, almost believing the jazzy eyes and pearl-white grin aren't really there. Then Dek jumps from the chair and we shake hands in the centre of the room, beaming.

'George!' he yells.

'Ringo!' I reply, curling an arm round his neck, and we wrestle a bit and nearly hug.

But don't.

'When did'ye get back fae London?' I say, stunned by how pleased I am to see him.

'About an hour ago.' His accent is odd and anglicised. He steps back, gives me the once-over, folds his hands back into his worn, denim jacket. Grins again.

'Looking good, Ringo!'

'Feeling good, George!'

George and Ringo are names we invented for each other at our cousin Tracy's wedding. Mum, pissed, was making elaborate theatre on the dance-floor. Dad was brooding like Satan with a hangover. Auntie Agnes, who'd re-mortgaged her house in order to construct the evening, doilies, cake, Beatles tribute band and everything, was sneering at us.

Dek half-laughing, half-grunting:

'If oor side ae the family wis in The Beatles we'd be George and Ringo.'

'Well!' he says, rubbing his hands together.

'Well!' I say, nodding at nothing.

'Well,' Dad says, scratching his jowls.

We all grin.

S Club 7 are on TV singing 'Reach' and the kids in the audience are clapping, happy as loons, as if Heaven's an eternal hologram of outlandish clothes, loosely-strung lyrics, a plastic backing-beat. Which it probably is.

Dad's fly is undone. I can see the purple Y of his Y-fronts and Dek, meanwhile, looks more like a Highlander than a banker. The paltry stump at the back of his head is the beginning of a pony-tail. His jacket is frayed at the cuffs, the elbows turning the colour of old men. He hasn't shaved, and his bum-fluff is growing in ginger, just like mine and Dad's does, and the overall impression is of Damon Albarn during the recording of Blur's *13* album. As if he's just split with Justine from Elastica.

'How was the journey?' I say, a fill-the-space question I'm disappointed with myself for asking.

'No bad,' Dek shrugs. He grasps a rake of bourbons from the

154

biscuit-barrel, shovelling them one at a time into his mouth while he speaks. 'Sitting next to this guy on the train – mind Handlebarus Moustachius?'

'Naw! Him that used tae sit ootside the Pakis? Eywis–'

'Pissin himself!'

We both laugh.

'It wisnae him, wis it?' Dad interrupts.

'Looked pretty damn like him!'

'Nae way! Whit did he dae?'

'He pissed himself!'

'On the train?'

'Never!'

'Always!'

We slot into the routine, Dad absorbing the contrast between old footage and new: caravan holidays; Dek bringing me home caked in mud; Sunday dinner and our grubby hands reaching out to grab the bread and Mum slapping them away and

Mum slapping them away and

Dad folds his hands on his stomach. Burbles softly with middle age. Something not quite fled from his face suggests he and Dek met at a strange, unwieldy angle. I realise they have been sitting in diametrically-opposed chairs, like facing statues in an old, sealed tomb. Like guardians of the dead.

'Ye see the Old Firm game last week?'

'Ah ken. Six-two. Poor Rangers.'

So much not being said. The absence hovering between us. We fill it desperately. The last time we saw each other – what *were* we wearing/listening to/on about? Who's number one in the charts just now? Have you heard it? It's *shite*. All of this sends emergency air into our punctured tyre, keeps the family unit trundling on.

And the three of us gathered after all this time, all that's happened. Polite. Nodding. Like the remaining Beatles meeting up on John

Lennon's birthday.

> you can't always get what you want
> no you can't always

take Dek to Comma Bar. 'Did this no used to be a bookshop?' he asks, as we wait for the waitress (not unlike Winona Ryder in *Heathers*, except prettier, not so pale). It did used to be a bookshop, called Inglis, and I can still picture the shelves, their ghostly spines emerging from the glamour. The Children's section, where a machine is now selling damaged lungs. Horror/Sci-Fi now a framed print of Manhattan at night, its lights unblinking, the clouds eerily frozen, and I remember Dolby buying his first Tolkien in that corner, rapt by its paperback immensity. He is a transparent vision beneath the Manhattan skyline, holding *Lord of the Rings*, hopeful as a child, turning, mouthing *Alvin Ah **huv** tae buy this* and as an oblivious waitress disperses him, it occurs to me just how many worlds are going on at once that you

> can't always get what you

don't notice. An untrendy town staggers past through trendy blinds and Dek orders something called *mocha*, gazing almost hopefully up at the waitress, who smiles, which is of course an *excellent* quality (Brian Mann thinks a good arse is important for bar-staff (hires accordingly), but I've always liked people who *smile* at their work. It makes a difference, it really does). I order a peach-schnapps and lemonade. Winona seems impressed, doesn't even *ask* for I.D. Usually the Lads buy me this stuff, Dolby dumping a mountain of crisps/Snickers bars/Irn-Bru cans into the back of Belinda, which our fingers forage.

Ordering drinks. Paying my own way. Handing over money.

Not being a virgin.

'Where's the bookshop in Falkirk now?' Dek queries, ripping a packet of brown sugar and guzzling its contents.

'That's disgustin,' I comment. Dek just shrugs and swallows the sugar, crystals of it catching in his ginger stubble, glinting. 'We've no got a bookshop,' I answer, slightly embarrassed.

'Falkirk doesn't have a bookshop?'

'Apart fae Bargain Books.'

'London's got about eighty Waterstones!'

'So? Falkirk's got about eighty . . . pubs!' I blurt, faintly annoyed, as if he's that Yank cousin in *Oor Wullie* that complains at how small everything is.

He grins fondly. 'You remember when you were ten, and you bought that novel about the boy who turns into a dog?'

'*Woof*?'

'An for two months after, *you* were tryin to change into a dog! Crouched on aw fours, yer face screwed up like ye needed a shite!'

'Christsake man,' I redden (the waitress is in earshot), 'Ah wis only ten!'

'And me an Alison Pearson bet you couldn't, and down you went . . .'

The memory hisses back, singeing my skin. Me with my eyes clamped shut, straining the word *dog*! into my sinew, then standing up, utterly the same, utterly embarrassed. Hallglen seemed greyer, more drained of mystery, after that day.

The waitress places our drinks down.

'Woof,' she says.

'Ah wis only ten!'

I remind him of the time he jumped from a tree in Callendar Woods, snagged his trouser leg on a branch, and swung screaming upside down for five minutes. Our laughter ripples.

It's good to see him. It is. I've decided.

157

Dek peers at the shoppers outside, their different shapes, bags, hairstyles, somehow worried, and he *so* much does not look like a banker. Do they allow him to go to work unshaven like this, I ask him, but he just shrugs and looks away, doing a double-take on a passing girl, suddenly scared/then not.

'So whit are ye daein back?'

Dek shrugs. Grunts. Just says, 'The streets of London are not paved with gold,' and seems

edgy, almost paranoid, resisting my attempts to find out about his job or London with shrugs and then a firm, 'Let's no talk about work,' and his face, which was always either a glinting humour or a sullen brood, has now settled permanently between the two. His boyishness is gone, lost a long time ago to responsibility. While my imagination was sponging up cartoons and TV, films and comics, books and computer games, his was thinking of ways to stop Mum and Dad from killing each other.

Dolby said once, when I asked him how he could be bothered getting up and fitting whirlpools every day, 'You just do it. You get up, put on the work head, and just do it.' And after he said it, I realised just doing it had pulled all of us – me, my family, the Lads – this far.

Broken.

But doing it.

And there is a quiet heroism which goes on every day.

Me and Dek chat about what I'm up to (exam-revision mainly these days) but he doesn't ask if I'm still a virgin, and though I try to tell him that Dolby has changed his name to Uriel, that Brian is supposed to be emigrating to California sometime soon, that Frannie's Mum and Dad are on the brink of splitting, Dek's somewhere else. Vague. Haunted. He's blinking, nodding, saying 'Aye?' and laughing in the right places. But not there.

'When I got in,' he whispers – interrupting my story about Kottsy and Brian – 'I found Dad in the garden, holding Mum's wedding dress.'

'What was he listening to?' I ask. This is a sight I've seen more often than he has. The meaning of it's in the music. Thumbs-down (and a night ignoring the study and telling Dad it's alright, I'm sure she loved us, I love you, Dad honest, no *honest*) if it's anything from London in the late seventies.

'The Sex Pistols,' Dek says, 'Pretty Vacant.'

I swear loudly, drawing arid glances from the old fuckers nearby.

'Ye ken that's Mum and Dad's song?'

'Yup. The bit in the wedding video when Dad does the Hokey-Cokey and spits at the camera.'

We laugh. But it's hollow this time. The sound of a coconut shell rocking on a table-top.

Dek recounts times when he found bottles of vodka hidden all over the house, or when he had to go out on his bike to look for her, see if she'd collapsed anywhere, only to come back and find her snuggled up in the loft with some Smirnoff. I stare at the mahogany knots in the table while he tells me this, wondering at the strangeness of the past, how if you drop it in the front seat of the present it does not land in the back.

'Ah'm amazed she survived as long as she did,' I say.

Dek looks at me.

'That's what I want to talk to you about . . .'

He narrows his eyes. The waitress comes over, but Dek hisses her away, and she withdraws, sullen, unsmiling, and just before he starts talking I notice a photo of Marilyn Monroe reading *Ulysses*, sitting in a swimsuit with her legs drawn up and her face slack with incomprehension, like a little girl trying to keep up with the teacher. The book is huge and heavy and has **JAMES JOYCE** on the front in big, bold letters, and I'm surprised she can hold the thing up, let alone read it. She is almost on the last page, and though I don't believe she's managed all that, I feel bad about not believing her, believing *in* her. The photograph disturbs me for the length of time it takes Dek to say:

'I think Mum's still alive.'

The three of us talk that night for the first time in years, dotted in separate corners of the room. One of us back from the wilderness, failure following like a cloud of flies. The others too tired to bother asking why. The wheels have come off us. Things are fraught with restraint. When we speak, cages are opened a crack. The beasts inside sniff, consider. Then retreat back inside. There's too much.

there's

too

much

blame almost attached and lifted just before the sting, and Dad plays an Elvis Costello song, 'Alison' flickering in and out of my awareness, making it feel as if he's strolling the room, crooning, knowing this world is killing me, and I can't concentrate on what Dek's telling me. I feel far away from things, behind glass, mouths moving but no sound coming out, a vague terror mounting, a feeling I get in Belinda sometimes as we cruise soundlessly in and out of Scottish new-towns like panthers in the night – when the Lads are talking about wages and shagging and beer and Rangers – as if I've gradually slipped down a crack between the seats and none of them can hear my plea.

Dek thinks Mum's been following him.

He's turned, several times, and glimpsed her standing on street-corners, staring coldly at him, then disappearing – *blink!* – and he reminds us (why? don't we know this?) that the police *never found her*, that *there was no body*, while on TV a male goat stands waiting to be castrated, which I watch on the edge of my seat, fearful. The goat blinks at the camera, stupidly chewing, making me wonder if it's, like, the *goat* version of Brian Mann, and has to return to its mates in the pasture dickless!

I feel like telling the two of them that hope is born, but lives in a short frantic burst like an insect, and then dies. But instead I find myself screaming hysterically:

'That's a lie! She *never* said that! You're a *fucking* liar, Derek Allison, you *cunt*!'

Sunday night.

The three of us not talking now, lurking in different rooms. Like the good old days. The walls feed off our resentment. The shower slow-dripping with sadness. The garden slabs broken. I head down to Dolby's with an idea for a new Clive Barker novel that I'm thinking of sending to his publishers. Dolby's Dad says he's at Frannie's (Dolby, that is, not Clive Barker), with videos and popcorn, but when I chap Frannie's door, nobody answers, though I want, *ache*, to head out in Belinda tonight, break onto uncharted roads at the speed of sound, shouting 'Heddy-haw!' from the sunroof, Limp Bizkit (or maybe some old skool metal like Motorhead or LedZep) playing loud enough to obliterate all this shit. I knock again, peering in the window. The lights are on, the standby button on the TV blinking red, and the video for *Casino* lies open on the floor. I knock a third time – still no answer – then, warily, like in a murder mystery, squeeze the handle.

Frannie and Dolby emerge from behind the couch, dusting themselves down.

'Aw. Alvin. It's you,' Frannie says flatly. 'How did we *ken* it wis gonnae be you?'

'Never mind that!' I laugh, 'Whit the fuck are ye daein behind the couch?'

'We, eh, thought it was the guy for the TV licence,' Dolby coughs, and Frannie nods earnestly. 'He's no paid the bill, ken?'

'No paid the bill,' Frannie mumbles.

'Ye forget Ah said Ah'd be doon the night?'

'We did,' they mutter, glancing at each other, as I excitedly tell them about the Versace top Tyra's been wearing recently, her nipples straining at the fabric, and my idea for the Clive Barker book which has a really cool baddie and should be made into a film and

Frannie yawns.

Next morning, the school assembly-hall is filled with universities plying their trade. Suits, stalls, clans of prefects all honing their careers over milky cups of tea. Mrs Gibson forces me to go. I was hoping to use that morning's free periods usefully, to watch *Scarface* or something. As I wander round the stalls, several scenes from the film keep

you know what capitalism is? i tell you. get fucked! dat what capitalism is. get fucked!

stuttering in my head. All the other local schools are visiting ours today. The hall is a tide of bobbing blazers. Campus photographs (rhododendron, squirrels, night-clubs) are arranged on the walls like a collage of wonderland. Tyra Mackenzie, who I've been following surreptitiously all morning, meets-and-greets boys from Graham High, St Mungo's, Woodlands, who she knows through the Debating Society, her face lit up for them. She is handing out invitations to her party, gushing, 'Oh I'd *love* it if you could come, guys!' but I can't get close enough for her to 'accidentally' find herself beside me and realise she hasn't given *me* an invite, so I manoeuvre myself secretly in and out of the crowd so that the *next* stall she visits (St Andrews), I will be there, casually perusing a prospectus, ready to exclaim, 'Oh *hi*, Tyra! St Andrews, yeah, I dunno, I suppose you just feel a *calling* to some places. What? A party? Oh I'd love to!' But *just* as she says goodbye to some Denny High prefect-stripe with awful acne, her hand lingering (too long?) on his sleeve, *just* as I start discussing with the rep the fact that no decent bands ever came out of St Andrews – *ever* – there's a tug at my arm.

'Alvin,' Mrs Gibson says, her smile glowing, 'There's someone here I'd like you to meet . . .'

and I'm pulled away from Tyra's light, like in a near-death experience, as she finds herself alone at the stall, glancing round (for me?), before her image is obscured by a drifting cloud of blazers.

!Fuck!

Mrs Gibson drags me to the Stirling display, giving it mucho pep-talk. Photos of greenery, rabbits, nancy-boys with folders grinning obsequiously outside lecture-halls. 'This is Alvin Allison,' she introduces me to the stiff behind the stall, 'A *very* talented student of mine. He sort of needs a bit of convincing to go onto further education, though, so if you could . . .'

I am only half-listening, scanning the crowd for Tyra, who is blowing through the far-end of the hall, shedding invites like sweetie-papers.

'Well, I think you'd really warm to the Stirling Uni environment, Alvin, blahblah blah,' the rep's blethering, 'It has *excellent* facilities, a *beautiful* campus, and . . .'

'Hmm. Yah. Supah,' I reply, rubbing my chin.

The Suit coughs, perturbed, looking at Gibson, who frowns and explains to him my keen interest in, um, *Gothic* literature. 'Alvin's Higher Still review is on *The Silence of the Lambs*, and it's quite an insight into . . . the, um, mind of . . . pathological violence.'

'Pathological violence,' I repeat, smiling.

'Excuse me a minute.'

Gibson draws me aside, glowering.

'*What* do you think you're playing at?' she snaps, hands on hips, 'Is your future some sort of a *joke*?'

'Oh come *on*, Miss!' I protest, 'Ah ken whit yer daein, an it's cool. "You *shall* go to the ball" an aw that. But mibbe Ah dinnae *want* tae go! University's full ae tossers like this . . .' and I sweep my arm around the pack of well-bred crocodiles, snapping for titbits at the Oxbridge stalls.

But Gibson's having none of it.

'Will. You. Just. *Stop*.' she enunciates, the magic wand dropped from her act, replaced by a whip. 'Think about your *potential* for once. This isn't a *class* issue, Alvin!'

'Everything's a class issue,' I mutter, switching to Smirk Automatic, as I wonder why Bernard Butler really left Suede (cos he would've sounded great on the *Coming Up* album), and shrug, walk away, strangely furious with myself but my fury dissolving, and I don't mention that my future seems like one yawning great chasm in which nobody loves anybody else and Scotland breaks away from the British Isles and crumbles pointlessly into the sea – *plop*! – since each of my thoughts is precious, hidden, hoarded and pored over like a gold prospector with booty and Mrs Gibson shouts something like '*Promise me you'll think about it*' but I can't promise anybody anything of the sort.

'Well if we're talking *forte*,' one of the prefects is braying at the Dundee stall, 'We'd be talking chemical engineering!'

'Would you recommend stage-school or are there active theatre groups at your institution?'

I start drifting round the tables, only half-interested in the patter while humming

> still haven't found what i'm looking for
> no I still haven't found

and realising that Tyra has left. Her invitations are given out. Her purpose is spent. Her perfume is only a lingering scent, which fades into mindless excitement for Business Law at Cambridge, Media Studies at Napier, Accountancy at Suffolk, and so I drip back to the

Stirling stall, which Gibson, exasperated, has quit.

> and i still haven't found what I'm looking for
> no i still haven't

Connor Livingstone beside me all of a sudden. He's had a haircut, and looks like one of the actors from the *Scream* movies. He says:

'Stirling?'

Shrugs.

'I suppose it's the right place for someone like yourself.'

And the weird thing is: *he means it as a compliment*!

And after my set-to with Gibson, my permanently uninvited status to Tyra's (the world's?) party, and a mother who has every right to be dead after all this time surfacing just when I need my sanity most, I'm spoiling for a fight.

I'll kill this bastard.

'Could you, um, *clarify* that, Connor,' I ask, gritting my teeth, 'That "someone like yourself"?'

Livingstone has total recall to the *Times Educational Supplement*.

'Well,' he begins, smiling like a toothpaste advert, 'It didn't make the top ten list of the best universities in Britain in the recent survey. It clings miserably to its left-wing reputation from the seventies. And if you compare it to somewhere like, I don't know, *Edin*burgh, it just can't compete in terms of resources and finances . . .' I'm nodding, encouraged by his insights. 'I didn't mean to sound patronising, Alvin. All I was *trying* to say is that for someone like yourself, who is obviously, um, *talented*, but not, how can I put this, *academically-minded —*'

'Academically-minded,' I repeat.

'—it would meet most of your needs. You wouldn't find it as stretching as, say, a Cambridge or a St Andrews, and most of the people there would be of your own cla . . . um, kind.'

'Of my own class?'

'Of your own kind.'

Connor smiles reassuringly, his prognosis delivered. Then he adjusts his hair, which, it has to be said, looks bloody marvellous.

I am totally sold on Stirling.

'Anyway, Alvin,' he appeals, patting my shoulder, 'I *really* have to go and see the Oxford rep, he's my father's—'

'Hang on,' I stop him. 'Can I ask one other question?'

'Of course,' he smiles, surprised but delighted at my willingness to learn (if only *all* the Hallglen scum would).

'Who the fuck do you think you are?'

He stares back at me, slightly startled. His gorgeous eyelashes blink quickly. As if I have jumped him on his way home from a fund-raising bash.

'Excuse me?' he says politely.

'Do you *know* me?' I snarl. 'Do you have any idea who I am or what I feel? How dare you dismiss me like that, you cunt,' and I say the word 'cunt' formally, enjoying the experience of it on my tongue. It feels like introducing a madman to a dinner-party.

Connor frowns. Picks some fluff from the shoulder of his blazer. Something – the word cunt? my challenge? – has riled him, and he lets slip that façade which I knew – *which I fucking knew*! – wasn't the real Connor Livingstone.

He sighs pityingly.

'At least I don't spend *my* nights boyracing with a pack of neanderthals. I'm—'

'You're *nothing*,' I sneer, smelling a kill, seeing visions of myself as a shop-steward inciting the workers to arms, to rebellion, to crush The Suits. 'You're an empty blazer. A prefect badge. A fucking haircut. *That's* Connor Livingstone.'

He takes a step back, and I like that feeling of power, that *reversal* of power, my hatred for him actually hurting, as I stare, *willing* him to test me, to force me to reveal the true seething nature of this outcast thing who dares litter the corridors of Connor Livingstone's school.

'You won't be going to Tyra's party,' is all he can say, shaken. 'You won't be going. I'll make sure of that.'

He stumbles, glancing back as if expecting me to bound after him, snarling like a rottweiler, and I form a confident picture of the moment he reaches the prefect hut, trembling, some girl handing him a glass of water while he shakes and tells them about this rabid thing that would

Take

No

More.

Then I think:

Fuck! I'm *never* getting into her party now.

I rush to find Tyra before Connor can, panicked, checking the places she spends interval duty, the Maths corridor, the refectory, the tuck-shop . . .

Then I spot her at the top of the stairs. She is with Louisa Wainwright and Jennifer Haslom, all chatting excitedly on their mobile-phones and I hear: '. . . *your hair down from all of this exam stress . . .*' and '. . . *Fran Healy from Travis, isn't he adorable . . .*' (which is good, since I don't look unlike Fran from Travis) her words floating like pink paper in a breeze, so I bound up the first two, three flights, energised, knowing that I have to ask her *now*, right now, but I

Can't.

Livingstone's right. I am a broom-pusher. A car-park attendant. My children are destined to work in McDonalds. She and her friends live in houses that have names. Money swirls and eddies about them like confetti. I gaze at her from the lower step and she is a promise that I will not reach. She exists in a dream at the end of a long corridor, in

167

some perfect, white, silicon future-world. The deft movement of her wrist as she talks. Immaculate brands coasting her body like pilot fish. Her mobile-phone is blue and

i still haven't found what I'm looking for

emits love-songs and right now I am the feeling you get when you switch on the TV and see that *The Simpsons* has just finished. Times one billion.

'. . . and *then* he said to me, "I can see that you are a *woman* not a girl", so . . .'

'. . . get your tongue out of my ear! But it's, like, this *silver* Merc. Cos he's totally taking over his Dad's company when he dies in, like, *five* minutes . . .'

'. . . What? Oh? Like, whatever. I mean he's a total dork-brain . . .'

Some people exist for the past. My Dad, for example. Some people exist for the present: ravers and extreme-sports guys and rich school-girls and bank robbers and the dead dead trendy and speedfreaks and boyracers. The present to me feels like candy-floss dissolving on the tongue; I can't quite hold onto its beauty for long enough. No, I think that I

still haven't found what i

exist for the future, the hope that it's as bright as they promise. But it's just that the faster I charge towards it, the further away from me it seems to stretch.

I traipse dejectedly away from school, unable to face Tyra and the rest of my classes, just desperate to return to bed, soft safety, not even in the mood for *Scarface* now, and all I can visualise, with stunning clarity, is the sticker I spotted on a car Belinda couldn't overtake which said

168

These are the Top Ten things Alvin Allison has looked forward to most in his life:

10. *The Blair Witch Project*
    (my generation's *The Exorcist*)
9. **Guns 'n' Roses reunion album**
    (even though only Axl Rose was actually re-unified)
8. *The X-Men* **movie**
    (at least they got Wolverine right)
7. *The Third Book of the Art* – **Clive Barker novel**
    (Book Two published 1994. Still waiting, Clive)
6. *Blair Witch2: Book of Shadows*
    (my generation's *The Exorcist II*)
5. *Spider-Man* **movie**
    (I should play Peter Parker, you know it's true)
4. *Kid A* – **Radiohead CD**
    (even though it was rubbish, etc.)
3. *Lord of the Rings* **movie**
    (possibly mankind's single greatest-ever achievement ever)
2. *All That You Can't Leave Behind* – **U2 CD**
    (classic me and Frannie bonding moment, oh yes)
1. *American Psycho* **movie**
    (there is an idea of a Patrick Bateman, some kind of abstraction, but there is no real me, only an entity, something illusory. And though I can hide my cold gaze and you can shake my hand and feel flesh gripping yours and maybe you can even sense our lifestyles are probably comparable . . .

    I simply

        am not

they're singing like they're winning – Frannie with the actual money from his wage splattered against the windscreen, lording it over all the passing skanks/weapons, and after we picked him up in Belinda with a poly-bag of Smirnoff Ice and Vodka Hooch (warm, but never mind), which Brian cracked open and handed round to the sound of whoops, cheers and classic Bon Jovi (yes, there is such a thing) and it's the end of the month and the Lads have just been paid and the four of us are rocking and we drive to:

Stirling Castle.

'*Dolby, Dolby, give us yer answer do . . .*'

Linlithgow Country Park.

'*We're half-crazy aw for the love ae you . . .*'

B&Q.

'*Been years since we had some nookie, and that was with a wookie . . .*'

Langlees.

'*But you're still sweet in the driver's seat, so pull us a skank or two!*'

as Dolby puts his palms on the ceiling of the car, laughs, 'Well one ae *youse* fuckin drive then!' and I grab control of the wheel, panicked, and Brian swaps Jon Bon Jobby for Deacon Blue, frog-singing away to 'Dignity' and soon we're all unleashing our throats on the bit that goes, '*Set it up again! Set it up again! Set it up again! Set it up again!*' like the Tartan Army invading the pitch at Wembley until I think some more about the words, pause, appalled, a wee bit, then say:

'Sortae patronisin that song, when ye think about it really.'

'How d'ye mean?' says Frannie, eyes weeping with laughter.

'It's patronisin tae the working-classes, in't it?'

Brian turns down the volume and I shift nervously in my seat. 'What the fuck are you talkin about now?'

'Well it's about this cooncil-worker, an everybody laughs at him cos he's cleanin the streets. But he's gonnae save up his money, buy a ship, an call it Dignity.'

Brian is waiting for the punch-line.

'Aye?'

'So it's sayin that ye huvtae have money to have dignity. That it's something ye can buy.'

'But he's no buyin dignity,' Frannie says, baffled, 'He's buyin a ship.'

'Aye. Called Dignity. It's a . . . metaphor for . . . aw never mind . . .'

'Oh, Ah wonder who's daein Higher English?' tuts Brian, 'Anyway, where *is* the fuckin dignity in workin for the cooncil? Cunt's cleanin the streets! Nae dignity in that. Let him buy his ship for fuck's sake, leave him alane.'

'How's there nae dignity in workin for the cooncil?' I reply. 'Why dis he need tae buy a *ship* tae hae dignity?'

'When did the song come oot?' asks Dolby.

'Dunno. 1986? 1987?'

'Thatcher!' I pounce on this, 'Only Thatcher could convince a Scotsman that working for the cooncil has nae dignity!'

'Here we fuckin go . . .'

'"Wages Day" is the same. Like, ye can only enjoy life if ye've just been paid.'

'Ye *can* only enjoy life if ye've just been paid!'

'*Ah* havenae just been paid,' I say.

'*You* dinnae work!' Brian sneers, wrenching his frame round from the front seat to take me, firmly, to task. 'In case ye didnae realise, aw these crisps and cans ae juice ye've been shovin doon yer scrawny throat are on us. Cos it's wages day and we've aw been paid an we're enjoyin oursels. You, *Runt*, huvnae even got a fuckin job, so dinnae talk tae us about enjoyment. Who's bein patronisin now, eh? Ye think we get up oot oor beds an work for the life-fulfillin experience eh it?'

'Ah'm no sayin that, but–'

'Once *you've* got a joab – wi nae seven-week summer holidays an nae study-leave – *then* ye can fuckin lecture us aboot dignity, wee man.'

Brian grips his Irn-Bru with result.

We stop at a red light. A council worker crosses with a lumpen rubbish cart, as dignity-less as anyone I've ever seen. Neither does he look like he's saving up for any. The lights change. Dolby speeds up. Brian rewinds the tape, deliberately, and I hear again

> you can have it all
> you can take it all away

'They're closing down the ABC and opening up a multiplex.'

Frannie utters this, monotone, as we pass the cinema for what seems like the millionth time this week.

Tonight it is showing the Oscar-nominated film TRIFFIC.

Rain starts to form little bodies on the glass. 'Think aboot aw the films that have been shown there ower the years,' Frannie sighs, '*Gone with the Wind. Star Wars. Robin Hood: Prince of Thieves.* It's sortae, like, a cultural history.'

'No it isnae!' Brian snorts, unimpressed, 'Ah'm sick ae this pish. It's *progress*. Sa shite picture-hoose anyway. The seats are uncomfy as fuck.'

> on wages day!

'Progress-schmogress,' I retort, still rankled by the Deacon Blue argument and sensitive to Frannie's vision of folks in old-style hats traipsing from a showing of *Calamity Jane*. 'Progress is a capitalist myth.'

'Capitalist myth?' Brian shouts, '*You're* a capitalist myth, ya cunt! Whaur wid we be withoot capitalism! A fuckin borin world that, eh Dolby?'

'Boring,' replies Dolby robotically.

172

'Nae Nike . . . Nae MTV . . . Nae McDonalds . . .'

'Nae Glasgow Rangers,' I goad.

Brian glares, at the same moment in which the veins at my temples (which feel as if they've been laced with fireworks and have been threatening gently all night) are set off.

'Whit ye tryin tae say aboot the Rangers like?'

It's bound to be more complex than this. Politics is, isn't it? But I can't grasp it, how can I, not really, be fair, and on *Star Trek* tonight Spock said, '*slavery can evolve into an institution, develop benefits, health-care . .* ' and then an advert for Doritos came on which had loads of mates laughing over a bowl of crisps and ended with the word FRIENDCHIPS and these years I'm living in now, should I forget, are The Best Of My Life, hey, so fuck it, fuck them all, I am *not* going to take Brian on because I've just

    stopping

          caring

               but before I know it I'm talking like this: 'Glasgow Rangers Football Club does *not* represent the working-man, Brian. They dinnae even represent Scotland.'

'Oh. And what *do* they "represent"?' Brian makes inverted commas with his fingers sarcastically.

'The Queen, the crown, greed, exploitation, the empire, Thatcher . . .'

'Thatcher!' he laughs, looking to the others for back-up. But they seem tired, bored, ironed-flat by the whole topic, '*Thatcher*! Come ontae fuck, Alvin, they're a fitba team, no a political party!'

'It's aw political,' I mutter, staring at him, my mean headache turning

did you ever listen to k billy's super sounds of the seventies

sideways.

'Yer arse is fuckin political!'

'My arse *is* political!' I laugh, hysterical and useless.

We pass the carcass of a dog strewn across the road. It has an eye missing and tyre-tracks across its back.

'So let me get this straight . . .' Brian is a fighter-jet screaming from Fortress Ibrox, 'Not only are ye a poof an a runt, but now yer a commie an a *Tim*?'

'A Tim?' I blink (really wishing Dolby would change this fucking Deacon Blue tape now), 'How's that likes? Because Ah dinnae agree wi your narrow-minded-Brian-Mann views, Ah'm a Tim! A Catholic? That makes sense!' Adrenaline surging and I'm making this a bigger deal than it is/pissing the three of them off simply because Frannie mentioned that the ABC was closing down, but I'm past caring, beyond the thunderdome, clouds are gathering on the horizon, things passing from simple to complex with frightening speed, and a heroine is screaming somewhere each time I issue words, as if I'm a lunatic brandishing a knife, my life passing for Chinese water-torture, incidents slow-dripping in my head: my unquenchable love for Tyra, Dek coming home a defeated man, Connor fucking Livingstone, the *Spider-Man* movie *only in pre-production*, Mum undead, losing my virginity (did I come too early?), Belinda needing a service, a broken leg in an accident at the Burnout which wasn't our fault – *I know it wasn't* – but which could result in some drive-by shooting outside the Callendar Arms bar, Connor-*cunting*-Livingstone, exams, U2 tour-dates *still* unannounced, the future (*I owe it to myself* repeated like a mantra in each of my dreams, each of which ends like a scene from a film) and during all of this I am trying to turn my squeak into a roar, become Russell Crowe fighting tigers in *Gladiator* while simulta-neously placating my horror at the crushing boredom of everything and everyone around me.

'See these part-time bigots like you?' – I am raging – 'Ah've less time for them than the full-time ones. At least Nazis and the KKK believe in it! You just switch it on an aff when it suits ye!'

'Naw Ah dinnae!' Brian retorts, 'Fuckin protestant through-and-through!'

'No yer no.'

'Aye Ah am! Twenty-one home games last season, ya bas!'

I ignore this, hammering on Thor-like: 'You live in a fantasy world called 'The Fortunes of Glasgow Rangers Football Club'. It disnae *matter* if they win or they lose! You're just a consumer – a means tae an end for the fat fuckers that own the club, who're gettin rich aff the stupit fuckin emotional attachment tae Rangers they've managed tae sell ye!'

'Listen tae it!' Brian laughs, '*Me* in a fantasy world? You're the cunt that reads *The Hobbit* and *Lord of the* fuckin *Jungle!*'

'*Rings.*'

'Whaur's the reality there? You cannae fuckin *deal* wi reality!' his tongue lunges into the tone of some angry beast, and though I'm out of order calling him worse than a Nazi, and though he's throaty with resentment, jabbing his finger at me from the front-seat, and even though this is one of my very best mates *and I really fucking love the guy*, what can I do?

Things are getting difficult.

'Now you listen tae me, *Runt,*' he snarls, 'Ye cannae just tag along wi us in this car and go–' (effects poofy voice), ' "*I tink tis is wrong and I tink tat is wrong*".'

'Tag along?' I say, startled.

'Yer too fuckin young tae be hingin oot wi us anyway! We've been tryin tae avoid you for *months.*'

'Brian!' Dolby barks, as I melt into the back-seat.

'Ye want tae know somethin else?' he laughs, blundering through my defences, 'You didnae even *shag* Shelley fae the pub!'

'Enough!' Dolby demands.

'You *couldnae* shag her, ye were sae fuckin pissed.'

175

Ice slowly spreads on my skin. On the street corner, a homeless woman hangs thin and bare, her hand out to me, her eyes pleading.

'Ye put yer head on her fuckin tits and asked her tae "hold" ye!'

We drive for the rest of the night in silence.

Frannie mentions once:

'Ah dunno where they're buildin the multiplex.'

We see nothing interesting that whole week. We meet nobody worth talking to. The chips we buy from Limetti's taste like vinegary pebbles. Each time we pass Rosie O'Grady's I find myself fascinated by the curl at the end of the 'y' – poised there, on the edge of space, seeming to mean something, be waiting for something. I can't think what. Then we've driven past; it's gone. Who cares. On Friday, we slam four doors, go four separate ways, and that night I argue with Dek across the kitchen table about his fucking stupid paranoia – Mum still alive? following him? the stupid, silly, fucking cunt – and he sucks up the spaghetti and replies that if I'd been more paranoid when she'd disappeared, phoned the police quicker, they might have *found* her, so I punch him, and he punches me back, then there's a flurry of punches, which Dad breaks up, horrified, and I run to my room saying I hate them both, knowing that I've missed *Buffy the Vampire Slayer* and that I also have no friends in the world, that Tyra doesn't – couldn't ever – love me, that my Higher exams represent my doom and that I am totally alone in this world, so I just listen to 'Stairway To Heaven', watching the rain drip transparent patterns on the window, marvelling at how they wrote such a song, so *intricate*, then read some of *Carrie* and just sleep.

I dream about aliens. Aliens and the Blair Witch. Frannie and Dolby picking them up in Belinda and taking them out and treating them right. The Blair Witch tastes haggis and Irn-Bru for the first time. She likes it.

Monday night.

I head down to Dolby's. Belinda is parked outside like an obedient dog, her rust flaking and falling with a quiet whisper. I imagine the Blair Witch in the back seat slurping Irn-Bru. Dolby is halfway into his dinner and *Babylon 5*, so I natter to his Dad awhile, who for some reason is keen to teach me 'House of the Rising Sun' on guitar. But I can't get my fingers round the frets, and have to pretend this is really funny, since Dolby's Dad looks like Lee Van Cleef in *The Good, the Bad and the Ugly* and is notorious for dispensing dead-arms with accuracy, so I try again.

'Gon,' he urges satanically, 'Play Layla . . .'

Later, in his bedroom, Dolby chucks me a package. I don't catch it instantly, having lost all feeling in my arm, but I do recognise the cover. It's the new release by Pink Floyd. *The Wall* recorded live in 1980, when Roger Waters was in the band!

'That's fae Brian,' Dolby says, 'He's sorry aboot the other night. Didnae want tae give it tae ye himsel.'

'Right,' I say, knowing it's a lie, that Dolby has bought this. 'Tell him thanks.'

'Cool eh?' Dolby nods at the CD.

'Cool,' I repeat, slightly disappointed that forever *The Wall* might remind me of Brian's mouth twisted with resentment, the *un*shagging of Shelley

but

I run my hand across the hardback book that accompanies the CD, the four faces of Pink Floyd on the cover, their eyes cut out like empty masks, while inside . . .

. . . *The Wall* concert explodes in a burst of stage-lights! David Gilmour's guitar glinting and his shadow, thrown by a spotlight, bleeding across the audience, and huge, marching hammers, and a nimbus of mist pun

ched through by lasers, and floating, malevolent pigs, and the head of a single, anonymous member of the crowd edged with light, saintly and insignificant in the vast, hallucinogenic dream of all of this, plucked from the fog of the past and made real. Apparent. Whole.

'Dolby . . .' I begin, but can't express any of it.

'Ah know!' he grins.

'Naw,' I say, 'It's just too . . .'

'Ah know!' he almost squeaks, his eyes screwed shut, 'Ah know!'

We listen to it.

For an hour and a half we lie still on the bed, watching the graphic-equaliser blipping up and down, his plasma ball flicking tongues of electricity, the shifting blues and greens of the fish tank and the spectral, gliding shapes of the fish. It is our own private Pink Floyd light-show. The scent of Dolby's incense (jasmine) curls in the air, revealing itself the way a pretty, stoned girl might take off clothes.

Outside the sky turns from grey to dark grey, the white concrete of the Hallglen housing scheme becoming dull alabaster, and we cannot hear the drunks shouting, the children baiting them, car alarms going off, on, off, bottles being kicked, smashed, while we lie on our stomachs with our chins in our hands, just listening to The Floyd.

Sometimes the world is too fine. Stuffed with good things.

The CD makes a small *shick*! sound as it spins to a halt. Dolby turns over, scratching his belly.

'If you make it away, Alvin,' he says quietly. 'Make it for the four of us, eh?'

And we both gaze down at the bedspread. Then we talk about the album: how Roger Waters is a pop genius, he really is.

On my days on study-leave from school, I try to work. I really do. This is what happens:

Dad makes me and Dek our tea, usually chips, egg and beans. We watch *Ricki Lake* (Dad likes the ones where someone comes on and says they're gay and everyone falls out and the audience boos the person who doesn't like the person who's gay and everybody feels sorry for the person who's gay because it's so hard in today's society and Ricki talks like a black person). But none of this resolves what to do about Tyra's party! It is the focus of my existence, the light above my bed, only a day away and going on without me. How can I concentrate on work? I am doomed to spend loose hours feeling my mind pinball from the new Top 20 singles chart to the wrongs of global capitalism to whether or not we should print DA BOYZ on Belinda to the question of Tyra's underwear (betcha it's white lace) to Stephen King's best book (surely *The Shining*?). Frannie's just off the phone. His Mum and Dad are finally divorcing. Maybe it's cos his Dad lost his job at Motorola recently, the contract punted off to Jakarta or somewhere else that sounds like a dance act. I dunno. He phoned me up, and when I asked him about it he fell silent for a good long while, only space crackling and hissing between us.

'So how's work?' I decided to say, and the silence mutated into a sigh.

'Ma hours are gettin cut in Tesco.'

'Seriously?'

Frannie sounded nothing like himself. As if he'd been body-snatched by some lurching misanthrope.

'It's a fuckin joke! See bein a guy these days? Women are too smart for us. This *lifestyle* dangled in front ae ye wi one hand, while yer work steals yer wages wi the other. Ah tell ye, we've been *betrayed*. Fuckin betrayed.'

before I heard what sounded like Frannie putting down the phone, walking around the room, and saying *fuck, fuck* to himself in an infuriated whisper.

'Fran? Ye there?'

'See the Rangers game last night?' he suddenly exhaled, 'Ally

McCoist wis commentatin.'

'Ah did, man,' I said, 'His patter's magic.'

so we talked about Coisty for a while before he went, in a better mood than he was, and, yeah, I suppose our story – mine, Brian's, Frannie's, Dolby's, Belinda's – is just another Scottish Fairy Tale, no more than a modern-day 'Fairies O' Merlin Craig' or 'The Brownie O' Ferne-Den', the sort of shite you find in big flog-it-to-the-tourist books with tartan spines and I'm not even sure if Scotland exists anymore. Or if it ever existed. Maybe Scotland was only ever a dream agreed upon by people who shared the same land and the same shit life, and that's it, and I stand before the bathroom mirror, seething with confusion, a razor poised at my cheek. I press it down. Red oozes from the blade. Then I make a quick slash and scream

'Post been delivered, Dad?'

I'm padding downstairs after a (for once) dreamless sleep, my stomach roaring for Coco-Pops (King of Cereals). The morning sun makes jungle-dapple on the floorboards. The neighbours exiting stage-left for work. Birds tweeting. The Sex Pistols drowning out Dek's complaints at the Sex Pistols drowning out Dek's complaints. I pass the front door, vaguely registering that the postman has–

Joy catches in my throat.

I pounce on the pink envelope, buzzing with hope.

YOU ARE INVITED TO THE
17th BIRTHDAY PARTY OF
TYRA MARY-LOUISE MACKENZIE

at

11 ALBERT ROAD, FALKIRK.
Friday 12th June, 8.30pm

And though my head is spinning like it's in a petal-filled washing-machine, I notice:

ps. Sorry I didn't catch you at school, Alvin. Would love it if you came!

the rest of the day shoots by like a torpedo! The drugged, soulless teachervoices – that drone on and on and on about transferred epithets, verb tables, isotopes – skirt the ground like dust in a breeze, while text-messages buzz back and forth between the desks and my mind soars upwards, whirls, becomes orchestral and limitless! I feel heightened, alive, muscle-bound, like Brad Pitt after being bitten by The Cruiser in *Interview with the Vampire*, the whole school alive with talk of Tyra's party, and I, Alvin Stephen Allison, am centre of the whirlwind, a god among inconsequentials. Everything is beautiful. First-years collared by Melville for running in the corridor have genius in their trespass. The word 'children' in Connor's Dad's notice on the PTA board – 'I request volunteers to organise more study-groups for the senior children' – strikes me as lawlessly funny, the way a swear-word leaps out in the context of a poem (would that be the same 'children', Mr Livingstone, who recreate the Grand Prix in Falkirk town-centre, masturbate like Duracell bunnies, and run up mobile-phone debt with each twitch of their hash-stained fingers?). Connor giving a letter from his mother to Mrs Pitcairn, complaining that the class tests are too easy, not stretching him enough. I can't bring myself to care about this for long, though, since I've just realised I have another eighty or so years left on Earth in which I can do *whatever the fuck I want* and I'm wondering what to wear to Tyra's party, or what booze I should bring, since I was sick the last time I drank. Brian *must* have spiked my peach-schapps and

Sorry I didn't catch you at school, Alvin. Would love it if you came!

we swagger from the shop at the bottom of the Glen Brae with two bottles of Famous Grouse and eight Strongbow (for the price of four). Brian and Frannie insist on singing 'Hello, Hello, We Are The Billy Boys' all the way up to Tyra's house, while I try to tell Dolby the latest on the *Lord of the Rings* movie. The evening is blue and clean and billowing. My stomach feels filled with circus performers.

The music pumping from Tyra's house (Abba?), the antiquity of Albert Road – its stoic, middle-class retirement air – filled with Europop and Rangers terrace anthems.

'So whit's the name ae the Birthday Bint?' Brian asks, thumping my shoulder with a Strongbow, 'Tie-Her-Up?'

'Tire-Her-Oot?' Frannie adds.

'No,' I say. 'Tyra.'

'Tyrannosaurus Rex?'

'So the thing about the film . . .' I carry on, my jaw tight, as we approach her door, '. . . is they're using the *same* technology as *Gladiator*, except they have to make you believe in a fantasy world, not a real one.'

'That's very interesting,' Dolby says.

'Tyra Shoelaces Together?'

'Tyrant?'

I ring her doorbell. The Grouse bottles are clinking gently. I can see dark shapes through the frosted glass: woozy, ghostly heads. I ring the doorbell again, and the music is turned down briefly. Someone says, '. . . at the door? but everyone's here . . .' then a grey shape swells towards the glass.

Brian growls, 'Ah could shag a whole *room* full ae schoolies . . .'

Frannie in a Vietnamese voice: '*You so honny*! *Two dollar*! *Sucky-fucky*!'

and as they make amused cartoon sounds, as Dolby asks, 'When's the movie due?' I shush them frantically and the door swings open.

'Alvin?'

182

I actually intake breath at how beautiful she is. Her hair, hazelnut-coloured, is cut in a curly bob. Her face is glowing from a study-leave spent sunbathing. The temptation to touch her hand, resting in the doorjamb, is overwhelming.

The Lads say nothing, dumbfounded by her looks.

'You, uh . . . you're *here*.' Her voice goes up on that last word, flecked with surprise.

'Well Ah'm a wee bit late, but uh . . .'

'Alvin?' she peers at my cheek, concerned. 'How did you get that scar?'

'Oh,' I fumble, 'Um, shaving accident.'

I thrust the gift at her, which she stares at for a second, as if unsure of something vital to the cogency of life. Then she shrugs awkwardly.

'Well, I suppose you'd better come in . . .'

We stride past her into the lobby, the Lads mumbling:

'Evening.'

'Happy birthday.'

'Hm.'

the same cowed way children speak to their dentist. Her hall is resplendent with balloons and streamers, littering the paintings and framed prints like clowns invading a serious arts debate, and (*I am in Tyra's house*) the mahogany thrums with drum'n'bass. The Lads spread sheepishly into the hall as Tyra unwraps her present.

'Oh,' she gasps, reading the words on the box, 'The Complete Albums of Pink Floyd?'

'Digitally Remastered!' I add, dying to let her know this cost me four months' dinner money and an *excruciating* afternoon at the back of the History huts, refusing vast quantities of dope.

'Thanks,' her small mouth utters. I was hoping she'd cry, but she's obviously too stunned and grateful.

'It's a real idea of how the band developed,' I point out to her, 'Over fourteen albums.'

The party is littered with star-names from the senior-school, the detritus of an exploded galaxy: Jennifer Haslom, ear-rings glinting, curls rocking gently on a slender neck, Louisa Wainwright brushing her hand fawningly down the arm of David Easton. All eyes turn as we enter, grinning like village idiots, hauling our Strongbow from the poly-bag to offer them round. No takers.

For most of the evening, we remain in a tight, defensive phalanx, moving from room to room as a unit. Brian's eyes goggle at Tyra's tanned, summery friends ('Cannae remember schoolies lookin like *this*!'); Frannie is horrified at evidence of Tyra's Dad being a Celtic fan ('A souvenir fae Dublin?'); Dolby scours the bookshelves for confirmation of his own good taste, his fingers resting on all seven of the Narnia books in hardback. The party shifts

up a gear. Someone plays Fatboy Slim's *You've Come A Long Way Baby*, Brian and Frannie rolling into an argument about lyrics. 'Does that song say "*Carol Vorderman is druggy, druggy, druggy.*" 'No. It's California.' Frannie cocks an ear, raises a finger. 'It's Carol Vorderman! "*Carol Vorderman is druggy, druggy, druggy*"!' 'Shut up,' Brian rumbles, as through the swelling crowd, I catch a glimpse of my mother's eyes watching me, the way they once looked balefully into my cot, and for some reason Louisa Wainwright is giving Gordon French a massage, her hands easing and rising on his shoulder-blades and a look of bliss breaks across his face, and a couple of guys – older blokes who claim to know Tyra (they wink) '*very* well' – ask about Dek. 'Is your brother home from London?/Sure I saw him the other day/What exactly is it he *does* down there?' and I half-deflect, half-ignore these questions, Fatboy Slim's loops burrowing a dull worm of pain into my skull, and Tyra is nowhere to be seen, and so, slurping at the syrupy warmth of the Famous Grouse, I go hunting, asking vague party-girls if they fancy my mates, cos they're, like, *all single*, glimpsing Mum several times – sipping gin on the stairs, helping

184

someone be sick in the garden, browsing the Mackenzies' CD collection – and when next I return to the living-room the hash-heads from the back of the History huts are talking to the Lads, Walenzic holding court like Shaun Ryder, his lit joint making the Lads stiff, wary, subdued. He is telling Frannie and Dolby about his idea for a novel called *Twelve Storeys High*, which is 'like *Trainspotting* (*puff*), except set in this high-rise (*toke*) in Fawkurt. And there's, like, twelve different stories for the twelve different storeys. And they're aw drug-dealers (*shrug*) so that's why it's cawed *Twelve Storeys* **High** (*puff*). Robert Carlyle'll play me in the (*toke*) movie.'

Doc, meanwhile, is imparting one of his prophecies to a rapt Brian Mann. I shuffle close, inconspicuous, hear Doc whisper in hushed tones, '. . . just tae let ye know, man, Ah've heard it said that Kottsy fae Camelon's gunnin for ye.'

Brian grunts moodily, retorts something about Kottsy having to fucking catch him first.

'What happened at the races, by the way? Ah heard somethin like yer mate ran ower some nutter fae Langlees?'

A monosyllabic reply from Brian. Doc continues, '. . . well *they're* keepin an eye oot for yese an aw. Kottsy's crew and the Lang Boys? Yese better stey aff thae roads for a while, man. They aw recognise that car ae yours. An mair important, they ken whaur ye work.'

'Fucksake!' Brian explodes, prodding Doc's chest and producing a brief splutter of smoke, 'Gonnae tell us some fuckin good news?'

'If ye like,' Doc shrugs, 'Celtic are winnin 2–0.'

I head (am directed? divinely?) to the garden to write a birthday poem for Tyra, trying to ignore the Slipknot slam-dancers who've colonised the living-room, one of them barging against me and dislodging a fantastic metaphor which I've just composed. On a low wall which borders the calm of the lawn, I listen to the gurgle of the fish-pool over the screech of guitars, raising my face to the sky, burbling with poetry. The sky is an irresistible velvet-blue, rippling

185

with stars and an indolent moon. I try to picture Tyra's face – just at her moment of ecstasy when she opened my present – then write on the back of a napkin:

> You are the moon.
> Celluloid-thin, white.
> Untouched by the silhouette of
> E. T.'s bike.

and get up to look for her, eager to impart these lines, my head swimming with whisky, romance and the Complete Albums of Pink Floyd, but over the pogo-ing heads of the Slipknot parade, between the prefects who smooch in drunken poses on the settee, beyond the pyramid which someone has built from Mr Mackenzie's golfing trophies, I cannot

see

her

but take the chance to steal carelessly left drinks (the tastes blending in a gloop on my tongue), but no-one knows where she is, not even, strangely, after I regale them with my joke about the Pope on a tour of Ibrox, which suddenly seems important – *vital* – to my quest. The party evolves into a vortex-shape, me anchored to the centre by the logic of my Pope joke as pretty, educated, drunken faces rotate around me then away before the punch-line, and someone

!

I am sprinting to the bathroom, hitting the porcelain and suddenly making a weird sound like this:

Blooooooouuuuurgh!

'. . . Bohemian Rhapsody will not be played on *this* piano, thank you very . . .'

Blaaarrruuuuurghhh! Uh! Help! **Eough!**

'. . . me, Jonesy, Doc, Frank MacAvennie and this bird with huge . . .'

Aah! *Aaaah*! *Heeelp*! **Booooaaaagghhhh!** (ohh)

'. . . invited that Alvin and those *awful* schemies . . .'

(fugg . . .) **Gooooaaaaghhh! Goooaaaaghh!** (ohfug)

'. . . *you are my Falkirk, my only* . . .'

then wipe my hand across my face, feel the slavers fall away in drips, and piss, making a 'Z' Zorro sign in the foam with my urine. In the living-room, people are gyrating hip against hip, kissing, and a copy of *Empire* magazine lies stuck to the table in a glaze of dried beer, so I pounce on it, ignoring the lovers crushed against me on the couch, their sex-crazed elbows digging into my ribs. Winona Ryder is on the cover, her face clear and white, like the moon above the trees on a fishing-night with the Lads last summer. Dolby, pencil-thin in the liminal dark, whispering so the fish wouldn't be startled:

'*Isn't it beautiful?*'

Winona has eyes which are a hazel colour. A sphere of reflected light glistens in the centre. Inside the sphere the photographer is visible, his sinister outline like a fleck of evil. There is a serial-killer in the chamber of Winona Ryder's eye. *Empire* magazine are advertising a **2-for-1 brilliant DVD offer**, and I lose myself in the glossy sheen of the pages, the glinting promise of each crisp edge, and soon I notice that the sky outside the room is the colour of slate, remember there's a street in Bainsford that has three – count them – *three* chip-shops and

All I want is to find a ruby in the trash.

Something that is true and good and right.

Every night we head out in Belinda like road warriors, avenging angels, and I search for it with *Terminator*-like determination, my eyes lingering on the actresses in the video-shop window and the drunks who appear randomly and who we ignore, laughing, nosing through a relentless shoal of streetlights but

I still haven't found what I'm looking for.

Dolby and Frannie are talking about some girl that Brian used to go out with – her name, believe it or not, was Victoria Wine.

'Mind ye telt her ye'd seen Noel Gallagher's willy in a toilet in Glasgow, and when she asked whit it looked like you said–'

'It's goat a big, bushy eyebrow and sings "Wonderwall"!'

They both crack up, and Brian tries to shush them, sorting out another pub crisis on the mobile (which I hope isn't Kottsy wrecking the joint) and I obsess upon that dark slice in the pure crystal of Winona Ryder's eye, then the fishing-night, where beside a fitfully flickering camp-fire we talked about Jack Nicholson movies and listened to the midnight hymn of the water, and Dolby, distantly, without emotion, mentioned that he would rather die than go back into Whirlpools Direct on Monday.

'Awright, Alvin?' Frannie frowns, lifting the drink from my hand, 'Bit green about the gills there, bud.'

My stomach lurches. I launch vomit onto his

> wish they all could be california
> (i wish they all could be california)
> i wish they all could be california

best of the sixties playing and what looks like a porno but is actually the new Britney Spears video flickering on MTV and an entire section of the living-room turned into a Hash-head Zone which the Lads have quit in protest at the giggling virginal dope-ridden faces of the prefects, and framed paintings of Scottish landscapes/glens/Tyra's modelling photographs (so soft-focus as to be hallucinatory) and row after row of Absolut Vodka/Omega cider/White & Mackay/Bacardi Breezers (such pretty colours) compete in my reeling vision and someone suggests heading out to Rosie's to which I snarl 'No I don't *fuckin* know what Dek does in London! Where's Tyra?' and Frannie shakes Brian's hand, congratulating him on Celtic's 3–2 defeat by Aberdeen and I can hear . . .

telepathic messages? . . .

saying? . . .

fuck knows what. Tyra's voice floats from the top of the stairs so I stumble towards it, my poem about her and the moon memorised. Someone – Frannie? Mum? Stephen King? – tells me they saw her slip away upstairs, and I creep towards a door ajar and behind it Travis are singing 'Last Laugh of the Laughter' and a voice, two voices, are moaning sexily, then spluttering, so I repeat the poem quietly in my head, picking up a photo of Tyra with her three sisters, who are all as gorgeous as she is, posing like the *Virgin Suicides*, kiss Tyra on the forehead,

open the door and

My eyes acclimatise to the dark. Someone is kneeling on the floor. Tyra is on her knees before Connor Livingstone. He has a sordid grin across his face and his jeans at his ankles.

Tyra turns. Her eyes are steely and hard as bullets.

'Alvin! Get the fuck out!'

I stand frozen. I can hear only the door swinging on its hinges. I am trying not to look at Connor's dick dripping with saliva or Tyra's face, vicious and twisted like an animal's.

'Well, fuck off then!' she spits, 'Shut the *door* !'

Dumbly, I retreat. Connor Livingstone's dirty laughter echoes.

The door closes, the room becoming a thin strip of dark. Downstairs

the party has become the universe at the dawn of time. Things fly, smash, die. Curtains balloon and fall. A window has been broken in the kitchen. People are standing around like dead-weights. The night roars in, black and relentless, while the room swirls in the breeze.

Brian comes over and fits a Becks into my hand. 'Aye,' I mutter to whatever he's saying, 'Aye,' and the next time I look at my hand the Becks is drained but I can't remember having drunk it. Then I'm sneezing, violently, the generous spray of flowers in the room launching my hayfever. For minutes afterwards, my germs are disseminating in the room, floating towards tabletops, beer-cans, CD cases, infecting every surface.

The smashed window has ended the party. People are fraught with concern, stomping to and fro, blaming each other, you drank this, you threw that. Someone has turned MTV over and a programme that nobody is watching is imploring us to look after our bodies, because as they get older:

'*By the age of 70 we have lost a third of our muscle strength . . .*'

'. . . new car if I pass my driving . . .'

'*the hairs in the cochlea die, leading to hearing loss . . .*'

'. . . play Eminem and I'll fuckin . . .'

'*cartilage rubbing together causes sharp pains at the joints . . .*'

'. . . starting salary of only, like, twenty grand . . .'

and computer graphics detail the cross-section of knee-cartilage grinding, gristling, twisting, like torture.

190

Tyra and Connor. Oh God.

I stagger outside, my stomach so light it feels as though it has floated away. Dolby follows, fearing I'm going to be sick again.

'Alvin?' he asks, concerned, 'Ye awright?'

My world pierced. The life escaping it in a thin, whining hiss. Everything resounding towards flatness. I feel functionless, totally fucked. Tyra belongs to him. I collapse onto a sun-lounger by the fish-pool, my hand dappling in its cold shallows, a smooth silver body brushing against my fingers, then away. The sky is huge and timeless and black. The point is there is no point, etc. Oh God.

'It disnae exist, does it?' I murmur to Dolby.

'Whit?'

'Youth.'

He doesn't answer. We stare at the shimmering black skin of the water. Things dance then disappear like phantoms.

'It's a con,' I say. 'A clear surface. It breaks when you touch it.'

There is a pause. Dolby blinks at me.

'It doesn't *do* anything,' I almost shout.

The cold wind in our faces. I lean back, realising how devoid that sky is of any secrets, how poor Oasis are now, all those Britpop bands, how fucking drunk I am, and after that all I can remember is Dolby stretching my jacket across me, the police arriving, maybe several times, and an anonymous kiss on my cheek, a brief waft of perfume, my name whispered once. Only once.

And then

Our living-room.

Me, Dek, Mum and Dad watching *Family Fortunes* in the dark. The light sharpening the corners of the ceiling. The TV makes everyone's face a flickering, aquamarine mask. I'm on my belly, jabbing at crinkle-cut chips, my sock dangling halfway off my foot. '*Name something,*' says Les Dennis, '*you would use in the garden.*' Dek passes me the 'George and Lynne' cartoon from *The Sun*, and we snigger sneakily at Lynne's melon-like breasts as she cooks breakfast, as ever, in the nude. 'Ah bet when she's in the shower,' Dek giggles, 'she wears a woolly jumper and a bodywarmer!' Simmering resentment from the couch behind us. Mum and Dad's blank faces crackle with light.

'Name something you can cut with.'

A contestant buzzes hesitantly. *'Paper!'*

Me and Dek trade punches to the arm.

'Enough,' Dad mutters.

He told us earlier tonight that he has been paid off from the oil refinery down Grangemouth. Being 'paid off' always sounds exciting in gangster films, like 'here's some pay-off money for ya ta keep ya mouth shut,' but Dek, his tone low, informed me that it isn't good at all. There was a lot of screaming and banging from the kitchen after Dad told Mum (though Dek took me to watch cartoons on the telly while this was going on). Mum always does the high-pitched keening. Dad grunts, sighs, asks, 'Whit exactly is it that ye want me tae dae?' Sometimes we can hear her sobbing in the middle of the night, along with Dad's rumbling monotone as he tries to reassure her.

Dek turns to Page Three and shows me Lena, nineteen, from London's 'boob-iful assets'.

'Her jeans are faded at the knees,' I point out, and Dek tuts and drags the paper away.

'Pepe jeans are *supposed* to be faded,' he instructs me derisively.

The TV fills the limp, blue darkness with chattering light, rising and falling across the cliff-face of my parents. Their eyes are lost to the loveless glow, the cue-track of laughter, the adverts flinging themselves into the hurtling path of the programmes, or the other way round.

'D'ye think Pepe jeans are better than Naf-Naf?' Dek asks.

'Pepe le Peu!' I say.

'Enough,' Dad murmurs automatically. Dek glowers at him

through the dimness.

'Name a country,' says Les Dennis, 'That you would–'

stairs rising to a glue-patch of darkness, and I can hear skulking, moaning sounds coming from it. Mum awake and roaming. Dek has a new haircut. He is being insistent about something.

'Listen, Alvin, Ah'm fed up. Ah'm gawin oot. Ah'm sick ae tellin ma pals that Ah'm no well, just cause ae–' He glances upstairs; there is a crash and some muffled swearing. 'Ah'm sick ae it full-stop. Ma pals are aw oot havin a laugh, gettin birds. Whit am Ah daein? Babysittin ma Mam!'

I gaze down at the carpet. A bleach-stain. An ill, white blossom of fibres.

'Whit time does Dad get in?' I mumble petulantly.

'Late. He's on the back shift.'

The darkness at the top of the stairs is silent now.

'If she tries tae get oot, lock aw the doors an windaes. Ye ken the drill. Then just put on a video or somethin. She'll soon faw back asleep. Ye've got Dad's number if there's an emergency.' He cocks his head. 'Okay, pal?'

I nod dumbly.

'C'mon Alvin. Yer eleven now. Auld enough tae help look after her. Cannae sit wi yer face shoved intae a Spider-Man comic aw yer life.'

I nod again.

He ruffles my hair. The hallway feels like a vacuum. The ear of the china dog on the phone-table is chipped. So are most of the ornaments in this house.

'One night oot wi ma pals. That's aw Ah'm askin.'

Dek opens the door and goes out into a hubbub of fifteen year-olds, hands thrust into his jacket, his fag making smoke graffiti in the air. I watch them cross the grass and clamber into a car, driving off, whooping. The throat of the stairwell is cold and narrow. Shaking, I climb the stairs.

She lies in bed like driftwood. Pale and forgotten. Her skin is thirty-four years old, but shineless, worn. Her hand clings to the edge of the duvet. Her eyes are her only motion, the only tiny, wet sounds.

A breeze makes a belly of the curtains.

'Son?'

I ignore her, tidying conscientiously. *Everything in its right place*, she used to say, when she could form whole sentences without difficulty. More chipped ornaments. A china donkey. A ballerina, on tippy-toes.

'Son, Ah need ye.'

Dust wafts through the light in the room. There is a smell of talcum-powder and stale nicotine. I raise the duvet so that it covers her bony shoulders. Outside, cars speed past on the main road, the sound a pulsing rush. Here, there is stillness. Here, there is only a blame refined over decades.

'Son, Ah need ye tae do somethin for me.'

'Whit is it, Mum?'

Her lips make a small clicking sound as she moistens them. Her pills lie scattered on the floor.

'Yer fuckin Dad—'

She coughs gutturally. The window is open too wide. I close it.

'Yer fuckin Dad willnae let me hae a drink. No even wan, the bastard.'

'Mum, ye ken why that is . . .'

She raises a hand, slim as a flower-stem, and points to the ceiling. 'But Ah've goat a wee bottle ae vodka in the loft. Ah just use it for a . . . for a treat. Will ye get it for me, son? Wid ye dae that for yer Mammy?'

I walk to the edge of the bed. Run my finger along the stitching of the duvet. She looks up at me, hopefully. Her tired lips are fighting with a smile. 'You were eywis ma favourite, wee Alvy. Ye mind me

194

takin ye oot in yer tartan shawl tae watch the stars? Ye mind the songs I used tae sing tae ye . . .'

Her eyes start to close. The spilled pills.

I pull back the duvet and get into bed beside her.

'. . . songs Ah used tae sing tae ye . . . Yer tartan shawl . . .'

I kiss her head. Her hair is papery on my lips. Her face closes.

'. . . just a wee treat . . . dinnae hate me son . . . dinnae . . .'

Outside, the cars hurtle past. The sound of air whooses and falls. Her mumbles finally cease. I sink towards the pillow and

wake in Tyra's garden.

The sun is fluttering its white wings. An orchestra of birds is practising somewhere, so I know it's either early morning or dusk.

Fuck, man.

Weak and shaky. My neck's complaining loudly. I lift a rose which has been soaked by beer and sniff it. The windows of Tyra's house hang tall and desolate and her garden is a mess: broken furniture, cans floating in the pond. I imagine groans shuffling out from sleeping bags all over the house. Maybe I'm the first one awake. Maybe everyone's died in the night and I'm the last man on Earth. The idea appeals to me.

I watch a butterfly for a few minutes, listen to the birds, feel the day warm up, the useless beauty of things. I think about nothing in particular, just look about, peaceful, swallowing, until eventually I stand up and head for home. Always home. There is no other place to go but home.

I bet if I could look at the street-plans of Falkirk Town Centre I'd see that it's shaped like a loop. I suppose that's why it's called the boyracer 'circuit', cos they just go round and round, like little Scalextrix cars. Round and round. Back to the start again. Which reminds me, shit, today me and the Lads had agreed we would be singing in unity – Brian's voice basso-rumbling, Frannie's high, squeaky, Belinda a clanking, disharmonious backing-track, while we eat, drink, be merry, blahblah, tearing down the motorway and stopping for a ripe pish every fifteen minutes. A competition soon starts over who can think up the most ridiculous insult – 'Unlicensed Bug-Lover' 'Juice-Laden Purse-Snatcher' 'Promiscuous Potato-Peeler' – but I win with 'Chrome-Plated Wife-Swapper' (my reward: Frannie's unfinished packet of peanuts), as we drive and drive and unfurl our collective, petroleum self and Dolby interrogates Brian about the chick he pulled at the party – a distant cousin of Tyra's called Morvern who had dragonflies painted on her shoes and a spider-web on her skirt – and Brian is describing *every* part of her anatomy except the ones we want to hear about. I ask Frannie if he pulled. 'Only my pole,' he grumbles, then relates to us his horror at Dolby introducing himself to someone as Uriel.

'Well it's ma name!' Dolby complains, adjusting the plastic Harrison Ford on the dash, which is in difficulty, hanging by one foot and a blob of Blu-tac.

'No,' Frannie tuts, 'It's not. Your name is Martin Dolby. You were *born* Martin Dolby. You will always *be* Martin Dolby . . .' Dolby's face closes and he shakes his head.

'You boys are skank-o-matic.'

Brian gives him the silent fingers behind his copy of *GQ*.

'Thing is,' I pipe up, 'There's probably some boyracer in Brazil with the name Uriel who's desperate tae change it tae Dolby!'

The three of them laugh – hearty, genuine – and a warm glow suffuses my chest until Brian growls, 'We're no fuckin boyracers.' And everyone goes:

'Harumph.'

accelerating across the surface of the land leaving a wake of crisp-packets/Springsteen lyrics/tyre-tracks to mark our passing while the Ibrox Twins discuss which Rangers Wives they (don't) want to shag

('Have ye seen his girlfriend? She could fuckin *play* for Rangers!') and I think about what happened at home.

My day at school had been abysmal. In my practice English essay I'd completely mixed up George Orwell, Orson Welles and H. G. Wells (how easy is that?). I'd had to endure a common-room on the boil with the news that Tyra and Connor were, officially, an item. On a desk at the back of my Modern Studies class, I'd written

IS THERE ANYBODY OUT THERE?

before initialling and dating it. Later in the day, I was summoned back to Mrs Costa's room and handed a scrubbing brush.

At home, I found Dek sunbathing in the garden, a Pina Colada in one hand and his pinkie extended. His ginger beard and chest fuzz have grown out of control recently, and he looked just like a comedy dope-fiend.

'Whaur's Dad?' I asked, supping some of his Pina Colada from the straw. Dek just shrugged, rustling through the *Daily Record*.

'Upstairs,' he said eventually.

'Have ye had a fight?' I said.

He didn't answer.

Our garden was slabbed with concrete in 1989. This was Dad's idea; it meant he didn't have to cut the grass and pull the weeds every summer. Now the paving stones are cracked and cock-eyed, lying at slants as if an earthquake's hit. Weeds creep through the gaps like bits of broccoli between teeth.

I pulled up a sun-lounger next to Dek, noticing Dad's slippers parked at the side. 'Does yer boss no want ye back at work soon?' I asked, pretending not to be concerned at all. 'Ye've been here three weeks.'

'Long holiday,' he said tonelessly. Sipping.

'Whit about yer rent?' I continued. My family aren't the greatest communicators, but I can guess their moods from only half-glances, since their faces, pretty much, unfortunately, match mine.

'Taken care of,' he mumbled, clawing at his beard the same way Dad does, the fingers hooked and inquisitive and quietly scratching out:

Get. Tae. Fuck.

I snapped, snatching his paper.

'Are you gonnae talk to me for chrissakes?'

Dek calmly removed his shades. His eyes were blazing. He leant over to me.

'Our Dad,' he whispered with a muted distress, 'is going *insane.*'

Upstairs Dad was face-down on the bed, spread like a starfish. He was surrounded by photographs. Dozens of them.

'Dad?' I said, and he made a surprised noise, turning round. His eyes were mild, red and ringed. He wiped at them manfully.

'Sorry, son,' he whispered. An effort to smile. 'Just me and yer brother havin words, that's aw. He sometimes disnae know when tae leave somethin be.'

I nodded, looking down at him.

Dad sighed and picked up the photos, an out-of-tune orchestra of faces.

'God, how did things get so fucked-up?' And he gave a short laugh, scratching at his beard, just like Derek.

'Dad?'

He looked up.

'Dad, don't go the same way as Mum. If you do, I will hate you. I will hate you completely. And there'll be no way back from it.'

He held my gaze, and it grew so icy and still that I felt the slightest motion from either of us would smash it to bits. He opened his mouth to reply, but I said:

'Do you understand me?'

And left.

and Frannie, meanwhile, is keen to head to Cally Park to 'check if

198

the flowers are in bloom – nyuk, nyuk!' his sex-drive emerging like a bee from the winter, so we stop at Haddows for Bacardi Breezers (where Dolby is asked for I.D. haha) then cruise into a slow swarm of sunburnt kids, relaxing our patter.

We get out and start walking. The Bacardi Breezers make a ringing clink as the sun flits across our faces. We climb the fence to the playground and lark about on the swings, pushing each other down the chutes. I feel like a kid. It's great.

A quartet of girls strolls past.

'Hey,' Frannie whispers, poised on the swing, 'Mind thae girls Ah gave ma mobile number tae?'

Wendy has clocked me, lowering her shades and smiling wickedly. 'Well we made a wee arrangement . . .'

I wander over, trying to subdue a grin.

'Are *you* Ally Ferguson!' she gasps, 'Can Ah have your autograph?'

'Very funny,' I retort, 'Where did they dredge you up fae?'

She tuts and adopts 'Wounded' look no.6. 'Don't forget Ah've seen your willy, pal.'

They burgle our Bacardi Breezers; we colonise their ghetto-blaster. It's all dance music, worse luck, save for one tape which is 'Brown-Eyed Girl' recorded twelve times (what is it with girls and that song?) and there's an easy feel to the proceedings, vaguely expectant. The Lads are acting like Roman gladiators being fed grapes by concubines; the girls preen like flowers contested by bumblebees. Each side thinks the other is doing all the running. Pointless chat fizzes like lemonade. Chilled-as-fuck lemonade.

'Whit song will be the first dance at your wedding?' one of the girls asks, running her hand along the grass.

' "In the Army Now" by Status Quo,' Brian replies.

' "Jump" by Van Halen,' says Dolby. The girls tut and urge them to think of their wives. Frannie shrugs, 'Okay,' closes his eyes, then says, 'Wow, she's fuckin gorgeous!'

I just laze, getting drunk, watching a kid watching a beetle, thinking and thinking about the Stirling University prospectus which plopped on my doormat this morning.

' "We Don't Need Another Hero" by Tina Turner?'

' "Hello Hello, We Are The Billy Boys"?'

'The theme-tune fae *Only Fools and Horses*?'

When I turn for a Breezer, Wendy is looking at me, her gaze heavy and true. Something clicks, a sort of tripwire deep in some primal place. Something shared and silent.

'Comin for a walk?' she says quickly.

We hold hands. Because of the trembling, I find I'm talking about Madonna albums louder than I should be. The ghetto-blaster drones at Wendy's side.

'Let me get this straight,' she laughs, 'Ye've never listened tae *Ray of Light*?'

'Is it better than *Like A Prayer*?'

'Miles!'

'Ah dunno,' I shrug, '*Like A Prayer*'s quite a standard.'

'*Quite a standard*,' she repeats, posh.

'Less ae yer cheek.'

She leads me into a shady bower, dappled with leaves and a quiet cool. I wave away a wasp. We sit, and she plays *Ray of Light*, lecturing me on its merits like a teacher, then she turns, puts her hand in my hair and the weight of our eye-contact drags us further down. '*Put your body close to my mind*,' she murmurs. Or something. Her words seem to melt in the heat, as she leans, kisses the space under my chin, and soon we are uncurling. Breathing. Our bodies, slightly slick, slide against each other. Birds are jabbering tiny sounds at the air and the sunlight is real and Wendy lies on top of me, her chin in her hand.

'Enjoy it?'

I nod, thoughtfully.

'Yeah, it was good. Had a nice beat to it. I reckon it is better than *Like A Prayer*.'

She pauses.

'The sex, you idiot, not the album.'

'Oh,' I say. 'Um . . .'

She slaps me playfully on the head, doing her bra-strap with an expertise which had totally eluded me ten minutes ago. Her back stretches, pocked here and there with tiny sticks, and I home in on the fine, red hairs which wisp at the base of her neck, the faint rouge tint in her skin, the tiny, bright mouths of sunlight which open in the green canopy above us. The scent of chlorophyll and sex. The distant, lazy drum of insect wings. The world seems to glisten with life, colour, choices. I think I'm in love.

Probably just hungry.

'Ken, Alvin,' Wendy muses, studying my face, 'You're actually no *that* bad lookin.'

'No *that* bad?' I repeat, aghast. 'Whit the fuck's that supposed to mean!'

'Ah dunno,' she sighs, cocking her head like a puppy. 'Another couple ae years . . . fill-oot a bit . . . decent haircut . . .' She muses. 'You could be quite a catch.'

My skin is starting to redden. I look away, doing up my buttons.

'Aye . . . well . . .'

I reach for a Coke and take a heavy, nonchalant slurp. Wendy stares at me, horrified. Murmurs:

'There was a wasp on the lip of that can . . .'

and I feel movement in my mouth. A dull buzz. I freeze.

'Spit!' she urges.

a small body grazing the inside of my cheek

'Spit!' she yells, 'Now!' and I

spray the Coke from my mouth, panicked. The wasp lies fighting in a dark-brown puddle, its stinger punching the air like a sewing-needle. I stamp it to mush, howling and covering my mouth.

'Ye ken whit would have happened if ye'd swall–'

'Ah ken!' I interrupt, raising my hand. 'Ah ken!'

Walking back to camp, we're laughing, but my nerves feel as if they've been laced with acid. One wee sting and I would have been a goner.

Wendy asks if it was my first time.

'Naw,' I say. 'Well, *aye*. There was this false alarm before.'

'Ye mean like a pregnancy scare?'

'Naw. Ah thought Ah'd lost my virginity when Ah hadnae.'

'Aw,' she says. Then: 'That's an *alarm*?'

We talk, daftly enough, about *The Broons*. I confess to her my secret fantasy for Maggie, she confesses hers for Joe. 'That waist!' I gasp. 'Thae muscles!' Wendy marvels. She asks what my favourite film is and I say *Jaws* and she says – get this, nearly ruining the whole moment – 'Which one?'

'Whit d'ye mean *which one*? There is only one.'

'No there's no,' she says, confused, 'There's four *Jaws* movies.'

'Naw,' I stress seriously, 'There is one *Jaws* movie.'

She punches at my arm – I let her, though she's clearly no *Jaws* purist – and it's fun and the world has a new and sudden brightness, but that

wasp. Its tiny sting sliding into the walls of my throat. My throat swelling, choking. The closeness of death. The sharks, the giant sharks. Wendy is pondering the shadows we cast, long and scrawled, in front of us, and then she is smiling at me.

'You've got a "look",' she says.

She has gorgeous eyelashes.

'A look? Like, whit sort ae look?'

203

'Ye look—' she cocks her head again, '—hungry.'

'Ah am hungry! Ah huvnae fuckin eaten since breakfast.'

'That's no what Ah mean. Ye look like ye . . . *want* somethin.'

'Have Ah no just had it?'

'No that. Naw, somethin bigger than that.'

'Hmm. So whit exactly *dae* Ah want?'

Wendy winks.

'Whit's comin tae ye.' Her hand snakes around my waist and stays there. 'Ye want whit's comin tae ye.'

and we split. Det

ach. Our fingers lingering. She fades across the lawn like a sunbeam as I bob back to the car with a helium grin. The grass makes a rustling noise, and I am impressed, just *convinced* of nature's talent as a performing artist, the potential for life to outdo itself just when you'd given up on it. Sweet. So sweet.

And that night, drunkenly happy, that state in which things bubble and pop with life and you wonder how anything could ever be bad again, Dek and me go wandering through Hallglen. Terrain sharp with memories. Its labyrinthine streets. Its ancient satellite dishes, like barnacles on a sunken ship. The lock-ups we used to smash footballs against and the places where we made dens or played hide-and-seek and the doors we chapped, and ran away from, shouting, booting garbage down the street.

I'm glad he's home.

But I still don't know why he's home.

The wind creeps between the shells of houses. The boarded-up windows are like damaged eyes. While I tell him about Wendy, her touch and her scents and her voice, and he nods, impressed, but doesn't tell me about a single girl he met in London, we wander into a swing-park where we both used to play. Now desolate.

'Imagine you wiping your dick on your t-shirt,' he tuts.

'What else could Ah use?'

'The last of the great romantics!'

Dek snorts and nudges an empty vodka bottle with his boot. Then he picks it up, weighs it, and hurls it against a nearby wall.

The smash rings round the scheme.

'I found her here once.' Dek gestures to the climbing-frames, which rear against the dark like dinosaur skeletons. 'She was lying unconscious. Weans had put dog-shit on her chest.'

I sit on one of the swings, rocking gently. The chain makes a comforting, nautical creak. I stare at him.

'Derek, why did ye come hame?'

He glances at me, then away, his eyes white marbles in the dark. He starts rolling a piece of the vodka bottle with his boot.

'She is alive, Alvin.'

He climbs onto the wall, gazes round at the unblinking lights of a place he once lived, but never called home, and Dek is the only one of us who followed his dream to see where it would lead. And where it led was straight back here. And I swing despondently, my feet making random pushes against the rubber slab. The glass shards of the vodka bottle lie waiting for a kid's foot, so I sweep them to the wall. Then I climb up, stand next to Dek, listen to the howl of dogs' separated souls while in the playground phantom children laugh.

'She's out there somewhere. I can feel her.'

My older brother – who always took care of me, who always knew exactly what he was doing, why he was doing it, or so it seemed to me – grown up into an unwound ball of string. And I can't help but think:

Weren't we promised something?

Sitting in our primary schools (little chairs, little tables), listening open-mouthed to the magic sounds made by the teacher, we could see something gleaming, just past her shoulder, out there beyond the playground. A rough-draft of the world. An artist's impression. But it looked *wonderful.* Something true. Something good. Something to run towards.

'Ever get the feeling you've been cheated?' Dek murmurs, hopping down from the wall, wrapping his arms around himself as

we soar in and out of the badlands and Brian makes slurping noises with his Irn-Bru while music from gleaming vehicles veers close then away and Frannie, hollering, obscene with laughter, ignores the crap rap music on Belinda's stereo (Asian Pub Foundation or something) to pose the question: 'So if Batman wis a pop star who would he be?' which is a tricky one since you have to think about Batman's iceberg-cool image and it's pointless comparing him to say, Robert Plant, the two just don't go, silly to even consider it, and we pass a sign saying DON'T FALL ASLEEP AT THE WHEEL and I can't believe how many beautiful women Frannie has ignored tonight – fortysomething trolley-dollys with their Mrs Robinson maturity on show, carrying shopping bags, parked at traffic lights – he's totally possessed with the Batman question, and he should be, it's an important one, crucial, and I can't stop thinking that it's been eight years since the last Floyd album/tour (do they do weddings and ceilidhs for Richard Branson and Bill Gates these days?) and Dolby is fighting with Brian to try and get some of the Irn-Bru but Brian's pulling it away, teasing him, bringing it closer, pulling it away, his cackling, and the sky is mottled red-pink, the clouds ridged and quilted like herringbone and the Scotland game hisses onto the radio (they're drawing 1–1!) and England were beaten 1–0 by Germany in their final game at Wembley and this holds deep, almost mystical significance for everyone (Dolby gives the loudest cheer and he doesn't even like football) and I answer the Batman question: 'Surely he's cool enough tae be Bono?' 'Bono yer arse!' says Brian. 'Naw,' Dolby adds, shaking his head seriously, 'Spider-Man's Bono. He's got the patter and the

206

charisma. Batman's The Edge.' 'Aah!' everyone sighs in agreement, this flash of insight illuminating the whole car, it's so convincing a statement. So Batman is The Edge and Spider-Man is Bono, 'But whit aboot Superman?' Frannie asks, concerned, plunging us into despair again, and mini-weapons throw chips as we pass The Golden Bird, Dolby not even trying to dodge them and one of the chips hits Belinda's rear-window, sliding greasily across its surface, then into oblivion, forgotten, down, and we rack our brains, the four of us, to solve this problem, somehow, and there are two girls in the car next to us, pointing and smiling (I'm guessing one of them is called Janice, she has that Strathclyde look, and, let's be frank, Janice is a Strathclyde name) but no Bobba Fetts for us, not now, the Superman issue must be resolved, and quickly, it's ruining the night. 'Elvis Presley!' shouts Brian, at the same time that Frannie, wide-eyed, shouts 'Cliff Richard!' then they look at each other, incredulous, and Brian says, 'Cliff fuckin Richard?' at the same time as Brian says, 'Elvis fuckin Presley?' and as they argue we screech towards Grangemouth, the refinery lights like an enormous art installation around us, pollution spewing from a crystal carapace, God's own mad-scientist experiment, which we zip through as a chemical compound, as Brian goes, 'Naw, Superman is yer Aw-American Hero. He *is* America. He's the King. He's tae super-heroes whit Elvis is tae rock 'n'roll.' 'Whit?' Frannie whines, 'Aw Brian yer insane! Superman's yer typical straight-laced, squeaky-clean, dae yer job wi the minimum ae fuss for fifty years, borin the tits aff everybody in the process, sort ae super-hero. He's no cool, dark an edgy like Batman. He's no funny and smart like Spider-Man. He is a personality free-zone. If he didnae have his job at the *Daily Planet*, mark ma words, he wid be releasing Christmas records every year,' and the argument continues like this, even though Dolby tries to arrange another fishing-trip to the Ness, even though Frannie's mobile chirrups Shaggy's 'It Wasn't Me' six times and even though I've got my baseball cap on back-to-front like a rapper and I'm making unconvincing Eminem noises and everyone laughs, with affection, and I tell Dolby I've reached the bit in *Lord of the Rings* (I'm re-reading it *actually*) when Frodo meets Shelob the spider and we discuss this, excitedly, like kids swapping stickers. 'How dae ye think they'll dae that scene in the film?' he asks, wiping his mouth twice, three times, as if preventing himself from salivating, and Bruce Springsteen reminds us that it ain't no sin to be glad you're alive and it ain't, and we honour him, raising our Irn-Bru in a toast, making plans to drive right across America when Brian emigrates, like Thelma and Louise, swapping these drizzly streets and *Daily Record* vendors and all of Scotland's crapness for wide-open desert land-scapes, Belinda possessed by the spirits of Red Indians like in an Oliver Stone movie, as we drink Wild Turkey and get sunburnt and slam our glamorous Falkirk patter at Yank chicks bored with Boston guys, and we live on the road, forever the people, the ones who had a notion, a notion deep inside, and the Scotland game finishes 1–1 (a difficult away game to Croatia) and drunk on our own youth, speed, LedZepness, we roll down all of the windows and start singing '*Bonny Scotland, Bonny Scotland, We'll Support You Evermore!*' as one single male chorus, one single Zappabeast and Dolby suggests, 'We should go abroad, support the Tartan Army,' his face bright with patriotism, which is weird, since the only places I've ever seen him patriotic about are Narnia and Middle-Earth, but Brian spews 'Fuck that! Rangers fans dinnae support Scotland abroad! Ye daft? We need oor money for the Champions League, man,' making me and Dolby shake heads, unimpressed by the Hun atmosphere in the car. 'So whit wid you rather?' I demand, 'Scotland win the World Cup or Rangers win the European Cup?' but Brian and Frannie just look at each other, wounded. 'Ah cannae believe you had tae ask that, Alvin?' 'That's good,' I nod, faith in humanity restored, briefly, 'Ah'm glad ye said that, Brian.' 'Aye,' they muse, 'Ah mean think ae the benefits tae the country if Rangers won the European Cup. National morale goes up, we attract foreign investment, Celtic cannae crow aboot the Lisbon Lions nae mair' and then Dolby's phone rings the theme to *Who Wants To Be A Millionaire?* but he switches it off, whooping and slapping, why? for nothing really, no reason, just cos he can, just cos he can do things like wrench Belinda's wheel and practise handbrake skids in a deserted street of Bainsford, grannies peering worriedly from behind net curtains at the screeching sound, the tyre-tracks imprinted in the road, our calling-card, since we're off again, too fast for them, too fucking fast for anybody, and then it's a debate about our fantasy night-out, our ideal drinking-partners, and names like Gary Oldman, Lemmy, Clive Barker, Judd Nelson's character in *The Breakfast Club* and Homer Simpson are bandied about and Frannie narrates like Richard Attenborough: '*as Lemmy and Homer sink their twelfth pint, Brian Mann and Dolby slide to the floor and Alvin talks shite to a bored Clive Barker*' and Brian's mobile beeps the *Top Gun* theme and Dolby says 'So who would be Wonder Woman?' and we all hiss 'Madonna!' as another Irn-Bru is burst open and

The headlights become jewels in the flow of night. Our car is linked to them. We drape onwards, jewel after jewel, life after life, glittering into the distance. The road ahead is all that we know. The thrum of cat's eyes on tyres. The beckoning throat of darkness. We keep good company against it, building a close, comforting fire with our laughter. To do this is vital.

Dolby halts Belinda on the forecourt. Her brakes whine. We stumble out, almost bewildered, into Sunday morning, blinking like cats after our overnight fishing at the Ness. Last thing I remember before falling asleep was a particularly gruelling debate about which hairstyle Brian should adopt for the States (when/if). Frannie favours a classic mullet. I personally think he would look very dashing with Tom Cruise's greasy do in *Magnolia*. Dolby reckons he should go baldy, right down to the wood and be done with it, which Frannie took as a slight

209

against himself, since, in the manner of Coisty or a moss-obsessed rolling-stone, he is constantly updating his own thatch.

'Why've we stopped?' Brian yawns, 'Whit's the story?'

'Morning glory.'

'Petrol,' Dolby grunts, wheel-fatigued, 'Belinda could dae wi a drink.'

'So the fuck could Ah.'

I stretch and look through the grey morning at toilet seats in the window of Carron Bathrooms, their mouths gulping at the cold air.

'Whit's yer favourite?' Frannie asks.

'That pink wan.'

'Whit! Naw, see that lilac wan. Lavender seat.'

'Frannie, yer insane!' I cry, 'A lavender seat?'

He shrugs, slaps a tempo on the car roof. 'Ach, it's aw shite anyway.'

On Friday, in class, I wrote a note to Tyra, telling her that I hope she is very happy with Connor. It took me fifteen minutes to write, probably missing valuable exam info. I wrote and wrote, my heart channelled through the pen, onto the torn page of my homework diary, while she rested her flawless chin in her hand and gazed across the class at Connor, lovelorn. Then I folded the paper, wrote her name on it, and passed it to her.

'It's aw shite!' Frannie hoots, 'Ye get it?'

She glanced up at me, took the note in her slim fingers, and unfolded it.

'Alvin, ye get it? It's aw shite!'

As she read, her eyes gave little away. I watched the balls, sheathed in smooth lids, flicker along the lines. She seemed to hesitate over certain passages, pausing to re-read them, her brow furrowing gently. When she'd finished, she picked up her pen, scribbled, and slid the note back across the desk to me. It said:

STAY AWAY FROM ME YOU FUCKING WEIRDO.

We slam back into the car, Belinda refreshed and the rest of us waking. Fingers of light creep across the morning's corpse. Brian guzzling at the bottle of whisky and Irn-Bru left over from the fishing. His brain revolves with hangover.

'Guuuuuh,' he manages. 'Fuckin Clapton solo in ma heid, man.'

'Nae hangovers like that in California,' I say.

'Tell me about it!' he visibly brightens, 'The hangovers ower there are like orgasms!'

On Friday night, after I slouched home from school, there was a doctor in speaking to Dad and Dek. I fumbled about in the kitchen, warming my tea, while she chatted politely, hands folded on her lap.

'Ah wish they aw could be California . . .'

'Ah wish they aw could be California . . .'

'Ah wish they aw could be California *giiiirlls* . . .'

After she left, I collared Dek upstairs, turning *Top of the Pops* up full so Dad wouldn't hear. 'He's having a nervous breakdown,' Dek told me, over the wail of Placebo's 'Slave to the Wage', 'He isn't mentally fit for work, but he can apply for disability allowance.'

I sighed and placed my forehead in my hand.

'And one of us can apply for a Carer's Allowance to stay home and watch him.'

I looked at Dek. He looked back.

'Hey, it's no gonnae be me!' I shouted. 'What if Ah want tae go tae university?'

'I thought that was for poofs.'

'But what if Ah decide Ah *want* tae go?'

'Well ye can't. Listen, I *took* ma turn. Years ago.'

'Aye right. You fuckin left! Who d'ye think's got him this far?'

'And a fine job you made ae it! He's had a nervous breakdown since I've been away! Oh you are one selfish wee shite, Alvin!'

'. . .'

'Eh? Come on, Alvin, whit d'ye say?'

'. . .'

'Alvin?'

Frannie shakes my shoulder.

'Alvin, yer a million miles away, man!'

'Sorry,' I grumble, 'Just tired.'

'Aye, well. Whit d'ye say, Alvin? Ye want tae go pickin oranges in California?'

'Oot Carmen Electra's bra!'

I look round the car. The three of them are staring, expectantly. I scratch my nose, slurp desperately at the bottle of whisky girders, which tastes flat/hot/Scottish and then I think I say something like:

'Um, every night Ah dream Ah'm in *Aliens*. Fightin monsters wi, um, big teeth.'

but they've started practising handbrake skids again. None of them hear me.

Later that night, Brian is picking the empty glasses from in front of his arse-nosed customers. Not that the booze-hounds notice, jammed into their *Sporting Life*, *Sun*, *Daily Record*, or even (one of Brian's regulars, Stoogie, fancies himself as a bit of an intellectual, wears polonecks and everything) *The History of Falkirk*. Me, Frannie and Dolby are hunched over the bar, like the Ochil Hills in miniature, Frannie watching *Friday Sportscene* on the telly, Dolby talking to Brian about *The Simpsons*, while I read an interview with Bono in *Q* magazine (he looks very cool for 40). Orange streetlights simmer outside, Falkirk on fire. The pub is quietly beery. Friday. Decent jokes. Scrooge still trying to cadge a pound for Neil Diamond songs. Frannie peers at my copy of *Q* during the lull of a Motherwell feature.

'Imagine Bono perched on the end ae the bar,' Frannie beams. 'Whit wid ye ask him?'

'Ah'd ask him whit the fuck he wis daein in Fawkurt.'

'Naw,' Frannie shakes his head, Coisty-eyes glinting, 'cos he'd be oor guest. We'd have bumped intae him backstage an invited him on a pub-crawl roon Fawkfurt . . .'

'Aye right!' I say, 'Bono in Behind the Wall? Bono in The Newmarket? Bono in The Welly?'

'Hiy!' Frannie protests, 'Bono widnae be seen deid in The Welly.'

The interview with Celtic's new Latvian striker (the name is unpronounceable – I'm not even going to try) ends and Frannie resumes watching *Friday Sportscene* as Stoogie clears his throat, officiously, wetting his finger and leafing carefully through *The History of Falkirk*, just aching for one of us to say:

'Interesting book, Stu?'

'It is that, Brian,' Stoogie nods ponderously, 'Oor fair auld toon has quite a chequered past.'

'Whit? Fawkurt?' Dolby screws up his face, 'Whit ever happened in Fawkurt?'

'Ye'd be surprised,' Stoogie replies, appalled by the ignorance/ arrogance of this generation, 'Youse boys should read aboot it sometime. It's yer hame toon.'

'Ach that's a lot ae shite!' Brian waves a dismissive hand, 'Nane ae that mettirs. The here an now's whit coonts, that's it.'

'Son . . .' Stoogie shakes his head wearily, 'Yer young. Ye've no been oan the planet that long. It's right that ye think like that. But ye'll learn sin enough that ye cannae ignore the past.'

'Fuck that,' Brian dismisses him, wiping the bar aggressively, 'We're the fuckin history ae Fawkurt, eh boys? This is oor toon!' His face shines with an almost fascist superiority, opposed by so much age and crapness. Brian Mann, king of the master race of youth. The three of us raise our glasses to him, and he bows.

'Tae the history ae Fawkurt!'

'The history ae Fawkurt!'

The front window shatters, spraying coloured glass across the tables.

Shouts from outside ('*ya fuckin*') and Brian is out with the speed of a cheetah. We follow him, confused, into the street, in time to see car lights disappearing round the corner and before we can even realise what's happened, Brian's hussled us into Belinda, handing Dolby a pint-glass, demanding that 'At the next red light, get oot and chuck this at their fuckin windae' then we're giving chase, like in a film, Frannie swearing uncontrollably.

'Who wis it, ye think?' I ask. Frannie with the pint-glass in his hand is like a

> finally
> you're paranoid
> but not a

statue of justice.

'Dunno.' He turns to Dolby, 'Kottsy?'

'Or them fuckers fae the races,' Dolby adds, screeching into the Cow Wynd and onto Comely Place, veering towards the traffic lights. Belinda roars righteously, and *I* want to be the one who throws the pint-glass, feel it leave my hand – just like the bottle-fight at school years ago – smash, damage, destroy, but

The streets are empty.

Dolby halts. Cursing. At the red light. And though we scour the roads like pirates for ten minutes, they've

gone.

Dolby turns, sweating, and heads back to Smith's. Behind the bar, Brian stands like a goliath.

'Yese get them?'

Dolby shakes his head. Kicks a post. Knowing he should have braked before he ran over that boy's leg at the Burnout.

'Right. The morra night,' Brian vows, 'We're goin doon the races tae see these'

214

cars revving, in heat, and the howling of chromium dogs. Engines noise each other up. Belinda slinks between them, sleek, fish-like. Eyes follow her through windscreens. There is fake cheering on the chorus of a dance track. The Central Scotland boyracer circuit gathered and beneath my Radiohead *Amnesia* top I flex scrawny muscles.

We park, disembark. Our hands thrust into our pockets, we walk towards a gathering at the far end, where weapons are standing with clipboards and there's even someone filming the whole thing. Swaz sees us coming and alerts Shiney.

'Ladies!' he enthuses. 'Didnae expect tae see any birds here the night.'

'Why's that?' Brian shrugs.

Swaz points to a weapon in a stookie, hauling himself on crutches towards a thumping VW. 'No eftir yer GBH on Chas there. Broke the boy's leg then fucked off, if Ah mind right?'

'Aye man,' says Shiney, staring, 'Ye mind right.'

'That wis an accident,' Dolby stresses guiltily. 'He didnae get oot the way in time.'

'Aye?' Shiney shrugs, drawing himself nose-to-nose with Dolby, 'Mibbe yer mate who runs the pub'll no get oot the way when we *smash it tae fuckin bits*!'

Brian places a hand on Shiney's chest. 'That's whit we're here tae talk tae yese about.' He eyeballs them nastily. 'Wan race. Eftir that, nae mair squads up tae Smith's. Ye'll leave ma fuckin windaes alane. Agreed?'

'Whit car?'

'Oors. Against your fastest.'

They consider this, huddled and swearing, inciting then calming each other, while Fran sits protectively on Belinda's bonnet, eyeing up weapons. Brian's arms are muscled and tense. I try to hang near the

215

front, my tendons expecting any second to spring.

Carer's allowance. A career carer. That's what I'll be.

my tendons expecting any second to

'Awright,' Swaz nods. We'll race ye fae there–' he points to the far end of the car-park '–tae there.' The finishing line is a high, brick factory wall, the word *Wranglers* in faded blue.

'Awright,' says Dolby, reaching for his keys.

'Naw,' Shiney grins, pointing to me, 'We want *him* tae drive it.'

'Me?' I say, shocked.

'He's no got a licence.'

'He cannae drive.'

'Me?'

'No take him long tae learn,' Swaz shrugs. 'Only got tae accelerate and brake!'

'Naw,' Brian says, uneasy, 'He's no–'

'Ah'll dae it,' I say.

'–auld enough an he's never had a lesson–'

'Ah said Ah'll dae it.'

'–no fair, come ontae–'

'Brian,' I say, something new and determined rising inside me. 'Let me dae it.'

Swaz and Shiney nod. Car horns make a ugly sound behind them.

'If he disnae, we kick yer heids in. Fair enough?'

STAY AWAY FROM ME YOU FUCKING

so Dolby slopes Belinda to a clear corner to instruct me, Miagi-like, in the Ways of the Pedals, while Brian and Frannie kick gravel across the ground. My blood is rich with adrenaline. It sucks and breathes through my veins. I feel – actually – amazing.

'Feel that wee nudge? That's yer bitin point. Hold that an then–'

'Now lift the clutch, an ye'll need tae slam yer foot ontae the–'

'An as soon as ye get anywhere *near* that wall, hit the clutch then the fuckin brake or–'

forty-five minutes I'm lifting and dropping pedals, testing biting-points, practising emergency-stops until I'm ready. Or ready enough to trail smoke for a few hundred yards then stop. Ready enough to prove something, as Bono, my own personal guardian angel these days, moans on the *Rattle and Hum* album

> come on . . .
> come *on* . . .
> into the arms of

the headlights blasting on along the track, and we're revving, furious, and though I don't glance at Swaz, I can feel his searing stare. No hate like young hate. And someone has turned a tape of UK garage way up, the tarmac pounding with off-time beats, and I am an anarchist, I am the antichrist, James Dean/John Travolta in *Grease*, ha ha, my trainers growling on the gas and Dolby is leaning in the window, reminding me of the pedal motions, speaking ('Ye dinnae huv tae dae this'), but I'm not really listening. Can't. I'm on fire

isn't mentally fit for work, but can apply for disability

and everything I've done, seen, fucked up at or obsessed upon, every time I wanted to talk to Tyra after English and that shimmering image of her kneeling before Connor, every time my *Dark Side of the Moon* CD sticks (on 'Money'), everything I ever wanted to say to my parents, everyone I wanted to kill or fuck is channelled now through my rigid hands.

Swaz draws his finger along his neck and mouths:

dead.

And Shiney raises the flag. And the stars behind him are like silver pepper. And the Lads are watching nervously, Frannie's hand over his eyes, as I flex the ball of my foot across the biting-point, and we're

[mum? mum, are you–]

alive. Belinda roars outrage in my hands and the headlights blink as the world slips past like fluid and the wall is growing. A side glance; Swaz's face. Focused. His eyes. Then the wall approaching quicker than I can
    (–the brake?)
    stab randomly at the pedals, panicked. A shout escapes then I'm screeching
    wailing
    bricks rushing towards me and I

Stop.

The world is still.

The world is very still.

And just ahead of me, a car (which car? what? where am I?) has met a wall, and someone is hobbling from the front-seat with blood on their face. His eyes are a mask of scarlet. And the slow, still world – so beautiful and within my reach – suddenly whirs back to speed, noise, screams, the scarlet face near me, hammering a bloody fist on the windscreen and leaving marks.

I stay locked in my seat-belt, watching him. Nearly fascinated. After what seems like a year of his hammering and screaming, people swarm the car. I am in a bubble. Their cries are dull. I start to shiver. Sirens are wailing and there are shouts and in the rear-view mirror cars are exiting, blue light splashing, as Belinda's door is wrenched open and Dolby is pulling me out – 'move it Alvin' – into the back-seat with Fran and Brian, taking off, hissing, hauling at the wheel, the world sliding to the side as noddies scatter like marbles and the police grab at

Stirling University is gorgeous. Green on every side. There's a loch shimmering in the middle and students coming and going across the bridge with folders and important-looking books with mind-boggling titles and they wear baseball-caps and yak into mobile-phones without – I stress this – *without* looking like boyracers.

The four of us are led by a bubbly young guide in a Stirling Uni tracksuit who keeps yelping, 'Great!' and 'Good question!' but she's nice. She looks like she'd be fun in Smith's after a couple of Aftershocks, 'Sweet Caroline' playing in the background.

'Fuckin students,' Frannie mutters, glaring jealously. 'Why don't they get a real fuckin job?'

Ducks splash oddly in the water, and sprays of violet flowers leap like effete muggers from the loch-side, while canoes slink and young couples walk hand in hand, stop, read books, walk on again, and our guide tells us that classes are suspended on Wednesdays for sports and bees buzz and people laugh and

you can't always get what

the Lads are just about impressed. Dolby nods thoughtfully at everything she says, asks a question, nods thoughtfully again. Brian checks out the girls gliding past like swans. Frannie wants to go to the sports-union to see the swimming pool, lithe bodies cutting its blue skin, and then Dolby takes us to the MacRobert Arts Centre (tonight showing *Hellraiser*) where a stall nearby sells posters of Kurt Cobain, Fred Durst, Eminem, Christian Bale in *American Psycho*, the Beatles recording *Sergeant Pepper*, and students amass and muse and laugh and talk about going to the pub or the Traffic-Light Disco at *Enigma*, or maybe not, maybe just watching the *Star Wars* trilogy at the Sci-Fi club. We visit the library. Three floors of books! I go to a terminal, type in **Stephen King** and see

Different Seasons	**IN STOCK**
Carrie	**IN STOCK**
The Shining	**Due 30th August**
Skeleton Crew	**IN STOCK**

and that one student who has taken out *The Shining* fascinates me. I fantasise about meeting (her?) on the first day of term over a peach-schnapps, talking about Kubrick's film adaptation in the Student Union, its flaws and strengths, where our tour-party is soon taken and where beardy intellectuals sup ale and trendy young clubbers touch their lips against crystal-clear drinks and rugger boys slam tequilas and the Chemical Brothers fill up the background with beats and people are brought toasties and hot-pots on steaming plates and a birthday party for a girl called Claire kicks off in the corner and

We sit by the loch-side, overwhelmed.

Bees investigate us in slow circles of sound. A group of tanned students roll a football across the grass, their shadows long on the lawn.

'Christ,' Brian remarks between mouthfuls of sandwich, 'This place is a fuckin holiday-camp.'

In the *Falkirk Herald* this week was a story which went:

INJURY AT UNDERGROUND CAR-RACE
Police disrupted an illegal car-race in Camelon last week, just seconds after a youth had been injured. Arrests were made. There

have been several races in the Falkirk area recently and police are
growing concerned. Mark Swanson (19) of Langlees was taken to
hospital with a fractured skull, after his car collided with a
Wranglers factory wall. Although several of the participants eluded
the police, Constable Eric Richards has promised that there will be
a crackdown on this dangerous activity. He said, 'These youngsters
think they'll be able to carry on like this forever but we're

taking shots at an imaginary goal. Hip-hop stutters from their ghetto-
blaster. Girls lounge in the afternoon sun next to half-open books and
silver mobile-phones and a light veil settles over everything – the
bridge, dotted with French accents, the loch speckled with white
birds, the Wallace Monument standing like a dazed sentry, the lulling
spell of an American woman reading a fairy-tale to her child. There is
a vague, summery work-ethic. From an open window I can hear a
chiming waterfall of guitar notes

> looks like we might have made it
> yes it
> looks like we've made it to the end

and I feel like I belong somewhere.

Everything is beautiful and vibrant. The campus rings with
tantalising laughter. Nobody looks like they might want to kick
my head in. Myriad windows, where students lean, chatting, smoking, so many people to meet. I keep the desire to explore close to my
chest – while the Lads yak about the Rangers game and a new clutch
for Belinda – until eventually it churns in me, burns, aching for them
to be gone.

Frannie's patter. Brian's disaffected grunt-language. Dolby's pop-
philosophy. My wide-eyed naivety. The rightness of our being
together.

But for the first time ever, *they* seem a burden to *me*, not the reverse. And though the shame of this goes deep, the louder they talk – the more 'fucks' and 'Fenian cunts' and 'Heddy-haws' – the greater is my need to be rid of them. I don't know what they have done to deserve this, but on the way home I will remember the translucent laughter that drapes the campus, I will close my eyes as Belinda chugs and splutters into the concrete jungle of Hallglen and a shoplifter tears from the corner shop with a bottle of Buckie screaming, '*Paki bastaaard*!!'

'Student poofs,' says Frannie, untouched by it all. 'Look at them. These arenae real people. Aw the guys are nancy-boys an aw the girls are up themsels.'

'Just as well,' Brian says. 'Cos *you'll* no be up them.'

Dolby shrugs, impatient with Frannie's attitude. 'Dunno, man. The Runt could dae worse.'

'Ye'd come up and visit me though?' I ask, a chill thought passing through.

'Wid we no just!' Brian says. 'Fuckin Butlins here, man!'

Dusk floats in. The sun settles orange petals on the water. But the Lads seem strangely sad, darkening like shadow, ageing right before my eyes.

'Hey! Whit's the coolest thing ye've ever seen?' I ask quickly, fearful they'll grey and collapse if I don't divert them.

'Brian's nipples,' Frannie clucks. Revenge.

'Dinnae be a dick. Whit's the coolest thing ye've ever seen?'

'That girl's arse.'

'Gonnae take this seriously?'

'Gonnae take this seriously! "Whit's the coolest thing ye've ever seen?" '

'Coolest thing I've ever seen . . .' Brian begins, surprising us all, '. . . was when Ah was walkin through Dollar Park one night as a bairn. The sun wis goin down, the sky wis lit-up aw different colours,

222

just like this. An Ah mind there was this guy . . . this auld guy . . . an he was just sittin under a tree . . . and he was . . .' He blinks, as if the character is flitting before him now. 'Playin the saxophone.'

Brian swallows his Irn-Bru, burps, hurls the can. I see it spin, the droplets falling like parachutists.

'An that's it. That's the coolest thing Ah've ever seen.'

There's silence for a while.

Imaginary notes curling between the Halls. The old guy treading carefully lest he tread on our dreams. My hands have grown cold, the fingertips numb, and my favourite episode of *The Simpsons* is still the one where Homer tried to join the Stonecutters (the Masons really). The fizz of the beer on the rim of Frannie's bottle and the two of us leaning against his bed, laughing so hard that his Mum banged upstairs.

Dolby turns to me.

'Sam Raimi's directin the *Spider-Man* movie.'

'Sam Raimi?' I gasp, shocked.

'He did *The Evil Dead*.'

'Whaaat?!' I whine. 'Whit happened tae James Cameron?'

Dolby shrugs. 'Jumped ship.'

'Ha-fuckin-ha.'

The old guy shedding languid notes across the dusk, and I know this:

I can't connect with the people I love.

'Ah hate that,' Brian mutters. 'Ah hate when you're lookin forward tae somethin an it turns oot tae be crap.'

We all grunt agreement.

'Anybody want tae know the coolest thing Ah've ever seen?' I ask, but Frannie snorts, stuffing a crisp-packet down my back.

'Alvin, two of your heroes are called *Brett*' (Anderson and Easton Ellis). '*Nothing* you've seen is cool.'

223

Everything must go.

Events are slowing down, speeding up, slowing down. Hour after hour spent cruising Polmont, Bo'ness, Dennyloanhead, stopping for petrol and *Loaded*, schmoozing half-heartedly with the girls behind the counter, playing the soundtrack to *Fight Club*. Patter is flat. Belinda has the feel of a once-beautiful film-star long past her prime. The streets hold all the fascination of an empty paper-bag rotating in a slight breeze. Frannie tells a joke; only one of us laughs. Dolby mentions that Whirlpools Direct might be shutting down. Brian reassures him that he'll get him work in Smith's, but this is forgotten in a debate about Al Pacino (does he over-act?) which also expires, uncertain of itself, unresolved. We whistle at the girls – shining white in GAP – and for a second the sky has all the brilliance of a summer's day, until grey clouds make everything concrete, dead. And nobody expresses disappointment at this, its predictability.

Brian says: 'California's takin longer than Ah thought. Havenae heard yet about ma visa.'

Dolby says: 'Ah'm thinkin ae takin an evenin degree in Philosophy.'

Frannie sings: '*If you steal my sunshine*'.

I say: 'Is anybody listening to me?'

. . . while anti-capitalist demonstrators in London break the windows of McDonalds, deface a statue of Winston Churchill, spray graffiti across banks and building societies, and William McIlvanney (who used to do the voice-overs for Celtic videos) writes in the *Scotland on Sunday*

The event has reminded us of the rights of the young to be subversive. But there is a question of how immature protesters can be and still claim to be expressing more than their own petulance. These caperings carried as much threat to the bastions of capitalism as a kindergarten sit-in. If you don't pay attention to us then we'll break our toys, they seem to be saying. Meanwhile, the protesters were distressed by the violence of the anarchists, the anarchists were distressed by the passivity of the protest, the right-wing papers were distressed by anyone who wasn't a statue, Tony Blair was distressed that Britannia had lost her cool. If you

steal my sunshine!

want to think of this event as a sort of cultural compass, then we are headed into a perpetual and vacuous present.

Brian starts drumming his fingers on his knee and talks about franchising his own pubs. I compose silent poems about graves. Frannie tells us Ace of Spads is thinking about a sex-change. Dolby changes the music, constantly.

but in the days when Falkirk was a blur to us, one long constancy of lights, pounding music, admiring glances, we used to discuss – *obsessively* – how we would do it when we were famous. It could only, surely, be a couple of years away. Would we be media-hugging icons like Robbie Williams, describing on *Parky* our years cutting the Falkirk tarmac? Or would we be interview-shunning enigmas like the Floyd, emerging from our ivory tower every seven years to a world that has mourned our absence?

It was never made quite clear how we were going to reach this level of stardom. Since we won't become famous for quoting Indiana Jones films whilst

snakes
why'd it have to be snakes?

225

complaining to Dolby about his chronic mobile-phone use.

I remember we went to this guitar exhibition at the SECC with Dolby's Dad (who really *does* resemble Lee Van Cleef). Guitars mounted all over like hunting trophies and I touched the strings of one. Gruff trolls in denim sprang immediately from behind amps to challenge my un-Def Leppardness.

'Wow,' Frannie remarked, 'Nice armpits!'

Dolby's Dad had paused at a stall where some poodle-haired rocker was lost in Gary Moore's 'Parisienne Walkways', his fingers performing frottage with the fret. Dolby's Dad turned to us, nodding seriously, and said:

'That's fuckin good music.'

Funny, I thought at the time, how overweight the world can seem. How if you pause and concentrate hard enough, you can hear it groaning.

It is the sound of Dek coming into my bedroom, as he is now, sitting, his face tight and troubled, about to confess everything.

He passes me a tray of bourbon creams. They're the biscuits we devoured by the barrel-load when we were kids. 'Eat them,' he instructs. 'I've went right off them.' He goes to my CD rack and draws out *OK Computer*, then puts it in the CD player and presses play and watches the lights, then sits again. 'Good album,' he nods, 'But no the best ever made,' and he seems to have shrunk in the years he's been gone. Outside it decides to rain

> down, rain down
> come on rain down on me
> from a great height, from a

nd Dek says, 'Know, Alvin, when I lived in this house, I wanted to do almost anything to get away. As far away as possible. There was a whole world out there, full of excitement. So I went to London, where the money is. Like Dick Whittington or something. Thought if I had enough money they'd let me in . . .' He shrugs. 'Didn't even know who "they" were. Didn't know where it was I was trying to get into. But . . .' he tails off, examines the six holes in the bourbon cream. 'Got the job in the bank. Couldn't bring in enough money to pay the rent. Moved to a bedsit. Could afford the bedsit, but it didn't leave me any money to go out or see a film or hire a video, never mind go to a club. My landlady didn't allow me to have visitors over, and I didn't complain cos the rent was so cheap, but if I wanted to see anybody, I had to wait for them to invite me over, which they never did. And I couldn't get a better job cos my CV only had on it this crappy post at the bank. And I couldn't get promoted cos there's millions of young folk down there with a better CV than you. They're like a pack of snarling dogs down there, these young guys. And every day all these rich folk are handing over their cash, giving me all the attention they'd give a hole-in-the-wall, griping about their mortgages and the rates on their savings, while I'm thinking, 'Do you know what a luxury a mortgage is? Do you know how few people have savings? You don't have a clue, do you?'

Psycho is on telly and Chapter VIII of *The Great Gatsby*, open, unrevised, in my lap, is beginning: '*I couldn't sleep all night; a fog-horn was groaning incessantly on the Sound, and I tossed half-sick between grotesque reality and savage, frightening dreams . . .*'

Dek breathes on the brass button of his denim jacket and wipes at it so it shines.

'And then I started seeing Mum. I saw customers who looked like her. Beggars who looked like her. Prostitutes who looked like her. She was everywhere. One morning I chased her down the street. I chased her, shouting, and she screamed and ran into a police-station, so I thought I'd better leave her alone.'

He leans back in his chair and folds his hands behind his head. His adam's apple floats up and down in his scrawny throat. My brother, all grown-up. Giving me a truth he had to leave to discover.

'Later that day, this woman came in. Middle-aged, middle-class. I was trying to count her money, but I couldn't do it. I kept thinking about Mum. And Dad. And you. And what was I doing there, alone, scraping out a living, roaming the streets in boredom every night, looking in the shop-windows at things I couldn't afford. This wasn't what it was supposed to be like! This wasn't what I was promised! And the woman starts shouting at me to hurry up. And I looked at her. And she looked at me. And there was nothing in her eyes. They were just like steel. She had so much money she'd become a robot, and I realised she could never connect with me, that it just wasn't possible, that there was nothing out there for me in the whole, wide world, it had all been an illusion, and I'd fell for it. Something snapped. I was just standing there, counting her cash, listening to her hissing at me to hurry up, like I was some kind of servant. Then I picked up her money, hurled it at the glass partition, and told her to go take a fuck to herself. It was all I could think to do as a protest. Silly really. But it was so funny.'

Dek smiles, cheekily, like the daredevil wee boy I remember playing chap-door-run, and as I picture some rich old bat watching her money swirl and flap through the air, while Dek picks up his copy of the *NME* and leaves, right there, while everyone watches, some part of me is proud of him.

'So,' I say eventually, 'Ye lost yer job . . .'

He raises an eyebrow, dabs with his tongue at a roll-up.

'The job, the bedsit, ma mind . . .' The roll-up is finished expertly and waves in his mouth as he talks. He searches his pockets for a light. 'All that's out there, Alvin, ma man, is the Withs and the Withouts. An it's worse bein a Without among the Withs, let me tell you.'

The fag is lit.

'That's why Ah came hame.'

His eyes pinch as he drags at the fag.

Tiny orange brightness.

'Dae ye really think she's alive?' I ask, my voice small and cold in the room. But Dek stands up, having said enough, and we hold our gaze, while Norman Bates twitches nervously on TV. Then we smile against the memories, somehow defeating them, and he shuffles off back to his own room in a hash-haze, quietly, as if

we're all in our private traps. clamped in them. we scratch and claw, but only at the air, only at each other. and for all of it . . . we never budge an inch

his appearance had been that of a ghost. In the scheme outside, an argument has erupted between the neighbours – something to do with a lawnmower and a dog. Their voices rise, becoming shrill and womanly, and there is soon the sound of someone kicking a fence and demanding, '*Shove yer Flymo up yer fuckin*! *dug's*! *arse*!' and I hear Belinda pull up outside the house, her horn calling, insistent. From the window I see Frannie bounding from the driver's seat (?) to my door, his steps athletic and his grin like fresh cheesecake.

'Guess whit?' he beams.

'The Martians have landed?'

'Nut.'

'There's nothing the psychiatrist can dae for ye?'

'Nut.'

'Ye've shagged Coisty?'

'Nut!'

'Whit is it, man, Ah'm studyin.'

Frannie pulls out a plastic wallet and at first I think he's joined the police or something. Then I notice the letters DVLA, the name **Colin Arthur Franton** printed beneath (Arthur?) and realise it's a driving-licence.

'Franman!' Our hands slap in mid-air. 'Ah didnae even ken ye were takin lessons.'

'Well Ah didnae want yese tae ken,' he shrugs. 'In case Ah arsed it up. Comin oot for a run?'

'Ah dunno, man. Loads ae studying tae dae. Big exams soon.'

Frannie is too cheery to accept this. 'Aw the mair reason! Ye stressed?'

'Aye.'

'Shitein yersel?'

'Aye.'

'Ye should be. Cos if ye dinnae come oot, Ah'll kick yer fuckin heid in.'

so we go on a maiden run to Cumbernauld and he's sky-high, gripping the wheel like a kid in a go-kart, *actually going* 'Wheeeeee!' as the evening roars dramatically past and I feel sick/exhilarated/ stressed/chilled all at the same time and at this speed something feels ending – this Robbie Williams song? my tether? the world as we know it? Brian winks and passes me a Becks, which I struggle with (beer, to me, still tastes horribly like beer), Fran guided through the motorway lanes by the wise Dolby-Wan. Frannie has a grin glued to his face, still going 'Wheeeee!' and I decide to play that Pink Floyd song called 'Several Species of Small Furry Animals Gathered Together In A Cave And Grooving With A Pict' (yes it actually exists) but Dolby slaps the tape away as if it's an amorous advance. 'Gie me one good reason why *you* should pick the music.' 'Ah'll give ye three. Robbie fuckin Williams.' And Frannie tells us about something weird that happened tae Ace of Spads: 'He's drivin up north, right, on this back road. An the mist's comin right at him, thick as, when he sees this thing running towards him through the fog.'

'Whit? Like a dug?'

230

'Well that's whit he thought. Then he realised it wis too big for a dug. Far too big. It's as big as a horse, except it looks nothing like a horse, obviously. But it's chargin right at him.'

'Whit wis it?' I ask.

'An ostrich.'

'Whit!'

'Get tae fuck!'

'Tellin ye. He must have been near wan ae thae ostrich farms or something. But this fuckin thing strides right up tae him, heid gawin like that . . . an then it just veers away. *Meep meep* ya bas.'

'That wis the road-runner.'

'Aw Frannie, fuck *off!*' scoffs Brian.

'Ah'm tellin ye!' says Frannie, 'Ask anybody in Tesco!'

'Aye right,' Dolby guffaws, 'The same reliable sources that said the floodlights at Ibrox are hotter than the sun?'

'Hiy!' Frannie notes, 'The *surface* ae the sun . . .'

'Ah bet there *isnae* even an Ace ae Spads,' Brian complains, knocking Frannie on the back of the head with the plastic Harrison Ford. 'Ah bet you've been makin it aw up.'

'Like Frannie's goat that much imagination!'

'Well . . .' Frannie shrugs, smoothing his hands down Belinda's wheel, 'Ah'm the wan wi the driving-licence, Mr Mann. You couldnae get a licence tae hae a *pish*.'

I listen, laughing, staring at the Irn-Bru can on the dashboard, the mystery which has evaded me all this time (if it's not attached to the car, *why* does it drop in a straight line? whywhywhy?) and realise:

How little everything's changed.

How much everything's changed.

We're still in the same car, on the same roads, inflicting the same patter on each other, lusting after the same girl, still trapped in an endless cycle of Abba choruses, *FHM* articles, arguments about what exactly the best Superman movie was (the third, obviously).

Except we're different. There's a hollowness to Dolby's *Star Trek* soliloquies, as if he's at last sensed they're lost on the other two. Brian is spending more and more time on the mobile-phone, trying to organise his emigration while keeping Smith's from being a hang-out for the cast of *Deliverance*. Frannie seems jaded, energy-less, like Coisty after he moved from Rangers to Kilmarnock.

And me?

I hate myself and I want to die.

as the argument over who has the biggest disc spirals out of control, and Bono yips on the new album

it's a beautiful day!

and Frannie accelerates, whooping, Belinda complaining deep in her intestines and the sky over Scotland is a cool vermillion and I appeal, 'Guys! Whit does it matter who's got the biggest disc? I dinnae even *own* a computer!'

'Dick,' Brian tuts. 'We're arguing over who's got the biggest *dick*.'

It's then I notice Frannie glancing in the mirror. Glancing again. His brow furrowing as a

car draws up beside us and

Kottsy leans from the open window. When he smiles, I notice the gap in his teeth made by Brian's fist at the Hollywood Bowl.

'Awright, gents,' he says, as the car veers close, making Frannie swerve and Dolby shout, gripping the wheel.

'Fuck sake, Fran!'

'Shit, Dolby, you'd better take ower! The fucker's gonnae ram me aff the road!'

'Forget it!' Brian barks, 'Stop the car an we'll take these cunts.'

Kottsy is holding up a knife.

'Mibbe no,' says Brian, 'Keep drivin.'

Kottsy's squad are crammed into their Fiat Uno, HARDCORE sprayed along the side. Dance choons blasting. Shiney and Swaz crack themselves up at Frannie's nervy swerving and my stomach goes that floppy way again and the muscles in my arms solidify for battle.

'Take the fuckin wheel, man!'

'Ah cannae, you're in the drivin-seat!'

Kottsy's car pulls close in, close enough for him to grab Belinda's wheel himself.

'You boys fancy pullin ower for a chat?'

Frannie hits the pedal and roars away. We must be doing ninety. I look back to see Kottsy wea

ving in our wake. Frannie is accelerating like a madman. 'Slow doon, for fuck's sake!' Brian commands. 'It's yer first time on the motorway.'

Belinda starts a violent shuddering. The gauges strain and bob.

'Slow the fuck doon!'

'The car cannae take it – slow the fuck doon.'

My heart retches, the four of us scream at once, and then this happens in crystal stages:

frannie clips someone's wing-mirror

kottsy edges up behind us

smoke erupts from belinda's bonnet.

dolby shouts *'get off the road*! *get off the road*! *get off the fuckin road*!'

then

things hurtle back to speed as our voices are lost in a prolonged moan

233

from Belinda's engine and shaking starts in the car's frame and our
speed starts to

    drop
        and

    we skim between two juggernauts

                off the road

                                      and
        plough up the grass at the side of the motorway.

    Kottsy shoots by, a jeering blur.

There is silence for ten whole seconds.

We get out, slamming doors. The sounds of cars whizzing past and a
hissing radiator. Frannie tries Belinda's engine, but she struggles for
breath, making gasping noises.

    'How long will it take them tae come back?' I ask.

    Dolby shrugs, gazing up the motorway. 'Five minutes?' he says.
'Ten?'

    Then he turns decisively and tells us what to do.

'Are ye *stupit*?' Frannie argues, holding Belinda's wheel protectively.
'That's the worst idea Ah've ever heard.'

    'Dae *you* want tae be here when they get back?!' Dolby retorts.

The A80 is bordered by a wire fence, which bars access to a steep
slope. We kick at three of the stakes like punk rockers, stamping the

wire to create a hole just big enough for a car. We laugh and make jokes. It begins to feel like playing.

Frannie is posted in the front, while we push and grunt against the rear. 'Bit more,' he encourages, 'Bit more . . . bit more . . . bit . . . 'Mo*aaaaaaggghhhhhh*!!!!'

Belinda disappears from our palms, trailing a scream, and we realise we've mis-judged the gradient. She hits into the bottom with a tinkling thud.

We charge down to see Frannie's teeth gritted, his face a terrified rictus.

Belinda cools and gives up her life, while we just stand biting our nails and the evening edges towards darkness.

'Fuck!' Dolby yells, hammering her bonnet, '*Fuck*! *Fuck*! *Fuck*!'

Then he stands. Stares at her. Starts tearing off the licence-plates.

'Whit are ye daein!' I say, baffled. He cuts me a look.

'We're leavin her,' he explains. 'Gie us the papers fae the glove-compartment.'

We watch him, stunned.

'Come an help then!' he commands. 'It's startin tae fuckin rain.'

So there Belinda is left, her bonnet crushed and curled like petals. Her windows cracked. Her headlights drawing slowly down on the world.

We stand there for a while. Just looking at her.

Then Dolby utters, monotone:

'Let's go afore somebody calls the polis.'

We head into the drizzly night, boxing our shoulders. Only once do I glance back at Belinda, to see her broken, alone. Dolby's hands are tight in his pockets, his face giving nothing, but I can feel him shutting down. Some part of him dying with Belinda. Rain patters on my brow. Sodium-light stretches on the surface of the road. I've started to shiver and feel cold. The four of us trudging in stark silence.

No more jokes. This – as David Bowie said at the Freddie Mercury tribute concert – is where the fun stops.

We have no place left to go.

And we have no place left to go.

When I traipse into the house, freezing, the phone is ringing. Dek answers it, as I shuck off my wet clothes, and as he says, '*Alvin? Aye, he's just walked in the door . . .*' he's seeing the state I'm in, seeing my clothes hitting the floorboards with a dull slap.

He hands me the phone. The room seems to sway.

'Hello,' I mumble, steadying myself.

There is laughter from the other end of the line. Disembodied laughter.

'Hello,' I say again.

'Hello,' someone repeats in a silly voice.

'Who is this?'

'It's a friend,' the voice answers. There's a host of giggles. 'Just wanted to, you know, ask if you enjoyed the party . . .'

Things are starting to swirl gently. I clutch the kitchen door to make it stop.

'Whit party? Whit ye talkin about? Who are you?'

'What party!' he says, a polite, clean voice. 'Have you forgotten already? Tyra's party! Your big night out.'

'Who are you? Whit big night out?'

'The one you weren't fucking invited to!'

('*Tell him, for fuck's sake . . .*' people snigger in the background, '*Put the wee mink out of his misery . . .*')

'Whit d'ye mean? Of course Ah wis invited.'

My hand is starting to tremble, rage or nerves or something else. My head is throbbing.

'Du-uh! Do you not know a fake invite when you see one? *Sorry I didn't catch you at school, Alvin,*' the caller repeats sarcastically, '*Would love it if you came*! Sound familiar?'

My legs are weakening. Someone driving bolts into the base of my skull.

'As if Tyra would invite y–'

I hang up, shaking, my teeth chattering in my head, Dek crossing the room to me, but all I can focus on is an advert on TV which is trying to sell me a car using a voice-over from *On The Road*, which becomes the news: Jim Baxter, ex-Rangers and Scotland legend, is dead.

And so am I.

'Alvin?' Dek peers at me, 'You all right?'

'Too much,' I think I say. 'There's just too much.'

and that night I spend caught between fire and ice. Curled, foetal, shivering. For well on five hours I am packed in my own sweat and carbon-dioxide. The room pulses in and out of view. My breathing shifts up and down gear. The curtains are not billowing, but somehow it seems they should be. So hot. So cold. Between the hours of 4 and 5 a.m. I discover Mum at the end of my bed. She is wearing a floral dress and her blonde hair is flowing and her eyes are shining with tears. I keep asking her why she is crying and tell her *I'm sorry. We should have been better kids. It's all our fault.* But she says, 'It was nothing to do with you. I know you blame yourself,' then becomes Dave Gilmour from Pink Floyd. I interview him about the making of *The Wall* album and he gives full, polite, elaborate answers, and sometime later I wake pouring tea for the writer Iain Banks, and Dad comes into the kitchen to find me naked and chatting to an empty chair, a stream of day-old tea spattering onto the kitchen floor and

calls the doctor. I feel tiny and huge in the corner of the room, watching him, watching the nation start to yawn and stretch on television. A royal variety performance. A bomb going off somewhere in Ireland. Brad Pitt, Jennifer Aniston. My teeth chitter like ice-cubes in a drink. I am fucked. Exhausted. *It's over*, I repeat. *It's all over. I'm dying.* Dad's eyebrows furrow, the phone gripped in his palm, his mouth not moving in time with the words, 'No, he *doesn't* take drugs . . . there *is* paracetemol in the house, but . . . well he's been under a lot of stress with his exams recently and there's been some family troubles . . .' I start singing, badly, aware of how badly I'm singing, the theme tune for *Brookside* and Dad

glances at me, repeats his urgency to the doctor. He starts to get me dressed and I try to stop myself laughing, hopping into the legs of my jeans, my chest cold and burning and exposed then I'm in the back of a taxi. Dad asking me questions, and I'm *trying* to answer them, but the causeway between my brain and my mouth is too wide and all that comes out is: 'I'm fine. Dad, I'm actually fine. Dad stay with me, I feel terrible,' and the stars are silvery and wintery, making me think I'm ascending, like E.T. My back hurts. My joints move like they're full of broken glass. Words dissolving on my tongue. The doctor feels my head and frowns. 'No drugs at all?' and I sing *now the drugs don't work, they just make you worse*, and laugh, but he doesn't seem to find it funny. No, not at all. A woman haunting the fringes of my vision. A vase of white flowers – the heads drained and tired like people at the end of a long, traumatic day in which their lives had felt ill-fitting. One of the nurses looks like Gwyneth Paltrow, a babe, and how annoying that she has to see me like this, as she withdraws the blood slowly, carefully, from my pendulous arm and I try to explain to her that I'm not mad or a junkie or anything I just have a head like a zeppelin on fire and the ghost of a wedding dress pulsing at the corner of my eye telling me something about misery and the wind and I turn to look but it is

gone

Rain falling against the window. Hospital radio playing Lenny Kravitz songs. The two things just not going together at all.

This is the infirmary where I was born. Falkirk Royal. Being here again makes me feel tiny, acorn-small. Nurses coming and going and doctors coming and going and me smiling like the professional patient.

I read the whole of *Moby Dick*, which is totally boring, since the whale doesn't appear until the second last chapter. Eight hundred pages of talking about the whale, and no fucking whale! There's a message there – which is probably crucial to life or something – but I'm just too tired to work it out.

I feel like I've been running for a long, long time.

Each night spent shivering out in the rain, gazing at the soft, blue light from Tyra's window, my head compressed with Suede and Floyd and *Parklife* (Pink Floyd and Blur are sometimes more similar than critics realise. I could go into this), my body numb to everything but my own inadequacy and that long, awful walk in the rain after we jettisoned Belinda, has brought me here. To this moment. Somewhere near the end of the line.

Mum has been drifting at the end of the corridor, glancing in my direction. Her smile is weak and sad. When Dek and Dad arrive, it's a family reunion of sorts. The faces are drizzly and faded, like a photo left out in the rain.

'When we get ye home, Ringo,' Dek smiles, 'Ah'll make toast an tea an we'll laugh at Dad's underwear drawer.'

'Cheers, George,' I manage, and there is much hand-patting.

'Whit's wrong wi ma underwear drawer?'

The Lads turn up just as Ahab spots the fucking whale!

I like Brian's new puffa jacket. Frannie is wearing my baseball-cap. Dolby is in a Nike t-shirt and trainers. They look more like boyracers than they ever have, bless them, and they warm the room as soon as they enter it, and to ease things along – me, the still centre of their swirling banter – Frannie and Brian start (might as well) slagging Dolby, Uriel, what the fuck was he thinking about, what a woofter. But he grimaces, holds his hands up apologetically.

'Ah'll come clean, boys. Ah've changed ma name back tae Martin.'

'Whit?' we all gasp. 'Why?'

'Naebody ever called me Uriel,' he shrugs, 'It was a silly idea in the first place.'

We shake our heads, tutting, but nobody mentions the coincidence of it, that Uriel died with Belinda. And Dolby – trying to laugh along, but out of sorts, mourning – looks like it's a double-suicide he won't recover from. Some tragic part of him out there on the road with Belinda forever, fluttering his wings.

They shuffle about my room, picking up flowers and cards and checking out the nurses' arses. None of them ask, but I want to tell them anyway. I raise myself up in bed, finger the U2 CD (which Frannie has bought me but which I can't play but has a cool cover anyway) then put it down and say:

'Ah know yer aw wonderin whit happened tae me. But Ah'm . . . no really sure. This last year, Ah've been fighting against . . . against . . . somethin horrible. There's been things gawin on inside me that Ah don't understand at all. Ah even thought about . . .'

The sheets are scrunched in my fist.

'But, em, Ah didnae. And I want yese tae know, that if it wisnae for you guys, Ah woudnae be here. Ah want yese tae know that. Ah would have . . .'

I pause, the tears rising.

'But Ah *didnae* dae it. Ah'm here. We made it. The four ae us. Tae the end.'

Dolby turns and faces the wall. Frannie looks at the floor and murmurs, 'The new U2 album's awright. Better than *Pop*. No as good as *The Joshua Tree*.'

242

Brian coughs, and when his voice emerges it is new and certain, ringing out.

'Next year for California, boys. Next year it'll happen.'

And I realise that I haven't said these things at all. Just thought I had.

And that now I never will.

And that's that.

The boyracers.

God's own Mario-Karts.

The summer has wound down like an old clock. The mornings are tinged with a bright, sharp cold. Birthdays have come and gone, Dolby's twentieth, my seventeenth. We did nothing special to celebrate them.

Dad helps pack the car. There's a battered typewriter he's fished from the loft for my essays, plenty socks and underwear, the copies of Kerouac and Kelman and rubbish critical books with names like *In Defence of Realism* which Mrs Gibson gave me, shining with pride, when I told her I'd made it onto the English degree course at Stirling Uni. Her notes in the margin, her pencilled thoughts forever adrift in the world. I open a page at random and find a line which says

as if there could be such things as true stories . . .

My rolled-up posters (Salvador Dali, Che Guevara, Clive Barker's *Hellraiser*) protrude from the mound of stuff in the boot, a papery arsenal, and in my pocket I have a dozen photographs to stick on the wall of my new room: the Lads in jubilant poses, me and Dek sharing cocktails on the back slabs, Dad glancing over the top of the *Daily Record* in his old Clash t-shirt, and

Mum.

We heave the stuff out from the house – me, Dek, Dad, the Lads – grunting and joking like workers, like men. Afterwards we stand about, just sort of chatting, pointlessly. When I ask what they've been up to in the last few months, Brian shrugs.

'No really seen much ae each other tae tell ye the truth.'

They all nod.

Through a heat-blanketed summer, I've met with them rarely. Since we've no car, our reasons for meeting up are few, though there's been the odd drunken mobile-phone call, boasting about some shag (not many of those actually) or raving about some film. Generally, I've been relieved when Frannie's said, 'Does your phone dae this?' and the

245

receiver's clicked down. Mostly, I've stayed in with Dad, listened to the clock's tick and the birds' chirpy nonsense, read books for my new course, watched *The Godfather* One and Two (not Three).

'Got everything?' Dad asks, closing the boot.

'Aye. Ready to heddy.'

We all stand, silently absorbing the moment. Cars shoot past on the main road. Our hands are in our pockets. It's as if we've just been introduced to each other and are desperately forming excuses to escape.

'Oh!' Dolby says, reaching into his jacket, 'Before Ah forget. We got ye a present for yer new room.' He hands me the plastic Harrison Ford from Belinda's dashboard. I stare at it, its wee arms and legs askew, blasting an invisible Greedo.

'Before we left her,' he adds. 'Ah managed tae salvage Han.'

'An this,' Brian beams, passing me a can of Irn-Bru. 'For the back-seat ae yer first car.'

'The front-seat,' I remind him. Never did work that one out.

We shake hands. Each of them wishes me well, promises to come up to Stirling Uni to visit. Brian asks me to set aside any tasty nursing students. The wind whistles the approach of winter and we huddle our hands further into our pockets and standing there with them, I feel older, grown. No longer a mild-mannered Runt.

I have to leave them.

But every second heartbeat is a scream to stay.

'Aw the best.'

'Heddy-haw.'

'See ye in the Hotel California.'

Just before I go, the mobile in Frannie's pocket beeps (*The Magnificent Seven* theme) and he draws it out to check his text-message.

'Alvin, it's for you,' he smirks, passing me the phone.

'For me?'

'She still has ma number . . .' It says:

SRRY I MISSD ALLY FRGSNS LST MTCH
TXT ME?
WENDY

'How dae Ah text her back?' I panic, fiddling with the buttons, 'Whit dae Ah–'

'Just keep it,' Frannie shrugs. 'Ah'm gettin a new wan anyway.'

'Ye cannae be a student if ye've no goat a mobile-phone,' Dolby points out.

'Fuck naw,' says Brian, 'How else are we gonnae get near thae wee posh tarts?'

'Thanks man,' I say, folding the phone into my pocket, where it sits, strange, like a little lump of the future and the past that has attached itself to me.

I move towards the car slowly. Things feel a bit like the end of *The Breakfast Club*. Simple Minds should be playing 'Don't You Forget About Me' in the background, highlighting the excellent crapness of the moment, and even that sounds like a good enough summary of the past year; I'll have to text that one to Frannie. THE XLNT CRPNSS OF THE MOMNT.

As I clamber into the front seat, Dek shuts the door behind me. He seems to want to say something, struggling with it.

'If there is anythin out there, George,' I say, cutting him off. 'Ah'll find it.'

'Away an take a fuck tae yersel, Ringo,' he smiles, ruffling my hair, and it's such a corny thing to do, like something a brother would do.

It's time.

Me and Dad pull away, and they're all in a line, everyone I've ever cared about, waving, smiling, flicking me the Vs. But already they seem in the past, already lost. And as the car gathers speed, it's too painful to watch them disappear behind me, so I don't.

I look to the future.

Ahead, the sun glows pink/orange/lime, like Bacardi Breezers, like a champagne supernova in the sky, and all the last songs on albums and all the closing scenes from films merge then part on a motorway in my mind, and everything under the sun is in tune, as I fiddle with the radio, settling on some crackling Highland channel with its comforting hills, heather, lochs and

> you'll take the high road
> an ah'll take the low road,
> an ah'll be in scotland afore

me and the Lads watching drunken Rangers matches, and I read Wendy's text. Read it again. Then again. And I'm not sure that it matters if I call her or not but I really think I will. This decision is made. I stuff the phone back into my pocket and stand Harrison Ford up on the dashboard and he carries the world on tiny shoulders.

Dad says, 'Ye ken you're the first in oor family ever tae go tae university?'

'Ah didnae, Dad, naw.'

Then he says, 'Did Ah tell ye Ah saw Elvis Costello at the Maniqui?'

He winks, and there's a grin I thought had died from his face quite some time ago.

'Naw, ye've never telt me that, Dad,' I reply.

ROLL CREDITS. VOICE-OVER. We are a generation who awoke to find all gods dead, all wars fought, only delusions to believe in, hope for, which we spend our whole lives racing towards, bright, shimmering on the horizon but then

We glance back. And the way we've come has gone. And we didn't stop, breathe, absorb any of it. It all zapped past. Like Grand-Prix adverts. Like a sitcom double-bill.

> where me and my true love
> will never meet again
> on the bonny bonny banks of

planet Earth, scorched with the touch of the sun, its rays appearing/ disappearing/appearing again and happiness becomes – *is* – attainable. It isn't this, but I know it's coming, making me chase it, frantic, like a greyhound after a rabbit, and who knows, maybe I've shot past it without even noticing, but till the day when all makes sense there is

THE XLNT

CRPNSS

OF THE MOMNT

'You an Dek are awright, Dad?' I ask. 'Ah mean, yer on the right track? Stirling's no far away if ye want tae–'

'We'll be fine, son,' he says, squeezing my hand. 'Yer brother's got that carer's allowance. He's gonnae stay for a while. We take care of each other.'

The road stretching out ahead. Cars firing towards mystery destinations. Those simple words *we take care of each other* and what they mean, what they do, and the world, I've decided, is a good place to be. Still fascinating. I have not exhausted its possibilities. It *ain't* no sin to be glad you're alive, and above all else it's this I realise, suddenly, like an epiphany, like the sun glowing through the clouds or the heady feeling we had in Belinda all those nights, boyracing together, together, so I roll down my window, turn up the stereo then just roar something triumphant at the sign rushing past which says

YOU ARE NOW LEAVING FALKIRK